Praise for *Good Husbands*

"An emotional and powerfully evocative story. Ray has expertly crafted a thoughtful and important read that ends with a stunning surprise."

—Liv Constantine, author of *The Last Mrs. Parrish*

"Multilayered, unflinchingly honest, and teeming with nerve-shattering suspense. Ray has created a much needed space for complex conversations surrounding consent and whether we really know the people we love. An absolute triumph."

—Heather Gudenkauf, author of *Everyone Is Watching*

"The most riveting and unflinching he said/she said novel to date. Absolutely staggering, insanely gripping, and wholly unputdownable, this riveting, unsettling suspense will leave you gasping for air. With her hypnotic, dazzling prose and captivating characters, Cate Ray is a masterful storyteller at the height of her powers."

—May Cobb, author of *The Hollywood Assistant*

"*Good Husbands* is both a gripping thriller and a thought-provoking exploration of toxic masculinity and female friendship. I couldn't put it down."

—Sarah Haywood, author of *The Cactus*

Also by Cate Ray

Good Husbands

THE YOUNGER WOMAN

CATE RAY

ISBN-13: 978-0-7783-6833-5

The Younger Woman

Park Row Books
22 Adelaide St. West, 41st Floor
Toronto, Ontario M5H 4E3, Canada
ParkRowBooks.com

Printed in U.S.A.

For Sally Pasche, with love

Loose tongues are worse than wicked hands.

—Proverb

Once she had made up her mind, there was no turning back—no mercy. Subtle attacks took as much strength as brutal ones, but were harder to prove. So she bided her time, looking for soft spots, weaknesses, waiting for the exact moment to strike.

He never watched the news, so she knew about the heat wave long before he did. He had no idea it was forty degrees out, and accepted her invitation. It was hot, she said, but there was a fresh breeze, perfect for a run before the temperature really soared.

The steep incline was not for the faint-hearted. People happening to look out their windows frowned at him as he soldiered on in the sweltering heat. She waited at the foot of the hill, bending over as though she had a stitch. Then she cupped her hands to her mouth. Later, a local resident said he'd heard her call out in concern. That wasn't true. It just looked like it.

Even if she had shouted at him to stop, he wouldn't have listened—not after the conversation they'd just had.

It was only as his legs buckled that she screamed. Running up the hill as fast as she could, she fell to her knees, crying out for help. A crowd gathered, an ambulance was called, but it was too late. His face was drenched in sweat, his lips were tinged blue—a corpse already.

The funny thing was his eyes were open, bulging, staring at her accusingly. Yet no one saw it that way, least of all her. She held his hand, cried, more than happy with her decision to kill him.

PART ONE

DIGGING FOR GOLD

1

How did we get here—when did things become so bad? There are so many triggers and alarm bells, I'm overheating with the effort of trying to pick just one. And now Alice is leaving and if I don't get a hold of myself I'm going to miss it.

Alongside our car, a student is saying goodbye to her parents, tucking in her camisole. Fred is watching her, instead of Alice. And I'm watching Fred, instead of Alice.

She's at the door of her accommodation block, about to disappear inside. And then, suddenly, she falters, looking back at us, twisting her fingers together. She may as well be in pigtails and a gingham dress on her first day of school.

My seat belt snaps off. "Gabby..." Fred says.

I'm already halfway up the path, pulling her into my arms, inhaling her hair. Alice, sweet Alice.

I don't want her to leave me. That's the truth. I don't want her to leave me with her father. I can't bear it. Everything is heating, melting, as my entire system gives way to emotion.

And then I stop myself. I can't do this to her. I pull back, grasp her shoulders, my arms rigid like tentpoles holding us together. "You're going to have a wonderful time, sweetheart. This is an exciting new adventure."

She's looking at me skeptically, but I don't so much as breathe. I can be a tower for her. It's only university; she'll be home again in ten weeks.

"Thanks," she says, her blue eyes filling, becoming sealike. I see my mother in her then and remove my hands from her shoulders in case I'm gripping too hard. "I love you, Mom."

"And I love you too… Now go." I give her a little pat, then watch as she keeps walking and this time she doesn't look back.

I think I'm going to die as the door closes behind her, and then it's me standing there, faltering, looking behind me, twisting my fingers together. Except that it's not my parents I'm in turmoil about, but my husband. There's a huge distance between us, much further than the twenty steps it would take me to reach him. He's not even looking at me. His head is turned toward two attractive girls sitting underneath a tree. I could be setting off a distress flare and he wouldn't notice.

Gazing at the door that swallowed Alice, I consider following her, hiding inside the laundry room for a few weeks. And then Fred honks the car horn and reluctantly I take those steps back to him.

Inside the car, I sit with my bag on my lap, staring straight ahead. He knows not to say anything, starts the engine. I'm glad he's driving, leaving me free to sob until I'm as dry as a raisin.

He's a steady driver, I'll give him that. We're at that stage after twenty-one years of marriage where I'm grateful for his practical skills. I'm sure he feels the same about me and my lasagna.

As we slowly pull away, everything becomes a blur through my tears. I don't know if it's my hormones, but I'm overwhelmed: missing Alice, worrying about aging, wishing Fred wouldn't look at this collage of youth as though I'm the crusty glue underneath that no one sees.

I'm uncomfortably hot, even with the air-conditioning on. It's very warm for September—shorts, strappy tops; a parade of gorgeousness. And just like me and my jumbled thoughts, Fred doesn't know which way to look.

Finally, as we pass through the entrance gates, he glances at me, patting my knee as though I'm man's best friend. "She'll be fine."

Our youngest has left home and that's all he can say.

"Aren't you upset?" I stop crying for a moment, curious about his response.

"Of course." He doesn't take his eyes off the road. "But this was what you encouraged her to do, wasn't it? And she worked hard enough to get there. What's the point in being upset? We can't keep her tied up at home."

I don't know about that. If there were a sane way to do it, I'd probably give it a go.

I hiccup, gazing out the window, adding emotional detachment to the list of differences between us. Here I am, breaking my heart. And he's tapping the wheel to "summer breeze, makes me feel fine," the salmon tint of his shirt making him seem pinker than he is. I bought that for him. And he needs a haircut. The ancient scar on his knee is shimmering where he's caught a tan from all the golf he's played this summer.

He's good for fifty-two—doesn't have to work as hard as I do to stay in shape, even though we're the same age, our birthdays only a week apart; both Taurus. I always thought this was nice, but someone once said *two bulls in one house? Brave!* And it was one of those things that went around my head for longer than it should have.

I don't think of myself as a bull; sometimes I find it difficult to ask for what I need. And Fred is too tall for a bull. He's less goofy and cheeky now he's middle-aged, but every so often I see the old him—the way he was, with curls, John Lennon glasses. I start crying again. And this time, it's for us.

"She'll be okay, won't she?"

He looks at me. "Yes."

We don't say anything after that. I cry behind my shades all the way home, sucking my lip. It's seventy-nine miles from Exeter to Shelby. It will be longer for Alice by train—nearly four hours. I'll send her money so she can come home whenever she needs to.

What if she never needs to?

I hiccup again, but Fred doesn't notice. I told him I was going to be okay today and he's taken me at my word.

I've been dreading it. It was bad enough when Will left for Edinburgh. And now he has a girlfriend, Zara, who wears cut-off shorts with the pockets hanging out. She's lovely, very polite; but she's twenty and in love with my son and there's a tiny part of me that wishes she weren't.

At home, I don't go straight inside but linger on the step, gazing at the baby oaks the children planted eight years ago when we moved in. The thing with trees is they stay where you put them.

Inside the house, it smells of Alice's perfume, which nearly sets me off again.

"Will you be okay if I do an hour's work?" Fred says, opening the door to the basement.

"Go ahead. I'm seeing Jam later."

He smiles. "Well, if she can't sort you out, then no one can."

But I wanted it to be you.

That's what I want to say. Yet it wouldn't sound right, not anymore. Too much has changed between us. There have been too many little betrayals, and some not so little ones.

"I'll give you a shout before I go," I say. "Would you like a coffee?"

"No, thanks," he calls out, already halfway down the stairs.

The kitchen seems bigger than it was this morning, the breakfast bar stools painfully empty, Alice's cereal bowl in the sink; I might keep it there for a few days. Opening the fridge, I remove a Pinot Grigio, pour a glass, taking it outside with a jar of olives. A breeze is rustling the palm trees on the patio, fluttering the surface of the pool. I take a seat, a cardigan draped over my shoulders like some Hollywood star.

Sometimes it helps if I glamorize the situation, imagining myself delivering lines, acting out the pain on screen. Sometimes it doesn't. To be honest, I feel a bit silly.

I put my cardigan on properly, unscrewing the jar lid, chewing an olive, my eye drawn again to the oaks lining the border. They'll be beautiful this autumn. It seems cruel that children fly the nest to university as the leaves begin to fall. Why couldn't it be spring—give parents half a chance?

I take a long drink of wine, twisting to look up at Alice's turret. She wanted a sea view when we moved in. Ten years old and she knew a premium room when she saw it. Suddenly, I want to be up there, to lie on her bed among her abandoned clothes and stuffed toys.

Upstairs, the room is surprisingly cool. I set the wine bottle on her dressing table, pouring myself another glass. "Well, cheers, baby girl."

Her bed looks inviting, despite the pile of ratty tracksuit bottoms. *Don't take those, Alice.*

I lie down, drawing my knees to my chest, hugging Big Bear, who smells of Alice's coconut shampoo. She still uses her bear as a pillow. I cry again, gazing at the photo stuck haphazardly on the wardrobe door: her and Will last year, by our pool, hands draped around each other.

My babies. Both gone.

I'm somewhere up high, on a clifftop, the sea crashing beneath me. It takes me a moment and then I remember that I've been here before, locked inside this ghastly dream, and then dread begins to drain through me because I know what's about to happen.

I wrestle to wake up, but can't. The rough gorse is grasping my ankles, locking me in place. I don't want to watch but have to, can't escape. He's there now, standing too close to the edge. Fred? Or Will? Don't let it be Will.

I writhe in panic, ripping my legs on the gorse. I call out, my voice lost against the roaring sea. *Get away from the edge! Get away from there!* I can't move or even turn my head away. I know someone else is coming, can sense them drawing closer. I struggle again, screaming, as they shunt the man forward over the treacherous edge.

I fight as hard as I can, my face wet with tears. And then I'm free.

Sitting up, I stare around me, the back of my hair wet with perspiration. Letting go of Big Bear, I gather the wine bottle and glass, tiptoeing from Alice's room. The house feels as empty and fragile as a greenhouse. Outside, the whisper of the sea sounds like passing traffic. I check the time on my phone: thirty minutes until I meet Jamillah.

In my en suite bathroom, I feel sick with fatigue. My tongue feels bulbous and there's a sleep line running all the way from my cheek to my chest, as though I'm a cardboard cutout that's been folded in two, ready to lie flat for the night.

I put on some makeup, fix up my hair, but that seems to accentuate my eyes—the fact that they're puffy, swollen—so I let it down again, telling myself that this is as good as it's going to get. I choose a T-shirt, jeans, and then head downstairs, knocking on Fred's cave door.

It smells of computer—that hot wire smell. "I'm off."

He looks up, removes his glasses, rubs the bridge of his nose. "Is it that time already?"

I nod. "There's pasta salad in the fridge."

"Thanks, my love." He frowns at me. "You all right? You look a bit..."

"I dozed off. And I had that nightmare again."

"It's okay. Everything's fine. I'm here. You'll always have me." He smiles, puts his glasses back on, focusing on the screen again. He works a lot of hours these days, more than he used to, but then so do I.

He's perfectly right though. The kids fly in and out like swallows, but good old Fred will always be here.

"See you later," I say.

As I go down the driveway to the side gate, I check my phone to see if Alice has messaged. She hasn't. I wonder what she's doing. I think about texting her, but don't. It's not going to help her to let go, move on.

It's a ten-minute walk to the seafront. I don't see anyone as I go. My thoughts swirl, froth about, and by the time I enter the bar, I know I'm going to have to tell Jam what I finally admitted to myself today about Fred: I absolutely hate him.

2

Rumors is one of those seafront bars that manages to look chic, even though it hasn't been refurbished since 2004 and doesn't have electronic shutters but plastic sheets that steam up when it rains. Yet it does have trendy cocktails with names like Anna Banana, and yacht-owning clientele with Rolexes and silk caftans that remind me of the meme *tell me without telling me*. That you're rich.

I love Rumors though. I was one of their first customers when they opened, and sometimes I'm one of the last to leave. During storms, I like being on the other side of the plastic, listening for the irregular toll of the bell buoy. On summer nights I rest in a deckchair by the firepit, watching the lighthouse blink. There's a rhythm to the bar that I'm familiar with and while I'd be exaggerating if I said everyone knows my name, it wouldn't be a lie that they know my drink.

I'll have what she's having, and that's when I always point to Jam.

As I head up the wooden steps two at a time, I hear her before I see her. She's in our usual place, a table near the bar that overlooks the sea while sidestepping its gusts. It took us a while to find this spot and we think of it as ours. Jamillah doesn't shrink from the challenge of evicting intruders, which is when I tend to make a quick trip to the bathroom.

Tonight, she's laughing with the staff, her hair in a high ponytail, her face flushed and shiny as she shouts something about liquid Viagra.

"Oh, hey," she says, leaning across the table to kiss me. She smells of cheese and onion—she can eat chips like no one else. "There's a new cocktail..." She lowers her voice. "And a new guy." She gestures with her thumb to the bartender. "Check him out."

"It's basically Jägermeister and Red Bull," he calls back to her.

He's handsome, but not much older than Will, the thought of which makes my tummy wilt.

"Sounds good. We're going for it," she calls back. And then I have her full attention. She places her hands flat on the table between us. "So, how was it? Catastrophic?"

"Worse."

She laughs. "Oh, come on. It can't have been that bad. And she is coming home again, you know."

"I know. But it's..." I shrug, setting my jacket on the back of a chair, running my hands through my hair. It only takes a few steps along the seafront for the air to batter it.

"It'll get easier." She taps my hand. "Or it won't." Biting open another packet of chips, she lays it out flat between us.

"It's all just so...I dunno...depressing."

"This..." she waggles her finger at me "...is why I didn't want kids. All that crap and hard work, just for them to leave you."

"There's still time for you yet," I say, as the bartender approaches.

She snorts a laugh. "You're joking! I have gray pubes!"

An older lady at a nearby table turns to look at us in disgust, but luckily the barman steps in front of me, blocking her from view. “There you go, ladies. Two Liquid Viagras.” He smiles, flicking his surfy hair. “Enjoy.”

“Oh, we will,” Jam says, lifting her glass speculatively. The liquid is blue, the straw radioactive yellow, a lime hanging on the rim. “Not bad.” She tastes it, winces.

I try mine. It’s not great, but it’s our ritual, working the cocktail menu. We’ve been friends for so long there are rituals aplenty, most of which we can’t remember. We met when neither of us had any family and agreed to fill the gaps. In Jam’s case, she didn’t want children, whereas I was focused on multiples—in the end settling for two, as reality bit.

She looks glamorous tonight in a Bardot top and PVC leggings she’ll have to peel off. I don’t know how she manages to stay in such good shape. She’s addicted to junk and only does Pilates on Fridays. That must be some class.

“Let’s not talk about the kids.” I sip my drink, watching the disapproving lady at the other table. Her husband looks like he could use this cocktail. He’s slumped over his pint, barely speaking. It must be so disappointing to get to that age and have nothing left to say.

“I wasn’t,” Jam says.

“Hey?”

“Talking about kids.”

“Oh.” I sigh. “So, how’s Nate?”

“Nate the Great?” she asks, even though there’s only one Nate that I know of and she’s married to him. “You know how it is.” She puffs out her cheeks. “If it’s on TV, he’s watching it.”

I nod, looking at the old man again, wondering whether his game plan is to slide downhill, very slowly, for the rest of his life—whether he has a plan at all.

A tiny ripple of appreciation for Fred forms: he does at least leave the house. But then the ripple stops; he plays too much golf. At least, that's what he says he's doing. Whereas Nate is like a teddy bear—loveable, inert. His reluctance to go out drives Jam mad and I have to say, she deserves more. So much more.

A tear trickles down my cheek before I can stop it. Jam stares at me, probably thinking she can't remember the last time either of us cried in public.

I expect her to glance awkwardly around the bar, but she doesn't. "It's gonna be okay," she says. "You've got this."

As she sets her eye on me, I know she's acknowledging that dark place in me that I spend so much energy hiding, and then she scrapes back her chair. "Sod this for a game of cards. Let's get more Viagras."

I watch her at the bar, bangles glinting as she sets her hands flirtily on her hips, throwing her head back to laugh so loudly that everyone turns to look at her, even the yachties.

By the time she's back with the drinks, I'm no longer teary. But something else is bothering me, something that needs saying, out loud.

"Jam..." I look around me, checking no one's listening in. "I have to tell you something."

"Ooh, sounds juicy," she says, slurping her drink.

"It's...personal."

Taking in the seriousness of my expression, she leans toward me, frowns. "What is it?"

I stir my drink, watching the liquid swirl. "It's Fred."

"What about him?"

"I want out."

"Out? In what—?"

"I want him to leave." I smile, my mouth tremoring. "I want a divorce and for him not to get the house."

She laughs dryly. "Well, that ain't gonna happen. But are you actually serious?"

"Yes. It's over." I look around the bar again, gazing at the miserable old man with his pint. "He makes my flesh crawl."

"Really?" She's looking at me curiously, head tilted. "It's that bad? I mean, I knew there were issues, but…really…?"

"Yes. I don't love him anymore. In fact, I hate him."

"Oh, wow." She bites her lip, leaving a trace of lipstick on her front tooth as she smiles, trying to make light of this. She likes Fred, is going to defend him, the way people always defend marriages when there are kids involved. But ours are twenty and eighteen years old. They barely count in terms of emotional damage. Which I know isn't true, even as I think it.

"Well, I get where you're coming from," she says. "He's creepy." Flicking her hair, she drinks her cocktail, avoiding eye contact.

Is she joking?

"What do you mean, creepy?"

She still won't look at me. "I knew you'd make something of this."

I reach across the table, touch her hand. "Jam, tell me what you mean."

She looks at me then, a full-on stare she uses when urging a client to buy a property they can't afford. I've seen her do it. "You know what I mean."

The barman approaches, towel slung over his shoulder, setting a bowl of roasted almonds between us. "On the house," he says.

We don't respond. The tension between us is too consuming, even though we're in agreement.

"Let's face it, Gabs: he's not been the same since you got the house. Everything changed then and it's taken you this long to be brave enough to admit it."

My face flushes. "Because of the kids."

"Because of the kids," she repeats, nodding.

Music starts to play—jazz for one of the yacht owners. There's a few of them scattered here tonight, in slacks and polos, knitted sweaters draped over their shoulders. And with them, dotted around the peripheries, like herring hoping to attach themselves to whales with their powerful suction mouths, are the beautiful young women who work alone, waiting to catch an eye, quicken a pulse.

This little patch here, the small town of Shelby, boasting the most expensive properties in the world and the second largest natural harbor on earth, is famous for gold diggers, or GDs. Jam deals with them at the real estate agency a lot more than I do. Whereas not many sexy young women wander into the Dorset council buildings where I work.

Despite my own personal history, I don't mind them all that much, have grown to accept them, but they get under Jam's skin.

Fred likes them though.

Ever since we got the house… That's the thing I haven't been able to admit. Jam's right: he changed practically overnight.

Over in the corner someone moves, catching the light, and I look that way, trying not to stare. "They get younger," Jam says, following my gaze. "And more pumped."

She's talking about the breasts—so firm they gleam. Dressed in a plunging slip dress, her legs demurely crossed, she's holding an old hardback with a plain cover.

"Yeah, right, like she's reading that." Jam scowls. "Bet the book's upside down."

I'm about to suggest another round of cocktails when her phone rings. "What," Jam answers flatly. "Hey? How d'you manage that?" She claps her hand to her head. "But I'm with Gabby. I… Okay. Just hang on."

She drops her phone into her bag. "He's locked himself out on the patio. What a tool bag." She turns to unhook her jacket from her chair. "I'm gonna have to go. Sorry. Want me to come back in a minute?"

"No, I'm leaving soon." Standing up, I follow her outside to the decking.

"Why not come now?" She looks at me suspiciously. "You're not going to wallow, are you?"

"No. Honest. I'm just going to sit here a while." I point to the empty deckchairs. "Get some head space."

"Well, text me when you're home."

"Okay." We hug loosely, tension still standing between us, and I know it's because of her *creepy* comment.

But Jam isn't one to leave things unsaid and before she leaves, she turns back. "Lunch, tomorrow? Continue the Fred talk?"

"It's a date." I sit in the deckchair, which seems a very long way down tonight. The cashmere blankets smell faintly of dog, but it doesn't bother me. I drape one over my legs, feeling a lot older than I am.

A lull of silence falls over the decking and then it's just me and the sea. No one is passing by, not even a boat. I'm always a bit morose in autumn, even more so when looking at this view. To me, it signals death, loss.

I'm so far into my self-induced darkness I don't notice any movement around me until she's suddenly there, dazzling, not a herring but a great white shark, capable of power and strength and anything she wants. All in a dress so slight I could use it to wrap my lunch in.

And then she smiles, bleached teeth glowing in the dark. "Hey, I'm Ellis. Mind if I join you?"

3

I'm so stunned I don't know what to say. Girls like this don't speak to me, unless it's for directions, or in life-and-death situations. They're not interested in my menopausal symptoms, the state of my marriage, what I thought of *Stranger Things* (didn't watch it).

All I can think is that she's not the herring; I am. I'm gulping and floundering, whereas she's already in the deckchair beside me and has summoned the bartender without saying a word.

"Liquid Viagras?" she asks, turning to me.

"I… Yes…that's right."

She looks up at the barman. "Two more, please."

He's gaping at her the same way I am. Or maybe he's looking down her top. "Sure thing," he says, retreating.

The door swings shut behind him, plunging us into uncomfortable silence. I wish Jam hadn't left in such a hurry. This is the same girl who was reading earlier. What was it Jam called her: pumped?

What is she doing here? Shouldn't she be inside, with the yachties? I can't offer her anything. That's how GDs make me feel: as though there's nothing about me that could possibly be of interest to them.

I fiddle with my wedding ring, twisting it. I took my engagement ring off years ago as it kept catching on my washing-up gloves—official excuse—but I never really loved the idea of a big rock. Not that it was big. But still, I'm more of a plain-wedding-band sort of woman, and even that's in question now.

"Do you come here a lot?" the young lollipop asks.

I turn in my seat to look at her properly, taking in the shimmering gold of her nightie-like dress, the way her breasts nuzzle against the material, her bronze hair impossibly lustrous and in sea air too. Not only is her face the most beautiful one I've seen in real life, her limbs seem flawless. Organic. She doesn't have a signature scent that I can detect, not even a whiff of fake tan. I bet her knickers are pure white. No, neon. A thong. Shocking against her sun-kissed skin.

I'm thinking about her knickers. This is what GDs make people think about when they see them. "What did you say your name was again?" I ask.

"Ellis."

"That's a pretty name." I don't want to antagonize her. Something about her makes me feel that she could beat me in a catfight, or any fight. I don't think I've ever seen such a toned body. "I'm Gabby. And do I, well...know you?"

"No. Not if you just asked me to repeat my name."

Fair enough. I look away, shuffle my feet, feeling shabby in my jeans and T-shirt, the blanket over me as though I'm infirm.

The drinks arrive and I'm glad of the distraction, wondering whether we're really going to sit here and drink cocktails together. Maybe she's lonely. I look at her again, thinking of Alice. If she were somewhere feeling vulnerable, alone, I'd like to think that someone would pull up a chair with her—not ignore her on the basis of her being about fifty pounds lighter.

"Do you live locally?" she asks.

"Yes." I swivel slightly in my chair to point behind the bar. "About ten minutes up there."

"Handy."

"Very."

"And lucky?" She inflects this as though it's a question, which surprises me.

"Yes. Probably," I reply.

She nods. "And this is your local drinking spot... It seems nice." She looks around her, reaching idly to touch a potted palm. Above us, Chinese lanterns are looped, softly glowing.

"It is," I agree.

"Then why are you so miserable?"

I almost drop my glass. "Excuse me?"

She shrugs a shoulder, her dress strap slipping down, affording a near-glimpse of her nipple. I go to adjust it, as though she's Alice, before realizing I can't do that. She isn't Alice. Nothing like Alice.

"It's obvious you're unhappy, even though you're trying to hide it," she says. "And not just in your current mood, but life as a whole."

I go to protest, because no one wants to be psychoanalyzed, least of all by a child. Yet she seems incredibly mature too. "You can tell that just by looking at me?"

"Pretty much." She lifts her dress strap back into place, crossing her shiny legs. Her toenails are painted bright coral. Alice bought that shade this summer too.

Again, the sadness. I have to stop doing this to myself.

"My daughter left home today," I say.

She sucks silently on her paper straw, tossing the slice of lime into a plant pot. I'd never have thought of doing that, although I suspect others have. There are probably all kinds of things in that pot other than soil.

"That must be rough," she says.

"It is. I'm now officially an empty nester. And according to legend, my life is now over."

"You have your marriage?" Another questioning inflection.

I twist the band again, wishing I could fling it off, into the plant pot with the lime. "To you, at your age, that might feel like a consolation—an end to all your problems. But trust me, it's not."

She stares at me. "You're saying that my aim in life is to find a wobbly rich man?"

"Maybe." I drink my Viagra warily. "Well, isn't it?"

She doesn't say a word, doesn't move. She has very long lashes that don't curl unrealistically like spider legs, but actually seem real. Her breasts do too.

These toxic blue cocktails are working. Everything this girl says and does seems real now.

"What do you do for a living?" I ask, having gleaned that she's independent, proud, or at least wants to come across that way.

She smiles, her eyelids growing heavy. "Now that you don't need to know."

I'm intrigued. "Yes, I do. Tell me."

She slips off her sandal, dangling it provocatively on her toe. It's not all that provocative in and of itself. But on her, it seems so. She seems so clean and dirty at the same time, the perfect body to eat from.

Now she has me thinking about eating off her skin. Those flaccid yachties don't stand a chance.

"Officially? I guess you could say I work in the fitness industry."

That explains the physique. "And unofficially?"

"I find ways to make men part with their cash. Sometimes with the help of these..." She points to her breasts.

I laugh in surprise. "So you do want a wobbly rich man then?"

She frowns. "No one said anything about wanting."

Behind us, the door swings open and the bartender arrives with two more glasses full to the rim. Has she had a word—slipped a credit card behind the bar? I go to say that I'm still drinking mine, when I realize I'm not. It's empty. He swoops, clears the glasses, the door swinging shut again. Silence falls.

"You're extremely attractive," I say. "It makes sense that you earn some kind of living from that. You should. I hope that's not insulting."

"It's not. Thank you. You'd be surprised how many women don't comment on my looks, aside from negatively."

"That's because they're programmed to see girls like you as the enemy. Don't be too hard on them. They know not what they do."

I don't know why I said that. I sound hammered. I think I even slurred a little.

She turns, places her hand on my knee. "Oh, I don't. Believe me. I never think that."

I'm trying to remember what I just said. She's so intense, staring into my eyes, I have to look away. I don't know what's going on, but there's a ringing sound in my right ear. I should call it a night. I want to go for a run at seven tomorrow before Alice—

Alice isn't going to her job at the crepe stand. That's over. She's gone.

Before I know it, Ellis is standing beside me, rubbing my shoulder. I'm dry-crying—too drunk for actual tears. It doesn't even sound like me. "My husband's a cheating bastard. He's cheated before and I know he's going to do it again. If he were to see you, he'd be dying to jump in bed with you, no matter the cost."

"Oh, I'm not a hooker, if that's what you're suggesting. I mean, maybe the odd blow job, but that's not guaranteed."

I splutter a laugh. "He'd settle for that, I'm sure. So long as it was with you. He wants someone young, not someone worn out and—"

Her grip tightens on my shoulder so severely that for one moment I think she's going to strangle me. I can't move; she's that powerful. Like an assassin.

"Don't say that. Don't ever build a case against yourself." She moves fluidly, crouching before me, dress rising, her legs sculpted and oily, a chain dangling from her neck. There's something small on it—a pendant, but I can't make it out.

"Look at you," she says. "You obviously take care of yourself, and I can tell you're smart. Any guy would be lucky to be with you. If he can't keep his cock in his pants, that's his problem, not yours."

She stands up straight, her dress falling back into place. Her nipples are hard where she got so fired up. I can imagine men queuing to give her their money, blow job or not. She's incredible, and I want to know everything about her. "Do you live near here?" I ask.

She shakes her head, sitting back down, picking up her glass. "I don't want to talk about me. Tell me about this dick of a husband. Why can't you just leave him?"

"He's not a complete dick," I say, feeling defensive about the man I hate. "He's attractive, and has money—all tied up in property. But…" I look out at the sea. I've barely noticed it since she joined me. Compared to her, it looks lifeless, the moon pale on its surface. "…It's complicated."

"How so?"

I pull the blanket from my legs, returning it to the basket. "Because it's my house. Or at least, it was given to me because… well, in compensation. But before then, everything was okay. Fred was fine."

"Fred? He's called Fred?"

I smile. "Yes."

"Bullshit name." The ice clinks in her glass as she lifts it.

"He was named after his grandfather. His parents are lovely. And I..."

"What?" She turns to look at me, raising her eyebrow inquiringly and I'm struck afresh by how beautiful she is. I don't think she's even wearing makeup, or at least it's not obvious without my glasses on.

"Oh, I dunno... I was an orphan and they took me under their wing, treated me like their daughter. I couldn't do anything to hurt them."

She shrugs. "If they're so amazing, they'll understand."

"I don't think so. Blood's thicker than water."

"I don't give a shit about blood."

I bristle, my skin goose bumping. "Well, I do. Maybe one day if you have kids, you'll feel differently. But blood matters, no matter what you might think."

"I guess." She taps her nails on the side of the deckchair—not fake talons like the usual GDs but a natural-looking manicure. "So you want to end the marriage, but keep the house, is that it?"

I sigh heavily. "I know it's not possible."

She's quiet for a moment. Behind us, inside the bar, someone laughs so loudly it makes me jump. I'd forgotten anyone was there.

"Everything's possible," she says.

"Only if he were to drop dead. That's the only thing my kids wouldn't judge me for. They're great, but they'd hate me if I broke up the family. They love him too much for that." I set my empty glass down on the decking. "Sounds terrible, but I'd be better off if he just died, slipped away. Sometimes I fantasize about that, you know. Fred, dying."

Did I just say that out loud?

I daren't look at her. Can't remember her name. Something unusual. How many cocktails have I had?

She's so still I wonder if she's awake. And then she speaks so quietly I have to strain to hear. "What if you made him leave?"

"What? How?"

"There are ways."

"What sort of ways? And anyway, it wouldn't solve anything. He'd still get half the house."

"But that's not all you care about, is it?" She loops one leg over the other, rolling her head to look at me. "Seems to me that what you really care about is the love of your family, and if he were to leave you, it would preserve that."

I have the strangest feeling that I'm hallucinating—talking to a divorce lawyer, and Alice. They're morphing into one, this person beside me with the perfect body and hair.

"Maybe you could buy him out. Is that an option?"

"I don't think so. I'd have to work it out, but probably not."

"But if you could find a way, you'd keep the house and your family's approval. And all you'd have to do is get him to end the marriage first."

"Just like that," I say, smiling. "But you don't know him like I do. He's not exactly dynamic."

"You know..." Her eyes become hooded again, slits of light. "...I could always be a honey trap. I could easily pull off something like that." Her sandal dangles on her toe again, bouncing gently up and down. I imagine Fred bouncing on her, hard, excited, more excited than he's ever been with me.

I finally catch up with what she just said. "A honey trap?" I laugh. "I don't think that's my thing."

"And condemning yourself to a lifetime of suffering is?"

I'm taken aback—would be if I were sober enough to process it. Instead, I bow my head, wondering why no one's entered or left the bar in all this time. No one's smiled and said hello, or maybe they have and I haven't noticed. I'm not sure that I remember what we've been talking about; there are gaps that feel like sinkholes beneath me.

"You know what? I should go." Getting up, I don't feel stable. I rest my hand on the deckchair, wondering whether I'm capable of standing without it. "It's been lovely meeting you, Alice."

"Ellis."

"Pardon?"

"It's Ellis. You said Alice."

"Oh, I'm sorry."

"Don't apologize. Never apologize." There's that scary intense look again.

She stands up, looking me in the eye. We're exactly the same height. Before I can stop myself, I draw forward to inhale along her neckline. She doesn't stop me, doesn't move.

"I was right." I pull away. "You don't smell of anything. You're like…tofu." It's the only word I can think of.

She laughs for the first time. Maybe she doesn't find anything all that funny. In her line of work, I can believe it. Although, I'm not sure that she's told me what her line of work actually is.

"Well, it's been a pleasure, Ellis. I won't forget you in a hurry."

"Oh, I think you will in the morning. Most people do." Reaching into a tiny bag that I didn't even notice was strapped to the side of her body, she pulls out a card which she slips into my hand. "Call me if you change your mind."

I'm confused. "About…?"

She smiles. "Goodbye, Gabby." And then she walks away as though she's walking across the sea, my eyes too bleary to see details.

I debate the wisdom of staggering home alone, but then reason that if she can do it, a girl half my age, then so can I. And it's only as I'm halfway up the street, my feet crunching on the sandy pavement, wondering why the sea is so silent, that I realize I didn't pay for anything. And then the thought's gone and it's just me and the moon.

At home, as I open the front door, I can still sense her presence and turn to look at the pool and the oaks, but there's no one there.

The house acknowledges me silently. I feel for the card in my pocket, sliding it through the torn lining of my bag, where no one would ever look for it. If it's meant to be, I'll recall doing this. If not, in twenty years' time someone will find it and dial Ellis for a blow job, only to find she's middle-aged and no longer does them.

In bed, Fred is curled on his side. I slip between the sheets, staring at the back of his head that I once loved. And then I'm falling asleep with the disturbing feeling that tonight, somehow, in some way, I stepped over a shaky line into very dark territory.

4

When I open my eyes, two things strike me. Firstly, that Fred isn't beside me; and secondly, the room is spinning.

I don't try to move, not right away. I close my eyes and will the room to stop. It doesn't. I try shifting up on one elbow, wondering why Alice hasn't burst in by now for her lift, yelling at me to hurry because her shift at the crepe stand starts in five. Five—that's all she ever gave me.

Now I'd settle for one, because I remember that she's gone.

If I keep torturing myself like this, I'm not going to survive. And alcohol isn't the answer. What was I thinking? Liquid Viagras? I'm not eighteen. I'm not sure that even eighteen-year-olds would touch them. It feels like the clue is in the name.

Rolling onto my side, I force an eye open to look at the clock. Ten twenty? Where's Fred? I check my phone.

Gone to golf. Didn't want to wake you. Hope you had fun last night.

Flopping back onto the pillow, I stare at the ceiling. I wish I knew whether I had fun. I can't remember half of it.

I text Jam.

Tell me I didn't do anything last night.

I wait for her reply.

Not that I know of. Why?

No reason.

Still on for lunch?

Yep. See you at Lloyd's.

Lloyd's is a sea-facing restaurant that serves overpriced fish-and-chips to tourists. I'd have thought we'd be tired of everything about it, but it's our favorite place to eat. Which just goes to show—

I put down my phone and run to the bathroom to be sick.

Jamillah looks at me as I pour my third glass of water. "You sure you're okay?"

"Perfectly fine." My hand's shaking so I slip it under the table, clenching my knee. The restaurant is near Rumors. I can see the bar from our window seat—can see where I sat on the deckchair last night. With…someone. I was with someone.

How much did I drink? Memory loss can't be good; I know it's not good. And I'm coated in perspiration. I'm stopping myself from picking up the water jug and drinking from it.

"Well, I'm not buying it. Something's wrong."

"Yes," I say, lowering my voice. "Something's wrong. My marriage is dead. And I don't know what to do about it."

There are no spare tables today and they always cram everyone so closely together, which normally we like because we're nosy. But today it feels claustrophobic, intrusive. Beside us, a young man keeps clearing his throat nervously as though about to propose to the woman opposite him. Out in the bay, the giant cruise ship responsible for today's influx of diners is gleaming like a set of teeth.

"I'm being obtuse," Jam says, picking up the menu, studying it, even though we've been here a million times. "Ignore me. Sorry."

"Don't apologize," I reply, my hand forming a fist on the table. "Never apologize."

She stares at me. I'm a bit taken aback too, as though someone planted the words in my mouth. And that's when I remember her.

I gaze over at the bar, at the deckchairs packed neatly away. No one uses them during the day—not chic or prominent enough. Instead, the clientele perch straight-backed on glassy stools, sarongs buffeting in the breeze. There are so many people there—a fusion of tropical prints, Ray-Bans and oversized jewelry glinting in the sunshine like bird scarers—that for one moment I think I see her. A beautiful young woman, too perfect to be real. A mannequin, a monster. Maybe somewhere in between.

"Gabby, what's going on?" Jam says, setting her menu aside. "You look like you've seen a ghost."

I look away, down at my menu, at the minuscule grooves in its leather cover, wondering how many hands have touched this today and over the years. Hundreds of thousands of hands, flicking the pages uncertainly, agonizing over choices like whether to have shrimp or cod, how many calories it contains, whether they need to lose weight, whether their lives are on track or about to veer off course.

Why does everything feel so exhausting, difficult? Why can't I just have the courage to say it?

I don't love you anymore, Fred. I want you to leave.

I could never say that to him, and I hate myself for it. I want him to say it first: to be brave and honest enough for the both of us. Because he has pushed me to this point with his behavior. And now he's going to be a coward and let me be the one to end it and take the hit. And the hit isn't pretty. I've seen it before, in the school playground and at work. Women who end marriages, causing damage to their kids, don't fare well in the long run. I don't know the stats but someone should run them because I think they'd find it's a problem.

"Do you want my take on this?" Jam asks, not waiting for my answer. "I think this is about Alice. You've just said goodbye and you're panicking and you need to give things time to settle."

She sips her water, lips puckering. It's so warm today, especially in here, we're in sleeveless T-shirts—Jam wearing a bright orange one with sequins at the neckline. I'm all in gray, no sequins, not even a logo. And it feels to me then that this has been my uniform my entire life.

"I don't think it's just that," I say, running my finger along the metal trim on the menu's cover. "I think it's really over."

She scrutinizes my face as the waiter arrives, pen poised on pad. "What can I get you, ladies?"

Jam is still looking at me curiously, gauging how seriously to take me, and then she snaps the menu shut, her hair fluttering, and orders for us because we always have the same thing: fish-and-chips, with a side of salad that we never touch.

As the waiter withdraws, I glance at the young man beside me, wishing I could tell him to think very long and hard about proposing, if that's what he's thinking of doing, because marriage is hard to get out of for the conscientious and kind. And I can already tell that he's both. He's way too concerned with his girlfriend's level of comfort, whereas she's way too into her phone.

Don't do it.

"When you said he was creepy..." I say quietly, watching Jam's reaction.

She doesn't look away, sets her eyes on me. She's a truth sayer and it's my favorite thing about her. Yet today her honesty is chilling my bones.

"...Were you talking about the letching?"

She nods. "Yes."

I'm relieved, my shoulders dropping. I gaze out of the window at the sea that looks like a worn-out tea towel, dappled with dull sunshine like a checkered pattern. I was worried she was going to say something worse. *Creepy* is one of those words. It could have been much worse.

Yet, my despair is growing—a ball of knots inside my tummy which is tightening, calcifying, on the hour.

"You've noticed then?" I can't look at her, but feel her eyes on me, still.

"Yeah, I have," she replies.

I well up, bite my lip. She reaches for my hand and we sit like that for a while as I absorb this. Ordinarily, I might have been embarrassed, but today I'm too hungover to care if people think I'm unhinged.

And besides, I am.

We've never really talked about it before, which might be surprising for two women who discuss their libidos in shocking detail, but there's something about this particular issue that's made us tiptoe around it.

We dissected the affair in even more shocking detail as it unfolded. Seven years ago, we spent the summer stalking his mistress on High Street and saw her buying socks (we were expecting more). Yet, we haven't touched on the way he looks at other women.

"When did you notice it?" I ask.

She considers this. "About two years ago?"

"Okay."

That figures. I noticed it then too. There was a lot of head-turning the summer we went to Cornwall. He barely knew what I was wearing—that I was even in the same room. And then when he met Will's girlfriend for the first time, I thought he was going to fall down her camisole.

Jam squeezes my hand. "I didn't want to say anything. I thought it might be a passing thing, a middle-aged crisis. It still could be, you know. By next month, it could all be different."

"Yeah. Of course." *Nice try.*

That's the thing about this situation. Checking out other women isn't validating in the same way that an affair is. It's a betrayal that can't be quantified—one that makes me look like an uptight old bag. The general opinion seems to be that a woman should just put up with it. It's a twinkle in an eye, a totally natural clandestine hard-on. After all, I'm all dried up, and she's twenty-two. Of course he's going to be into her. What's the big deal?

"So, what are you going to do about it then, Gabs?"

I can hear her voice, but it's muted, blocked by my own thoughts. I would love to believe it's a phase, but I know it's not. He's available; his green light is on.

"Gabby..."

I used to obsess about him and Daisy Day. That was her name, like she was a cartoon character. I don't know what her parents were thinking, or what Fred was thinking, but the day she rang to tell me about the affair, she sounded so young I thought it was one of Alice's friends. I never did find out her age, but someone told me she was older than she looked—in her thirties. All I knew was that Fred was sleeping with her within six weeks of her joining Pixel8D Designs.

Bullshit name.

"Gab," she whispers.

"What?"

Jam narrows her eyes at me. "Put the fricking knife down."

I'm holding my fish knife upright. "Oh." I drop it with a clatter, the nervous man next to me jumping in surprise.

I remember everything then—that girl, that stranger, what we were talking about… Pushing back my chair, I excuse myself, the man looking up at me with baby deer eyes.

"Gabby, where you going?" Jam shouts after me. "The food's here!"

In the quiet of the ladies' bathroom, I enter a stall, standing with my back against the door, my heart racing.

I told her I fantasized about Fred dying. I told her that I would be better off if he were dead.

Something else comes to me then and I reach into the lining of my bag, feeling around for the sharp edge of a card. I take in the curly script, trying its hardest to look stylish.

Ellis

Mobile PT services

I don't even know what that means. What was I doing, forming a connection with this person—telling her my secrets? Ripping up the card, I drop it into the toilet bowl, press the flush. Flapping the back of my T-shirt, I apply a futile dab of lip gloss before returning to Jam, trembling all over.

She's glowering at me as she attacks the golden batter of her cod. "Seriously, Gab, can you just sit down and have a proper conversation with me, instead of this…" she's trying to think how to describe it—waves her fork at me, cod dangling "…this weirdness."

It is weird. I never drink that much, but these are extreme circumstances. I have an empty nest and I'm trying to navigate it with grace and failing. "Maybe you're right. Maybe this is about Alice and it'll blow over. Maybe I am imagining things."

She looks at me with a strange expression. "Did I say that?"

"Well, yeah." I pluck up a chip, nibbling it, testing my appetite.

She sets her cutlery down. "Look, Gabby… It's real, okay? The checking-other-women-out… It's real. I just didn't want to hurt your feelings. But Alice is also a factor. You're feeling vulnerable, bereft. But…" She glances around the room, even though everyone here will be a tourist "…That's even more reason why you should feel close to him, not more distant, you know? I mean, your actual words last night were that he makes your flesh crawl. And if that's true, then you have to deal with it. It's that simple."

Simple? Maybe it is.

Dear Fred, you make my flesh crawl. It's over.

"Now eat something," she adds. "You look like crap."

Sighing, I'm nibbling another chip, when my phone lights up. I glance at it, so stunned that I swallow the chip prematurely, burning my throat.

It was great to meet you.

It's not the message that shocks me, but something else. It takes me a moment to work it out in my current state, and then I've got it. Her name—it's in my phone.

She's there: Ellis. Snuggled dangerously close to Fred in my contacts. I don't remember adding her, which means there are other things I don't remember too.

Fear seizes hold of me and I freeze, staring at her name until it blurs. What did I do last night?

5

I take the long way home, along the seafront. With the sea sparkling and the breeze lifting my hair, I wish I could wind back the clock to when the children were small and we used to spend almost every weekend at the beach. I wish more than anything that Will and Alice were here.

Sitting down on the wall, I watch two tots building a wonky sandcastle, their dad lying underneath the sand where he's been buried. He isn't letting on how uncomfortable that must be, sand hoppers jumping against his skin.

Fred used to be good at that stuff too—letting the kids jump on his stomach like a trampoline, or sit on his shoulders and hold his ears.

As Jam and I parted ways just now, she told me to just tell him—to take responsibility and not be a victim. She's absolutely right. I want to take responsibility, but that means being the one to end things. And I want Fred to do that. I refuse to take the blame.

At some point, I'm probably going to have to though. I can't remain sitting on a wall, watching families, seagulls, white horses, anything rather than going home to him.

I remember then that I said I'd see his parents today. Pulling my phone from my bag, I scroll through my contacts, ignoring Ellis as I pass her name. I wait as the call connects, banging my shoes against the wall, sand gently cascading. "Hi, Len. How are you?"

"Oh, hello, love." My father-in-law sounds out of breath, fragile, my stomach churning guiltily. "Just mowing the lawn. How are you?"

"Good." The lie makes me immensely sad. Len and Monique have been married for fifty-something years. How can they make it work, and we can't?

I watch as a silver-haired man in rolled-up chinos passes by along the shore, a GD hanging from his arm, practically gliding along in a maxi dress. Coming toward them, the opposite way, is an almost identical match, right down to the clothes, height, and age differences. Aren't they embarrassed—do they even realize or care?

"So, how was it?" Len asks. "Brutal?"

I nod, looking out to sea, a white yacht passing by. "Yeah, you could say that."

"It'll get easier, Gabby. I promise."

The way he says this brings a lump to my throat. So gentle, tender, exactly how I wanted Fred to be yesterday. I kick the wall a little too hard with my heels, punishing myself for even thinking about hurting Len. He's solid, decent. People like him are the furniture in families no one realizes they need, until they go to sit down and smack their tailbone.

"I'm sorry, Len, but I'm not going to be able to make it to see you today." My voice wobbles. I clear my throat. "Hopefully next weekend?"

He's not the type to drill me for a reason why. "Okay, love." And that's it.

I continue my way along the front, and then at the end, when I can't go any farther, I turn around and head slowly toward home. It's time to face him. Chances are he's not there anyway.

He isn't. The house is hauntingly quiet. Yet, I notice as I make a cup of tea and take it out to my usual chair by the pool that I don't feel as lonely now.

I'm halfway through my tea before it dawns on me that I could have deleted Ellis's name from my contacts, yet didn't. And it occurs to me then that she's the reason why I no longer feel so alone.

No matter how close I am to my family, they wouldn't understand this—my feelings about Fred—like she did. I didn't have to explain, didn't have to divulge the darkness in my past that led me here. I didn't have to justify myself at all, at least I don't think I did.

I also didn't have to tell her that our house is the second most important thing in my life, after the kids. She just got it.

I try to picture her face, but can't. It's a blurry mix of Alice and Daisy Day. I hated Daisy for a long time. Yet, eventually Fred and I went to couples' therapy and I was able to get past blaming her for ruining my life.

But him? I told myself I forgave him—told him that too. That's the official line we went for, but sex was never the same again. It became a calendar event that I marked in pencil, so I could erase it if I felt like doing that, and often did.

I withheld sex whenever I wanted to, and he resented me for it. And in the meantime, we did the school run and went to work and had lunch with Len and Monique and bought a dog—lost a dog—and got grayer and softer and now we're here.

There's a noise out in the road and I look up to see the electric gates opening, Fred's BMW appearing. I lift my hand in a stilted wave, feeling guilty, even though he's the one pretending to play golf. But I'm the one with a woman's name in my phone who knows I'd prefer him dead.

"All right, my love?" he says, approaching along the path. "How was lunch?"

This throws me. "How did you know I was going to lunch?"

He sets his golf bag on the decking, crouching to talk to me, grunting with the effort. "Don't you remember?"

"What?"

He lifts my shades, looks into my eyes. "Must have been a rough night… You woke me last night, said you were going to lunch with Jam."

"I did?"

"Yep." He stands again, running his hand through his hair. He looks good today, in chinos and a pale pink polo. He looks like the Fred I once knew. "So, have you heard from Alice yet?"

"No. I was wondering about calling her."

"Maybe let her settle in?" Lifting his bag, he swings it onto his shoulder, heading for the patio doors.

"Yes, you're probably right," I reply, wondering if all this is about to change—these seemingly casual conversations that are in fact priceless because we value each other's opinion, knowing no one else cares about our kids as much as we do.

Of course it's about to change. That's why this is hard. It's another loss at a time when I'm not sure I can face any more. Middle age isn't about filling out, as people think, but thinning. My life's contracting and I'm going to have to find ways of plumping it—making it seem full again, like blowing up a tire.

He's passing through the open door, when he turns back, stops. "You said something strange last night."

My heart skips a beat. "Oh?"

"Something about honey."

Honey? As in trap?

Holy cow.

I can't look at him. I watch the surface of the pool, a dragonfly skimming, dipping its wings. We used to get a lot of them when we first installed the pool, Will running around the edge with his butterfly net. I was always petrified he'd fall in. I was neurotic, obsessive back then—saw death in every drop of water.

"You know I'm allergic to honey," Fred says, smiling.

"Oh, right. Yeah." I pick up my tea, hoping he can't see my cheeks burning.

He's about to disappear when he pokes his head back out again, pointing both index fingers at me. "Fancy a fresh cup?"

I've not seen him do that for a long while. He used to point his fingers at social gatherings—a playful gesture that he never quite pulled off. It always made me feel a bit sad. He was handsome, charming, didn't need to feel awkward.

I don't want more tea, but can't bring myself to tell him no. I know he regrets everything—wants company too, misses the wife who used to curl onto his lap and deep kiss him until his ears overheated.

"Yes, please," I say, my mouth trembling a smile.

I well up for the hundredth time since Alice left, and then Fred returns with the tea and I brace myself in case he comes too close, touches me. Sometimes I use dripping washing-up gloves as a barrier, or the laundry basket, especially when full of Will's pants. But I've been caught short on this occasion, a sitting target.

"There you go," he says, setting a package on the table beside me, stooping to press a kiss onto my cheek, turning me to stone. "A little something for you."

There's so much to process here I can't take it all in. "What is it?"

He rocks on his toes. "Open it and see."

My hands are clammy, leaving marks—traces of guilt and fear. I pray it's not jewelry. My reflection looms in the metallic packaging as I untie the ribbon, removing the lid.

"Pralines," he says. "Your favorite. From the new deli in town."

What new deli? I don't know what my face is saying, but I'm confused. He never buys me chocolates. And the pointing fingers? Why the sudden awkwardness around me?

"Right," he says, rubbing his hands together as though he's just sealed a deal, and then he turns away, heading for the patio doors.

"Aren't you having tea too?" I call after him, surprised.

"No. Had a pint at the club. Gonna take a quick shower."

As the door slides shut, I put my hand to my heart, feeling it race, watching the steam rising from my tea. He chose the mommy mug that Alice bought me, which was right at the back of the cupboard.

I can't do this anymore. I have to find a way to force him to make the first move, so I don't lose my family in the bargain.

Only one person has offered to help me do that. Because it's not a job for a best friend, or someone with any kind of moral code. There's a reason why executioners made the victim wear a sack over their head before chopping it off. Or was it the other way round? Did the axman wear the mask?

I pull up the last message on my phone, pressing Reply.

It was great to meet you too.

Once it's sent, I panic. Why did I do that? She knows my most twisted secrets. No good can come of this. I have to delete her from my phone.

Yet, my life feels less painful with her there in the background. And so I don't.

6

She was about to submerge herself beneath the bubbles when her phone pinged. She always kept it beside her on the bath rim because it made her feel more secure, knowing she could make a call if someone broke into her hell pit of an apartment. It had taken her the best part of a year to learn to sleep through the sound of slamming doors, crying babies. She wasn't going to gripe about it though. There were plenty of people with less than her.

It was great to meet you too.

She read the message several times, not that it was challenging or begged another look. It was clear enough. But still, she read it over, looking at the letters, how there were two *e*'s in a row, followed by two *o*'s, and how pleasing that was to the eye.

But it wasn't just the letters. It was the sentiment. It was great to meet her. Not *lovely*, the polite word. Not *amazing*, the fake. But great. A direct repetition of what she'd said first. It couldn't be more perfect. It was exactly the response she had been hoping for.

Holding the phone above the bubbles, she licked her lower lip, feeling the way it bobbled and dipped, as though there were tiny shapes under the skin, peas in a pod. She liked her lips more than any other part of her—the way they drew attention more than anything else, now that it wasn't as socially acceptable to stare at her chest.

She read the message again, placing her phone on the floor beside the bath. It wasn't on charge, but she never took any chances where her personal safety was concerned.

It was a dangerous world. She never left home without a blade. It wasn't legal, but no one ever heard the police praising a woman for her law-abiding ways after her corpse was found at the end of an alley.

Cupping her breasts in her hands, she slipped underwater, holding her breath before surfacing again, watching her nipples pop. She never tired of admiring herself—appreciated her immense efforts.

She trained hard, harder than anyone else. Maybe there were others out there like her, but she hadn't met them yet. She was always first into the gym, didn't stop until she'd worked out for an hour and a half. Mat work: dead bugs, shoulder taps, bird dogs, Russian twists, rocking planks… And then treadmill, rowing, weights. They called her psycho behind her back, but they could have said it to her face because she wouldn't have minded. She liked it.

Sitting up, she reached for her towel, gently nuzzling her face into it. She'd learned from a young age to respect herself—that you taught people within five minutes of meeting them how you wanted to be treated. And what they got from her was do not touch.

She knew they wondered what her secret was—cosmetic surgery, more money than sense, vile personality, that kind of thing, not that anyone would ever ask her. They were too busy judging, ogling, shooting daggers—you name it, they did it.

But if they were to ever come over and have a polite conversation with her, she would say, *Well, thank you for asking, madam or sir, and the answer to your question is self-love.*

It was easier when you looked like her, for sure. But she liked to think that she'd have worshipped herself even if she hadn't been physically flawless.

Toweling herself off, dabbing moisturizer on her thighs, she stared at herself in the cabinet glass, drawing closer to look at the tiny freckles on her nose. They came every summer, left by Christmas Day.

Her necklace had swiveled round, the chain almost a choker at her neck. Pulling it straight, the pendant swung into place, landing just above her breasts.

She had almost messed up. It was so unlike like her to be careless that she wondered if maybe she'd done it deliberately, giving the subtlest of clues. She thought she had been caught out, held her breath. But then the moment passed and she knew she'd got away with it.

Next time, she would be more careful. She hadn't come this far to make one stupid mistake.

Going through to the bedroom, she crouched on the floor, pulling a shoebox from underneath a dresser. Wrapping her necklace in tissue paper, she hid it inside the box, sliding it away before returning to the bathroom to clean her teeth, gazing at her bare chest. It didn't look right. She would have to get something else to go there. A pendant with the initial *E* this time.

In the cramped living room, she picked up the old hardback she'd lifted from the bar last night and took it to the bedroom, where she flicked on a lamp without a shade and began to read.

The trap was set. Now all she had to do was wait.

7

Fred was up early and working in the basement before I even stood up this morning. I don't get one-day hangovers anymore but a whole week of it. My body temperature hasn't rebooted yet and as I take a seat at my desk, calling hello to my gem of an assistant, Claire, I'm uncomfortably sweaty.

Without saying a word, she turns on my desk fan and hands me a cup of cold water. I smile gratefully, peeling off my jacket. I could do all this myself—the fan, the water—but when she does it, it makes me well up, as though she's my mom, even though she's only five years older than me. I rely on her more than she probably realizes. Every year at salary review time, I put in a word for her, listing her assets. The biggest one, however, is the one I don't state: that she makes me feel it's okay to be a hot mess.

I didn't call out bye to Fred before leaving—didn't ask if there was anything he needed picking up from town. I work in the council offices on High Street, handy for chores, bad for compulsive shopping. I'm going to have to find a reason to keep away from the shops.

The new eco center on the seafront is overdue a visit. I'll go there.

Logging onto my computer, I wonder what Fred thought when he heard the front door slam. I've never left before without speaking, but today it felt more natural to do so than the other way round. That's how I know it's over.

That and the fact that when he tried to spoon me last night and stick me with his penis, I was so horrified and weakened by my hungover state that I lashed out without thinking. "Get off!"

He didn't say a word, but turned over, taking half the cover with him.

It was a cold night in many ways, but an important one. Tonight, I'm hoping he will move out to the spare room.

I look up as Shaun enters, looking like he's just got up. Sometimes I get the feeling that by bending the dress code, he's saying he doesn't respect me, as though putting on a jacket or combing his hair would give me more authority over him than he's comfortable with.

We've both been working here in this same office for over thirty years. There's a photo somewhere of us both looking geeky, not long out of school. We used to get along, but when the environmental manager role came up, our relationship deteriorated at record speed. I threw my cap into the ring, thinking it was worth a try, and I got the job. And there's not a day goes by that he doesn't let me know what a laughable decision that was.

"Morning," he says.

I know he's late. He knows he's late.

"Morning, Shaun." I always do this special polite voice for him, the one I used for Will when his room was a mess. It's like there's this giant pair of scales in the office and one of them—my side—is unfairly weighted. So through the day, I have to build up his side, adding little treats, compliments, kind words. It's exhausting.

"Did you have a nice weekend?" I ask.

Claire looks up, waits for his response. "Nope," he says.

She rolls her eyes at me and I smile, trying not to look too vexed. In fact, I'm glad we didn't get into a discussion about weekends because I'm not sure what I would have said about mine.

"Actually, Claire..." I say, pushing back my chair, resting my hand on her shoulder. "Do you think you could shift that meeting for me? I'm going down to the eco center today. I've been putting it off for weeks."

"Absolutely," she replies, smiling.

I spend the rest of the morning lost in a coastal erosion report and then at lunchtime I tell Claire that I'll be back shortly.

Outside, it's eerily quiet, a seagull pecking about, barely any shoppers. It's only five minutes to the seafront, yet time enough for me to become fully absorbed in thoughts of Fred.

And I'm so focused on him that when he manifests in front of me, I'm so shocked I almost fall over my feet.

Diving into an alley, I try to stay calm. Was it him? I'm sure it was.

Why is he in town? I think back to this morning. I assumed he was downstairs; he works from home on Mondays. Has he changed his hours? Even so, he's a long way from his office.

I straighten my jacket, inching forward, gazing at the deli on the other side of the road—the new deli, the one he mentioned yesterday.

He's inside, leaning on the counter, talking to the sales assistant. I recognize her: Paige, one of the renters at the end of our road. She came to our neighbor's summer party, wearing a skimpy dress. I didn't know Fred knew her.

Withdrawing into the alley, I hold my hands to my face, flustered. It makes sense now: the chocolates, the awkward finger pointing, the mommy mug. He's either sleeping with her, or trying to.

I don't know why I'm so upset, shocked. I knew this was going to happen. I just didn't know how or when—didn't know it would be right under my nose, near my office. Somehow, when it happened before with Daisy Day, it was in another universe, one that I didn't have to visit.

Standing with my back against the cold wall, I hug my arms around my waist, gazing upward at the sliver of sky, unable to stop the tears flowing.

My upset breaks my resolve, cracks it, and like an addict I have to hear from Alice. I pull my phone from my pocket, dialing her before I can stop myself.

"Mom?" she whispers. "You okay?"

Her voice brings me to my senses. I stare at the wall, watching a wood louse making its way along the line of cement. "I'm fine. I just—"

"I'm in a lecture. I only answered because I thought it was an emergency. Call you later." There's a click as she hangs up. I lower the phone, looking at the faint moisture of my tears on the screen.

This is the new Alice. She's really left home for university, just like I wanted her to, because I didn't, couldn't, do it myself.

I breathe in, inhaling the dank air of the alley. Hemmed in on both sides, a puddle by my feet, a shiver rattles my frame. The fear is overpowering—the prospect of being fifty, alone. But I always knew the facts: knew I'd have to be strong to cope with an empty nest and a cheating husband.

Maybe someone else could handle this, turn a blind eye, but nothing about that phrase ever sounded comfortable to me. Creeping forward again, I watch him. It takes five minutes, but when I get what I'm after, I bury my face inside my jacket, casting my eyes down as I set off along the road again. At the seafront, a gust of warm salty breeze meeting me, I take a deep breath and set my shoulders back.

He rubbed her arm, kept his hand there.

★★★

I used to love sitting by the pool on warm evenings, when the kids wanted to let off steam after a day at school. I'd pour a glass of wine, sometimes throwing a hoop for them to dive for, but mostly just sitting, watching.

I always thought those times were about being with them, yet I'm enjoying it almost as much tonight on my own, listening to the palm trees shaking. Palm trees can bend to the floor and not break. I planted them in the back garden when we moved in—thought they would remind me to be resilient, a survivor.

But bending isn't always great. Sometimes a straight spine's called for.

Picking up my wineglass, I cross the lawn to the summer house, going inside where the air is warm, stagnant. There are dead spiders and flies on the windows. Shuddering, I stand still, the gloom embracing me.

Fred's car isn't in the driveway, but I glance that way just in case and then up to the top floor of the house, scanning for a light, even though he won't be there. He's somewhere else, again, and now I have to be brave enough to put an end to this the only way I know how.

I scroll down to her name, my heart racing. As the phone rings, I take a long drink of wine, justifying myself. This isn't my fault, what I wanted. If it weren't for seeing him with Paige, I wouldn't be doing this. But something's broken now that can't be fixed and my desperation is real.

To my disappointment, I get voicemail. Hanging up, I nibble my thumbnail, wondering what to do.

I ring again, listening to her greeting.

This is Ellis.

That's all she says. It is so short, I'm caught off guard, blurting my message. "Hi, Ellis? It's…it's Gabby. Can you call me back? It's about… Well, you know what it's about. I've changed my mind. And I...I want to go ahead or at least—" There's a beep as the phone cuts out, her voice storage full.

Damn. I didn't want to leave it like that. I could text? I drink more wine, thinking, and then decide to leave it. She knows how to reach me.

Sitting back down by the pool, I feel cold. Sometimes, I can hear the roar of the sea from here, but tonight the trees are rustling loudly, a thousand dry voices whispering.

The sky darkens, pink tinged clouds racing by. I pull my cardigan closer around me, looking all around me again, feeling unsafe. I don't want to be out here anymore but inside the house where I can turn a key.

As I close the French doors, checking the lock twice, I think about how strange it was that Ellis appeared on exactly the same day as Alice left—so neat a handover, almost as though it were planned.

8

I've been thinking a lot about the timing of Ellis's appearance and Alice's departure—the synchronicity of it. Not to be paranoid, but their names are strangely similar too. Then again, lots of names are samey, especially girls'. She hasn't got back to me about my blurty voicemail last night though. It's Tuesday now, and with every passing hour, I'm starting to get the uneasy feeling that she isn't going to get in touch.

I don't like that she's the one in control, as though there's a threat within her silence and in my lack of memory. There are gaps in Saturday night that are troubling me, a nasty pulse at the back of my mind that won't stop beating.

What if I said more to her than I can remember; something worse? That's if there is anything worse than wishing Fred dead.

It's not easy trying to focus on work with a disturbed mind. By lunchtime, I have a migraine, so I take a walk along the seafront. Sitting down on a bench, I'm about to unwrap my sandwich when my phone rings and I jump so much I bite my tongue.

It isn't Ellis; it's my mother-in-law.

"Hi, darling," she says. "How are you?"

"I'm fine, Monique. Couldn't be better."

That's such a stretch; I imagine her nose wrinkling. "Even with Alice gone?"

"Even so."

I don't know why I can't tell her the truth. Maybe I just don't want her to think of me as vulnerable, with everything going on with Fred. I don't know what lies ahead, but being seen as a pushover isn't going to get me very far.

"Well, I'm glad to hear you're not moping... When Freddy left, I was so distraught. And then I joined a choir and my life opened up... Have you thought any more about that?"

We've had this conversation many times. I'm not very musical.

"You don't have to be musical," she intuits. "I think you'd like it. It would give you a sense of belonging."

"We'll see."

The difference is that Monique didn't work, but I don't want to say that. It's not really about working or not working. It's about happiness and we all get that from different sources. For Monique, it was choir. For me...well, it's environmental reports.

Something else is bugging me though: she thinks I'm missing a sense of belonging. I don't think I've ever given her any reason to think that, so it's presumptuous, patronizing. Yet, I can count my family on one hand, so I let it go. Even though as I'm thinking this, I realize this is exactly what she's getting at.

Aside from Jam, and Claire at work, I don't have many people on my side. And Monique knows it.

"Anyway, the reason I was calling was to ask what you're doing about Saturday?"

"Saturday?" I draw a blank, can't think past the end of today.

"Your wedding anniversary." She laughs.

Oh, crap. That's this week? "I don't think we're doing anything. We don't normally do much."

"Exactly. Which is why I'm inviting you over for lunch. It would be nice to see you."

When I don't reply, she presses on. "There's no pressure, if you'd rather get a burger and watch the sun set." She's referring to last year. That's what we did, but Will and Alice were with us then. I can't see that happening this year.

And that's another reason for us to split up. Without our children, there's nothing holding us together.

"So, would you like to come?" she asks.

"Okay," I say, trying to sound cheerful.

"Perfect."

"Great," I reply, hanging up with a sense of dread. The last thing I want to do is spend my anniversary with my in-laws. She's never invited us before. I'm struggling to think of a time when she's even acknowledged the date. In fact, she once said that wedding anniversaries were private, just between the couple.

As I unwrap my sandwich, I have the horrible feeling that she knows about me and Fred. I thought I was doing a good job of acting, but maybe he's confided in her. Yet, said what exactly? That he's cheating on me?

And now I've lost my appetite. I'm just about to go back along the seafront when I see a flash of bronze hair that makes my stomach do a loop the loop. It's only a GD, clutching the arm of a yachtie. But for one moment, I thought it was...

I can't let this spill over into work. I need to be able to concentrate this afternoon, and every day after. I'll give her until tonight and then she's out of my phone, out of my life.

9

Lying on the sofa, I check my phone for the hundredth time, pulling up Ellis's name, gazing at her number as though it might reveal some terrible truth about her. What I find odd, aside from our meeting in the first place, is that she was so switched on, so fired up, only to then ghost me.

She seemed very confident, in control, doing whatever it is that she does. I've looked up Mobile PT and she's a personal trainer. Officially. The unofficial bit seems very murky. Maybe she decided that I was too flaky, unsure. I didn't sound sure when I met her and I certainly didn't sound sure when I left that fumbling message. I'm not even sure what I want now, other than to end my marriage without losing everything else.

Maybe I'm selling my family short, coming at this the wrong way. I could sit Will and Alice down, tell them I don't love their dad anymore. Then do something similar for Len and Monique.

Surely, I could manage it. What was it Ellis said? If they're so amazing, they'll understand.

Parts of our conversation stand out like sea glass in the sunshine, or splinters, the sort I get when I walk barefoot along the boards to the beach. And other parts are gone, and even though I know they're gone, I can sense that I don't have the full picture.

It's those gaps that are scaring me the most. That and the silence that has fallen since we met. Somehow, I know she's not going to contact me, no matter how long I wait.

My hand hovers over her name and then I press Delete. Sitting back on the sofa, relaxing my shoulders, I exhale, feeling lighter. That wasn't so difficult. What could she have done to help anyway? She was lying, surely. I'm not sure that I believe she isn't some kind of sex worker, even if she does only offer occasional blow jobs. Why even tell me that? I didn't need to know.

Out in the hallway, there's a rhythmic pattering as Fred runs up the stairs from the basement. "All right, my love?" His head appears around the door.

He still calls me *my love.* A habit.

"Just a bit tired. Been a long day."

"Coastal report due?"

I smile stiffly. "Yep."

He knows my schedule, just like I know his—or thought I did. And I realize then that yesterday, when he took a gamble by flirting with Paige so near to my office, he thought I'd be doing my usual Monday paperwork. My trip to the eco center threw things off-kilter.

"Your mom's invited us over Saturday for our anniversary," I say, not completely without malice.

He nods, two red circles forming on his cheeks. At least he has the decency to blush. "I know." He hesitates and it's what is said in these silences that is so important, to both of us. "Are you okay with going?"

Even though I'm sniffing around a thirty-year-old? Again?

"Yes," I reply. "I don't think it's worth upsetting your mom."

"And Dad," he adds protectively.

They're close, father and son. And mother and son. There are no weak points in the family chain anywhere. Only between him and I. This rusty link that has finally fallen apart, breaking the circuit.

A tear escapes and I'm glad it does because somehow years ago I was designated the role of strong one. I had to be strong through all the hospital runs with fevers, rashes, broken limbs, while Fred paced the floor, mumbling to himself, as if that's ever helped anyone.

He was loved too much by his parents. That's a thing. I've seen it first-hand with him.

Sighing heavily, he sits in the armchair opposite, removing his glasses to rub his eyes. He wears them more often than contact lenses lately; I like them, their boyish charm. He's the sort of man who can wear a knitted cardigan and look Beatle-esque. He's handsome, still. But none of this passes my lips. Not now.

"The thing is, Gabby..."

I straighten my back, holding my breath. This is it. We're going to have the talk.

"...I love you."

That wasn't what he was supposed to say. A hot wave of agitation washes over me, as I sense him trying to lure me back in. Maybe if I hadn't been pretending for so long, I could have hung on in there for a while longer. But I can't do it anymore.

I'm going to have to be the one to pull the emergency cord. He's never going to do it.

"Cut the crap, Fred. I saw you with Paige."

He has the cheek to attempt a confused frown. He's not very good at it, never was. When I accused him of sleeping with Daisy, he denied it for a month every night, like a witch on a dunking chair, refusing to drown.

"Don't play games. I saw you with her yesterday at the deli."

My voice trembles and I lower my head so I don't betray how much of a big deal this is to me. "I deserve honesty, if nothing else."

He stands up, knees clicking, and that little noise of aging saddens me. I'm not rejecting him because of what nature's doing to him, but that's exactly what he's doing to me. My body doesn't excite him now, no matter how many miles I clock on the beach (three daily, to his zero). He's not going for women my age, but younger women. It's a flat-out rejection of my years, an embracement of their youth.

Sitting down beside me, he sets his hand loosely on my knee and I stare at his flesh, the bones protruding, the dull metal of his wedding ring.

"Nothing's happened, I swear," he says.

"You swear?" I push his hand away, shifting as far along the sofa from him as I can get. "As if that means anything." I fold my arms tightly. "So, is it just her or have there been others? They always say the wife's the last to know."

"Don't be daft, Gabby. There's no one else. And she doesn't mean anything."

"That makes it worse. The fact that you're willing to throw everything away for some trashy piece of skirt."

I stop short of calling Paige a slut or whore, but even so, I hate the way I feel about her, about myself—the way my insides are shrinking. This is what this does to a person in middle age, or any age, but it's worse now that time and the mirror aren't on my side. I don't want to shrivel up, wither away.

So I do something that a year ago, last week or even four days ago, I wouldn't have been capable of doing.

"I want a divorce."

He stares at me. "What?"

"Oh, don't act surprised!"

"It's not an act. It's real. You want a divorce? Why?" He has the balls to let his mouth fall open, as though stunned.

This agitates me so much I jump to my feet, hands on hips. "Are you playing some kind of game—trying to push me to do this so you don't look bad in front of your parents? Or the kids? Because that's not fair, Fred!" I stamp my foot.

"What?" he says, gazing up at me. "I don't even want a divorce, Gabby! This is all you!"

"Exactly!" I yell. "You're pushing me to this. Well, that's fine by me. Because I don't care what your parents think anymore. And the kids will stand by me, when they hear about Paige and Daisy and—"

"There is no Paige. I told her it wasn't going to happen. That's what I was doing yesterday."

His calm silences me. I stare at him, the carpet wobbling beneath me. Reaching for the mantelpiece, I hold it, weighing his words. Could it have been a breakup I was witnessing? I hadn't considered that—was too caught up in the fact that it was happening at all.

"But you admit you were having an affair?"

He says nothing, looks away, lips pursed.

I shake my head. "If you think I'm going to stand by while you run around chasing girls, then you're deluded. That's not happening, Fred. I'm worth more than that and I won't stand for it, not after everything that happened with—"

I close my jaw with a snap of my teeth; I didn't mean to say that.

It's his way out, his alibi, and he knows it. He looks at me slyly, as though a light has come on. Standing up, he almost smiles. I take a step backward, bumping into the mantelpiece. "This is about your mom," he says.

"It has nothing to do with her. I want a divorce, plain and simple."

He rocks on his feet, hands in pockets, more sure of himself now. He's on safe territory. I should never have mentioned my mother.

"I'll move out to the spare room tonight then, if that's what you want..." He trails off, fixing his eyes on me and I know what he's saying: that he's going to let me have what I'm asking for. And he'll let everyone know that I asked for it too.

"It is, yes." I'm gripping the mantelpiece as though it's the only thing propping me up. The other day, I was on my way to work when the pavement turned upside down. I had to sit down on the curb, wait until it passed. Since then, I've been mistrustful of the ground beneath me, wondering when it's going to flip.

Vertigo, hot flashes, palpitations, headaches, yet somehow I'm still running every day, working full-time, managing a team of people.

I mustn't let him shrink me. I still matter.

I can't believe I'm even having to tell myself that.

"Have you thought this through?" he asks.

"Of course."

"Really?" He hesitates, the long pause making my mind whirl. When he finally speaks, it's so soft I think I'm imagining it. "What about the house, Gabby?"

I look up at him, biting my lip to stop it from quivering. "What about it?"

"Well, you don't think I'm going to just walk away and let you have it, do you?"

I study his face for a sign of misinterpretation—a playful smile. Yet, his face is blank, aside from a firmness, a microaggression around his mouth that I've never seen before. "But..." I begin.

"But what?"

"I..." It's like I've been muted. How is this happening? I said I wasn't going to shrink and now I can't even speak. Instead, my past flashes in front of me, reflected in the bright lights of his spectacles as we stand underneath the fancy chandelier that we chose together when we first moved in.

All those times I stood in this same spot, wondering whether to go to bed or wait up for him, wondering what I'd done wrong. All the mistrust and paranoia, wondering whether he really was playing golf or working late. All the times he swore undying love and loyalty.

"I want a divorce as soon as possible," I say, walking from the room, closing the door quietly behind me in an effort to maintain some dignity.

As I climb the stairs, he pulls open the door, shouting up at me. "You're going to lose the house, Gabby!"

In the bedroom, I pace the carpet, contemplating tipping his wardrobe onto the lawn or, better still, into the pool. But I have to be cleverer, less predictable than that.

Getting into bed, I draw my knees to my chest, going through everything in my mind until it's a carousel of thoughts, fears. Things have shifted a gear, becoming sharper, bare facts floating to the surface.

Len and Monique will take his side. Nothing I say will change that.

Will and Alice… They're my everything. All I can do is try to protect them and consider their needs as best I can. There are no guarantees.

Closing my eyes, I feel sick, his voice bumping around my head. *You're going to lose the house, Gabby.*

I can't lose it.

I can't.

10

I leave the house for my run at seven o'clock, the same time as I always do. Nothing has changed. At least, that's what I want him to think. I jolt down the footpath that leads from the top of the cliff to the beach. If I turned and ran uphill, I'd meet Len and Monique's road. It's like a vein, connecting us to each other and ultimately to the sea. I'm so familiar with the overhanging buddleias, ankle-snapping nettles, and sandy borders that I could run it in my dreams, often do.

This morning, there's a breeze billowing up through the lane like a wind tunnel. I always run with my hair in a ponytail so it doesn't bother me, and I listen to music so I don't have to hear my footsteps. I've run for all my adult life, since eighteen. Back then it was for a different reason. I ran in the primal sense, because I was scared. But now it's a part of me, like cleaning my teeth.

As I reach the beach, I slow down as I hit the deep fluffy sand, making my way to the firm shoreline. I'm running toward the early sunshine, which helps because on the way back when its rays are stronger, it will be at my back.

Through my music, the sea crashes, hisses, a friend by my side and an enemy. I will always have this complex relationship with it, the same as I have with Fred. I'll always love him as the father of my children, hate him as my husband.

Sometimes, I see interesting or sad things—shells, dead fish—but I try not to stop for anything or anyone. Not even the runner who's coming toward me now. We normally meet at this spot, near Rumors, but because we're both wearing headphones it's never awkward, even though I find him very attractive.

He's older than me, with dark features. He could be from anywhere, but I always think Italian. I know only two other things about him: he's a routine person, like me, and doesn't get red-faced from running anymore, like me.

In my fantasies (because I have them too, Fred, only they feature age-appropriate people) we stop and chat, and he asks where I live and I point up to the house just poking out behind the trees and he says maybe he could come back for coffee. I used to cut the dream there, out of loyalty.

"Morning," he calls to me, as he runs past.

"Morning," I reply, continuing along my way.

As I draw parallel with Rumors, I turn my head, imagining Ellis standing there in her golden dress, strap dangling down. And then I blink and she's gone and there's just a pigeon perching on the stacked deckchairs.

She's no use to me now. The honey trap was only helpful if I wanted to protect my family's good opinion of me, but everything changed the moment I blurted out about wanting a divorce.

It doesn't matter who cheats, legally speaking; I've checked. There's no wrong party, aside from in extreme circumstances, such as financial negligence, stabbings; things that are unlikely to happen to me in Shelby town. As it currently stands, if I file for divorce, he'll get half the house. Which is why I'm going to wait, mull it over some more.

Continuing along the beach, I pass Lloyd's restaurant, thinking of Jam; and then past the eco center, keeping my eyes fixed on the white rocks at the end of the headline, the sun bouncing off spectacularly onto the sea.

Our house came along at just the right moment, even though we weren't looking to move and were happy living the simple life.

It didn't feel like a blessing at first. It felt painful, complicated. I don't think there's a worse gift than one that comes because of death.

As I pass the lifeguard station, I feel momentarily uplifted. This part of the run always goes quickly. There are less people along this stretch of sand, save a few beachgoers in the dunes. My running becomes fluid, startling sandpipers and kittiwakes. Out to sea, cormorants dive-bomb the waves, and seals bob up and down. I settle into my thoughts, the rhythm of my steps.

I knew the property very well, as it happened. No. 23, Ocean View Road, cherry blossom trees lining the pavements. Burnt orange bricks and tiles, Narnia lampposts.

Fred wanted to install a swimming pool—make the place our own. Will was twelve, Alice ten. Before I knew it, the kids had taken over: a rope swing in the trees, flippers by the pool. It felt like no one else but us had ever set foot in the place.

At the end of the beach, I touch the slippery rock before turning, heading back, the sunshine warming my shoulders.

The house changed us, or Fred. I did all I could not to let that happen—took legal advice and had the house put in both our names. I didn't want him to feel displaced, emasculated; I was already earning more than him as it was.

But he cheated within six months of our moving in. It's possible that it would have happened with or without the house. For all I know, he might have been cheating while we were at the old place. That's possible, but I liked to think I'd have known.

I knew he was having an affair—knew one day at dinner, while we were all chatting about our days and he kept his eyes fixed on his plate, didn't join in. Yet, I didn't acknowledge it, not even to myself.

It took several months for the situation to come to a head, and that was only because she called me.

I was about to serve dinner, when the landline rang and I answered it, thinking it would be Monique, and instead a young voice said, *Hello, is that Gabby?* She told me she was sleeping with Fred and thought I should know.

Still, even after that, he wouldn't confess. It took many arguments for that to happen.

Running up the pathway to home, I enter the side gate into our garden, dropping the metal catch into place. I pull off my headphones, gazing at the garden, a butterfly resting on the birdbath. And then there's a whirring sound behind me as the electric gates open and I realize that Fred's in the garage. He's going into work earlier than usual, breaking with routine again.

I can't help but turn to look as he reverses the car, offering him a sad smile. Yet, to my astonishment, he doesn't even glance my way.

Inside the house, on the hallway table, there's an ominous-looking note, a paperweight trapping it.

We've both been unhappy for a long time.

This is my lawyer, as suggested by Mom and Dad: DJ Crawley & Associates.

Please let me know if you're happy to apply jointly.

I don't know what to be most shocked about—that he's being proactive, has already got a lawyer, or has told his parents what's happening.

So that explains Monique's invitation. She's trying to mend our marriage. Or keep our divorce friendly.

My phone's ringing… Alice.

I'm out of breath, not just from my run, but from the enormity of this moment: the dissolution of my marriage. I answer the call, still clutching the piece of paper.

"Mom?"

My heart melts, just hearing her voice. "Alice, how are you?"

"What's wrong?" she says. "You sound—"

"Nothing." I flap the paper to my face. "Just been for a run."

"Oh. Sorry… I wanted to catch you before my nine o'clock."

Her nine o'clock. So grown up.

"That's okay. You can call me anytime. So, how is it? Everything all right?"

The line crackles as she exhales. "It's amazing, Mom. I love it."

I well up, flapping the paper harder. "That's brilliant. I'm so pleased for you. Is there anything you need? I can—"

"I'm fine, Mom. I just wanted to ask if you'd like to speak on Sunday?"

"Yes." I nod. "Sounds great."

"Okay. I'll text you a time." And then she's gone.

I'm back there, on the cliff edge, struggling to wake up because I don't want to witness this again. My legs are weighted, entangled in gorse. It's too dark to see how close to the edge I am, but the man is there once more. I'm screaming at him to stand back, but he can't hear me and it's going to happen anyway. He's going to fall and there's nothing I can do about it.

The whole cliff is starting to slide, the earth turning to liquid under my feet and everything is tilting, propelling forward. I can't stop myself from being dragged toward him. And then, just as he's about to fall, he turns and grabs my arm and I see that it's Fred.

★★★

Sitting up with a gasp, my head rushes, stars appearing in my eyes. I try to get my bearings, before realizing it was that nightmare again and I'm safe in bed.

I reach for the bedside lamp, flicking it on, taking in the soothing details of my room. The light's only been on for a few seconds when my phone pings the arrival of a message.

It's two o'clock in the morning. Who would be contacting me at this time of night?

It's from a withheld number. I read it, unable to see much without my glasses. Grabbing them from the nightstand, I read it again.

Don't worry. Your secret's safe with me.

I stare at the screen, my heart racing. What secret? What does she mean?

This has to be from Ellis. Who else could it be? Without thinking, I press the button to connect the call, but it immediately disconnects. Has she blocked me?

Why would she do that?

Turning out the light, I try to sleep but it's impossible, fear pinning me in place. In the dark, her words dance, taunting me.

I don't know what I'm supposed to say or do, if I can't contact her. There's a part of this that is deeply disturbing. And I realize then what it is: the message arrived as soon as my bedroom light came on.

She's watching me.

11

It's a steep incline to my in-laws' and the hottest of days. I'm wobbling along in heels, carrying a bouquet of lilies and every so often I glance back over my shoulder, scared we're being followed. Since Ellis's message three days ago, I've been checking my phone incessantly, looking all around me whenever I leave the house, sleeping fitfully.

I didn't expect a romantic anniversary stroll, but we're going way too fast, Fred several strides ahead of me, carrying a Tupperware tub of salad, which will be well shaken by now. And then a cat jumps onto the wall beside me and I give such a start, gasping, that I almost drop the flowers.

I rest a moment, catching my breath. "Wait, please," I say, tugging my dress straight. I shouldn't have worn black, the sun's rays soaking into it; nor high heels, but I wanted to feel smart, in control.

He stops, but doesn't look at me. "What?" Impatience in his voice as though I'm a real drag.

"Are you sure this is the right thing to do—go to your parents'?"

"You said you were fine with it," he replies.

"Well, that was before you left me a note about divorce lawyers."

"I thought that's what you wanted, Gabby," he says, gazing up at the sky, bored.

"It is. But isn't it all a bit sudden?"

"Again, that's what you said you wanted. In fact, I think your exact words were 'as soon as possible.' I'm just following orders, like I've always done."

I feel my cheeks burn. "You call cheating on me following orders?" I shake the lilies slightly at him, pollen spilling. They signify purity and innocence, which is why they're popular at weddings, so the florist told me. The irony wasn't wasted on me.

He sighs, glancing at his watch. "I'm not arguing with you. We're late."

"I'm sure your mom can spare us a few minutes." I shift my weight, my shoes pinching my toes. There's a dusting of pollen on my sleeve, which I try to rub off, only making it worse. I don't know why I agreed to come today. I don't know what Monique's intending and should have established that first.

But I'm used to going with the flow, accommodating everyone else's needs. Which is why trying to change direction is going to be so difficult for me now.

"So they know everything?" I ask, trying not to make my voice small, but it happens anyway.

He turns to look at me then, worried I'll start crying. "Not really."

"But your note? You said—"

"I had coffee with Mom yesterday. You sounded determined, so I wanted advice." His face takes on a pinched look, as though he's the victim here.

"I see."

He didn't waste any time getting them on board then.

"They won't take sides," he says. "Which is why Mom still wants to do this lunch—to keep things as civil as possible."

"You think sausage rolls are going to do that?"

"Don't be a child." He turns away, starts walking again.

"I'm not going in there," I call after him. "Not until you tell me exactly what's going on."

"Nothing's going on, Gabby," he says, turning round, his nose creasing in irritation. Some people might have missed it, but I don't—know every line on his face, and its purpose. "You won't listen to reason. You're paranoid about me cheating because you never forgave me for before. Even though…"

"Even though what?"

He hesitates, looking down at his feet. Brown leather sneakers, the sort that could pass for shoes. All the graphic designers wear them at Pixel8D. He's part of a trendy set of middle-agers who dress like twenty-year-olds. How did I not notice this before, or realize what it meant?

"Well, Mom thought you were…distracted at the time, depressed."

"She knows about Daisy?" My mouth falls open, as something else occurs. "Wait, did she know about it back then?"

"Yes."

"But she never said anything." I set the flowers down on the wall, humiliation drying my mouth, the start of a headache pulsing my temples. "Why didn't she say something? I could have used the support."

He smiles ever so faintly. "I guess because I'm her son."

Whereas you have no one, Gabby.

This was what Monique meant the other day about me not having a sense of belonging. She didn't really mean that though; she meant family.

"So she blamed me?"

He shakes his head as though he is wise and I am not. "That's not what I'm saying."

"Then what are you saying?"

"I'm not getting into this now. It's rude. My parents have—"

"I'm not setting one foot inside that house unless you tell me."

He turns on his heel, waving the Tupperware salad that I painstakingly prepared. "Then I guess you're going to have to go home." And then striding up the path, he turns the corner, disappearing from sight.

Sitting down on the wall, I knit my fingers together, wondering what to do. Too much information in one shot, or maybe too little. I feel overwhelmed, undermined, don't know what to focus on.

It takes me ten minutes of watching bees on the overhanging buddleia to decide. I'm not going to skulk off, as though I've done something wrong. I will show my face and if things take a turn for the worse, I'll politely excuse myself and go home to cry where they can't see me.

Their front door is ajar, waiting for me. "Hello?" I call.

My tummy shifts nervously, and then there's a fluttering noise as Monique appears in the doorway, wearing a bouffant crepe skirt. "Quick, come with me," she says, installing me on a kitchen chair, handing me a glass of champagne. "The men are in the garden. We've only got a few minutes… Cheers." And she clinks her glass against mine.

I'm always docile around Monique, do as I'm told. She takes a seat at the table opposite me and I study the hazel ambiguity of her eyes, the beetroot tint to her lips.

"Fred and I had a frank conversation this week," she says. "I know he cheated on you with that girl and I'm very sorry that I never said anything. Because maybe with my support, you wouldn't be where you are now."

I don't know if that's true, whether her input would have changed anything. But I nod. "That's okay."

"No, it isn't, but I didn't want to make things worse. I

thought ignoring it would help it to go away. I knew he loved you, still does."

Behind her, Fred appears in the French windows, making his way toward the pond with Len to feed the fish. I envy him the simplicity of his familial bonds, the unconditionality.

"This latest girl..." she says, reaching for my hand, setting it on mine "...it will all blow over. Wait and see."

She means well and I'm thinking this is a brave talk for her to have with me, but something is troubling me. I glance around the kitchen, at the food platters covered in plastic wrap, the spotless surfaces. So neat and tidy, no one would think she'd been cooking in here all morning. And that's when I realize how off everything is. "What do you mean: latest girl?"

There are so many things wrong with this; she sees it too, meeting my gaze, her pupils shrinking.

There have been others.

She knows about them, as well as this one.

Fred has told her there is someone, meaning that it must be serious.

She squeezes my hand. "He's being very stupid, but he still loves you, Gabby, in his own way."

"It's not about that anymore, Monique. We're past that point. It's not about love now, but..."

"But what?" she says, examining my face, trying to read it before I speak.

I inhale, squeezing the stem of my glass. "Divorcing as amicably as possible, to protect the kids."

"So it's true, then. You want a divorce."

"Yes." I badly want a gulp of champagne too, but daren't move. She's watching me so closely.

"And there's no hope of reconciliation?"

"I'm afraid not."

Her shoulders sag and she recoils into herself. I've never seen her do that, but then I don't think I've ever crushed her before.

Several moments of silence pass. I watch Fred and Len outside, tossing food flakes on the pond.

"Listen, this isn't going to change anything between you and me," she says. "I love Fred, that goes without saying, but I love you like a daughter and I will not lose you over this." Her eyes brim with tears and then she blinks rapidly, jumping up, going to the oven as though the timer just went.

I don't know what to say. I don't want to lose her either. But if it's a choice between our relationship or my personal well-being, then I choose the latter—have to.

"I'll do everything I can to keep things the same between us, Monique. But you know it's going to be difficult. Fred's your own flesh and blood, and—"

"He's a cheating dickwad who can't keep his tackle zipped up," she says, slamming a hot baking tray onto the counter.

I would laugh, but it's not funny.

Outside, the men are strolling toward the house, lost in conversation. "This new girl…" I say hurriedly.

"She's not new," Monique replies, forking chipolatas out of the pan. "I said latest. This one's been around for some time."

"Really?" I frown fearfully. "He said that?"

"In so many words." She sets the pan into the sink, runs the tap. "It was more of a hint than anything else."

"So what made you think it would blow over?"

Sitting back down, she cocks her head ruefully. "Wishful thinking?"

We have about one minute until they're here. They must have stopped on the patio, looking at Len's clematis. "Have there been many others?" I ask.

She nods, sipping champagne, shuddering as though it's sour. "Perhaps."

"Many times?"

"Possibly, yes." A mother's way of saying dozens.

"And this latest one…is she called Paige?"

"Paige? I'm not sure," she whispers, as the door handle goes. And then they're with us and Len is kissing me hello as though I'm the one person in the world he's happiest to see. And then Monique is smoothing Fred's shirt, tugging it straight, and I realize in that one tiny action that she's going to stand by him no matter what. The ties between us will be cut the moment he tells her to do so.

This is what I didn't want to happen, this orphaning for a second time in my life. This was what I would have done anything to prevent, but it's been taken from my hands.

As the three of them launch into a conversation about the neighbors, I have the strange feeling that I'm already a shadow—not in colored pen like them, but a pencil sketch who has already been erased.

Excusing myself, I slip through to the bathroom, standing there breathlessly as though the walls are about to narrow and squash me. This is all starting to feel very wrong. I only made up my mind last week to end our marriage, only just admitted it to myself. Why the sudden rush? It was supposed to be a slow operation, under my control, my instigation. He doesn't get to choose what happens when. And yet that's exactly what it feels as though he's doing.

On my way back down the hallway, my phone pings a message and I know without looking that it's from her. Returning to the bathroom, I close the door behind me, reading the text, holding my breath.

They don't deserve you. Don't waste your precious time.

I look all around me, even though I'm in this tiny room with frosted windows. She can't possibly know I'm here? Did she follow me earlier?

Trying to think straight, my headache thickening, I ring

her. But again, the line disconnects. I chew my thumbnail, my heart racing. Why does everything about her feel like a threat?

A sudden laugh from Monique makes me give a start. Turning to the mirror, I dab concealer under my eyes, trying to mask my insomnia, and then I return to the kitchen, my heels snagging on the carpet, reminding me of the gorse in my nightmares.

I wish I'd never met her. What have I got myself into?

"Oh, there you are!" Monique says, topping up my glass.

Picking up my champagne, I sip it, swallowing fear with the bubbles, thinking about the message hiding in my bag.

My precious time…

Is she saying it's running out?

12

9 months earlier

"Have Yourself a Merry Little Christmas" was playing, the Judy Garland version. One of the few songs that made her cry, she changed tables so that she couldn't hear the music as clearly. It reminded her of things she didn't want to be thinking about—people who didn't have any right being in her head tonight of all nights.

Outside, it was starting to snow, fat flakes that would go to waste because the pavements were too wet. She checked her watch again, a knockoff that left a faint rash on her arm, but no one would notice.

He would be here any minute now. At least, he'd better be. She couldn't afford any more drinks at this price and the barman kept looking over at her empty glass.

It was a sad place to be on the last Tuesday before Christmas, or any day, but this time of year made it sadder. She gazed at the tinsel fluttering above the door, the plastic Christmas tree with uneven baubles, fairy lights dragging on the floor. She hated it when people couldn't be bothered to do things properly.

The barman was looking at her again, so she pretended to

be drinking, prodding the ice with her straw. When he turned away to serve a customer, she relaxed, subtly slipping a finger between her foot and heel to scratch an itch. One thing she had learned was that these men didn't want any fidgeting, cellulite, lipstick on teeth, any kind of sass.

The men who came here—married, too lazy to remove their wedding bands, even in a singles' bar—were a type. They checked women out, but balked at the sight of a tampon box. They thought women shouldn't play men's sports—asked for the TV channel to be changed if it was on—but swiveled to watch a girl making a shot at the pool table. They had so much in common with each other it was like a club. For letches.

Most of the girls in the bar knew the rules and also fitted a type: gold diggers in cheap skin-tight outfits, escorts, plus a couple of older women who were legitimate singles and couldn't be more out of place. They wouldn't be setting foot in here again, only fell for the neon sign the once, thinking it actually was a nice place to meet a divorcee in a turtleneck.

There were no turtlenecks. The men were in designer leisurewear. Some of them talked to each other about yachts, golf, otherwise there was a stillness in the air, a sense of waiting.

She had sat here for weeks, keeping a low profile, observing the routine. The girls knew when and how to strike, timing it to perfection. They made their move, the men glancing appraisingly at them before pulling out a credit card or a spare barstool—something to lock them down. Like putting a rein over the head of a horse, fixing it to a post. The men were in charge and they never moved for sex. It always came to them.

"So have yourself a Merry Little Christmas now..." As the song ended, there was a blast of cold air and she looked up just as he entered the bar in the cool pause between music, their eyes catching.

He tore himself away, unwinding a scarf—one she hadn't seen him wear before—and made his way forward, stamping snow from his shoes, ignoring her. She had guessed he would do this. No one ever moved fast around here.

As he approached the bar, she willed him to look back at her, but he didn't. Opening her bag, she checked the contents, playing for time, hoping the barman wouldn't come over and ask if she wanted another drink. Lip gloss. Phone. Condoms. Blade.

If the stupid barman left her alone, she could stall awhile longer. She watched the TV, a cage fight going on silently. Then she watched him again as he took off his jacket, placing it on the stool beside him, drumming his hands on the bar as he ordered his drink.

And then he turned as though pretending to look out at the snow, and glanced at her. She didn't let on that she had noticed, continued to watch TV. He turned back around, thinking he'd got away with it.

Half an hour was the sweet spot. Any longer than that and he would think she wasn't interested; any less and she'd seem too easy. These men didn't like their women slutty, or for anyone to think that's what they liked, even though everything about this setup said otherwise.

She pretended to suck her straw again, the ice almost melted, keeping her eyes on his back. She had thought a lot about how to approach him, trying to work out whether he'd be turned on by a flash of no panties as she crossed her legs, or whether he would want conversation, connection.

She was almost certain that he'd want connection and her panties on, at first. He was unsure of himself—the way he hunched his shoulders, tried to start a conversation with the waiting staff. Needy, looking for affirmation.

He didn't look round at her again, which was disappointing, but not the end of the world. Maybe he was drunk already, had forgotten her. She would remind him.

At ten o'clock, she stood up slowly, walking toward him,

heads turning to look at her. "Excuse me," she said, "is this seat free?"

He tried not to look stunned, but was blushing. "Yes. It is."

And there it was: the hand. Pulling the barstool back for her. The rein around her neck.

She smiled, sat down, smoothing her dress as though proud of it. In fact, it was a piece of crap from the charity shop, a velvet slip with spaghetti straps, two sizes up so it wouldn't cling. She had bought a new nude lip gloss too. Something that seemed accidentally sexual. The last thing she wanted to do was look like a whore.

Next came the wallet. "Can I buy you a drink?"

She hesitated, pursing her lips, weighing up whether to accept. Then a glance over her shoulder, as though there were some place else she should be, someone else who wanted her.

It just so happened that this was the key that unlocked him. He glanced that way too, frowning. Less than ten seconds and he was all hers. She congratulated herself silently. "Okay, then," she said, loosening her shoulders gratefully.

He didn't seem to be able to believe his luck. He feasted his eyes on her, reluctantly turning away to order the drinks. She always went for a Flirtini, ever since she read that it wasn't as innocent as it looked—was way stronger. And besides, sucking that cherry really turned them on.

"What's your name?" he said, turning to look at her again as the barman begrudgingly fixed her drink.

She cast her eyes down, as though pleased he'd asked. "Ellis."

"That's unusual," he said. Beside him on the bar, curled into his scarf, were trapped snowflakes, not yet melted. She really wanted to touch them, set them free.

"And what's yours?" she asked.

He hesitated. "Nigel."

Oh, wow. Awful choice. She almost felt bad for him. Did she look like someone who would pick up a Nigel?

The barman set the Flirtini down, slopping some of the orange-tinted liquid on the napkin, and there was no cherry either. No surprise. Men fell into two categories when faced with the prospect of her in a short dress. Some killed themselves to be nice, making fools of themselves; others treated her like dead meat, a waste of space.

"Ellis…cheers," he said. "Happy Christmas."

She forced a smile. *Happy Christmas? For real?*

As they clinked glasses, he looked at her breasts, then her legs. He didn't try to disguise his excitement, even licked his lips. He didn't totally repulse her though. She eyed the golden curls that were grainy with gray, the biceps trying to bulge and failing. He was wearing a pink polo shirt that she'd seen him in before, and gray chinos—pastels that reminded her of chalk. It suited him. Chalk was nothing but dust.

"So…" he said, turning to face her fully. "Tell me something about you that would surprise me."

She sipped her cocktail, licking sugar from her top lip. "I could kill you with one flick of my hand."

He looked shocked and then laughed, slapping his knee. "Good one!"

Idiots. She always gave them the chance to see who she really was. And they never took it.

Discreetly, she checked her watch. It was going to be a long night. Just stick to the plan and get it over with.

13

For the first time in Rumors, instead of saying, "I'll have what she's having," I look at the cocktail menu, choosing a piña colada in the hope that it's milder than the rest. I want to stay in control, alert. Glancing about me, I position myself so I can see the door in the mirror behind the bar—can watch who's coming and going.

"I'll have what she's having," Jam says, stealing my line, smiling at the barman, then turning to me. "I'm glad you decided to keep that on." She tugs at the fabric of my black dress, letting it snap back into place on my hip. "You look fantastic."

"Well, it is my anniversary," I say, pulling a stool out at the bar, glad to rest my aching feet. "But I don't feel fantastic. I'm feeling pretty ropy." I glance at her, hoping she'll press me for details because I'm longing to tell her about Ellis and the messages and the sense of being followed. Yet, at the same time, I'm scared to say anything.

Jam doesn't pick up on it—is preoccupied with the yachties who are sitting at our special table. After a long hard stare, she decides to let them be, turning her back to them. It's busy and hot in here tonight behind the plastic window sheets, one of those evenings when the rain smells musty on the pavements.

"So how did it go with the in-laws?" She rests her arm on the bar, charm bracelet gleaming.

"Awful." I watch the barman moving the cocktail shaker like maracas in time to the music. "I give them one week before they hate me."

She touches my arm. "And then the kids will come for you."

"Yep." It was a joke, but I swallow awkwardly, looking away.

"It's going to be rough. You know that." She leans in, her hair brushing mine. "But you've got me, and…well…"

I pull back from her to examine her face. "And what?"

She shrugs a shoulder. "I think you should tell the kids about the cheating sooner rather than later."

"No, I can't do that. It'll derail Alice. She's only just got there."

"I understand what you're saying, Gabs, but you can't protect them forever. They need to know who he really is and what he's put you through." She runs her finger along the bar as though checking for dust. "Promise me you won't wait too long."

"Promise," I say, as the drinks are set before us in frosty glasses, a wedge of pineapple on the rim.

Jam draws her glass toward her. "Whatever happens, don't take all the blame. I hate how women are blamed for everything."

"Tell me about it." I rotate my cocktail slowly on the bar, watching the beads of moisture running down the outside of the glass.

"You should hear them at work. Whenever I'm doing a showing and doing all the spiel about family and what each room might be nice for, blah-blah, I always wait for it. And then…bam! There it is!" She slams her hand onto the bar. "The diatribe about the psycho bitch who's controlling everyone, ruining their lives. The monster-in-law, sister-in-law, evil ex-wife." She slurps her cocktail through the straw. "'Course, some of them are more subtle about it—little digs, snide comments, but it's always there, in every family, every time. You'd think all the men were perfect. And shit, it drives me crazy."

She breaks off, straightening her batwing top, plucking up the cocktail menu to fan herself, and then laughs. "Wow, was that me? Did I say all that?"

I laugh too, feeling a rush of gratitude, and I reach for her hand. "Thanks for being here for me, Jam. I'd be in a coma or something if it weren't for you."

She smiles. "Right back at ya, sister. You'd do the same for me."

"Absolutely." And we clink glasses, some of mine slopping onto my dress, right where the lily pollen was. "Look… I finally got rid of that stain!"

We're both laughing when my phone lights up and I remember that I mustn't let my guard down. My stomach is in knots as I read the message, but it's only Will asking me about diary dates.

Relief fills me and I position myself again so I can watch the entrance, giving a start as the door swings open, only to relax again on seeing it's not her.

This time, Jam notices that something's wrong. "You okay?"

I pick up my drink. "Yep."

"It's just that you're all jumpy, like you're expecting someone. You got something going on that I don't know about?" She nudges me.

"No, there's nothing going on."

"Then stop twitching. You're freaking me out."

"Sorry."

I don't look again, not until Jam's in the bathroom and then I turn to face the room properly, pretending to play with my phone, looking up systematically to take in every face. No one's outside; the rain is dripping down the plastic sheets, forming puddles on the decking.

She definitely isn't here.

I'm about to order another round of drinks when there's a voice close to me and I look up to see the man from the beach, the runner. The one I find attractive.

"Hey," he says, flicking his finger between us, from his chest to my body, stopping short of touching me, "do we know each other?" His eyes crinkle as he smiles.

I smile back at him, even though he's out of my league. He's too handsome to be interested in me. We're about the same age by my reckoning. Has he not seen those young GDs over there?

I hate myself for these thoughts, and in my best dress too.

"I think we know each other from the beach, from running," I say, fixing my eye on the barman to get his attention. I'm not interested in this guy, not close up, not in real life. He's a fantasy, an ex-Italian professional footballer, or chef. I don't need to make him real. "Two piña coladas, please."

Glancing at the bathroom, I wish Jam would hurry up. It's so stuffy in here. I lift my hair away from the back of my neck, flapping it to cool myself down.

"What's your name?" he says, resting his arm on the bar, leaning in to me in a way that I don't love. There's a whiff of something on his breath. Garlic. I wish I'd never spoken to him.

"Hey, hun," Jam says, clamping her hands on my shoulders. "Everything all right?"

I flash her a look. In response, she uses her body artfully to slip between him and me. "Are the drinks on their way?"

"Yes." I glance past her at him. He's none too pleased, taps her on the shoulder.

"Excuse me. That was very rude. We were having a conversation."

"I'm so-rry," she replies, holding her hands to her chest as though astonished. "I didn't even see you there. I'm myopic."

"That means you can't see long distance. I'm an ophthalmologist. Or an eye surgeon, to you."

She stares at me for a moment, her eyes widening. And then spins on her stool to face him. "Oh, to me? You think I can't handle big words?" She slides off her seat, standing at her full height. "What I can't handle—" she waggles her finger at him "—is small little men."

I never noticed his height. He'd seemed much taller when jogging.

"You ought to see someone about that anger problem," he says, turning away.

"Or we could just take it outside now," she yells after him.

I watch as he disappears into the crowd and all I can think is: *Great, now I'm going to have to change my running route.*

"What a slimeball," she says, wiping her hands on her jeans.

"Definitely," I reply, stirring my drink.

"What?" She narrows her eyes at me. "Too much?"

"No. I'm glad. Thanks."

"Then, what?"

I blink slowly, clasping my hands together. "It just felt like I didn't know what to say to him, how to handle it myself... It's as though I'm shrinking."

"Hey? What do you mean?"

"It's since this whole thing started with Fred. I feel as though I'm disappearing."

She curls her lip. "Then don't! Stop it! You can handle it! You're not going to shrivel up and die because of this. You're going to come out stronger. Wait and see."

"Okay."

"Okay? That's all you've got?" She picks up her glass. "Here's to coming out stronger."

We clink glasses again. "To coming out stronger."

It feels hollow though, despite her best efforts, despite mine too. Because the truth is that I needed her to fight my battles for me tonight, just like I wanted Ellis to do. If that weren't so, I wouldn't have got involved with her in the first place. Yet, I wanted to enlist someone young and empowered to help extricate me from my mess, probably because Fred's using youth as a weapon too, through his string of mistresses.

Ellis offered me a way out and I took it, or thought I had. Only somehow it was lost in translation. And now I have the nasty feeling that it's my happiness that's on the line, my life in jeopardy.

Four piña coladas later, I'm cursing myself for drinking more than I meant to, fiddling with my key in the lock, when there's a snap of a twig behind me. I twist around dizzyingly fast, holding my hand against the wall for balance, peering in the direction of the noise. A bat is skimming across the lawn, rising above the trees. Otherwise, everything is still.

I know what I heard though. Going inside, I lock the door, crouching to draw the bolt at the bottom and then dragging a chair to bolt the top one too.

I'm kicking off my heels, rubbing my sore toes, when my phone pings. I can read the message without my glasses because it's in capitals and only two words.

WELCOME HOME

The words merge, the longer I stare at them. She must be out there, watching my every move. Panic squeezes my chest. What do I do?

Go back out and try to find her—confront her? Yet, that feels like a bad idea. She could be unstable, dangerous. In fact, I'm sure she is. I remember that intense look in her eyes, the assassin-like grip.

I'm scared of her, of what she's capable of.

The house is so quiet. Fred didn't leave a light on upstairs for me. Maybe he's not even here. That doesn't help—the idea that I'm all alone and have no clue where my husband is, who he's with.

Whatever I'm going to do, I'm not going to solve it tonight with a head full of cocktails. As I climb the stairs, I text Jam, hoping I'm not going to regret this in the morning.

I need to talk to you xox

14

"Here, eat these." There's a rustle of paper as Jam reaches into her dinky knapsack and pulls out a bag, setting it on my lap.

I peer inside, although I can already smell the sugar. Six doughnuts. "Are you kidding me?"

"Just do it," she says, reaching for one, taking a bite, raspberry dripping onto her jeans. "Woops."

I smile, my skin tight. It's colder today, the first time it's felt like autumn. I dug out my puffy jacket from Will's wardrobe, running in and out of his room before I could get sad. Behind us, distant church bells ring, calling the congregation. I'm half-tempted to join them. I have a lot to pray about.

"So what did you want to tell me?"

I open my mouth, hesitating. "I…don't know where to begin," I say, doughnut on my lap, untouched.

"Just pick a place, any place. I'm a fast learner."

She is, but I don't want to blurt this out. For a start, I haven't made sense of it myself. But, if I'm really honest, I'm scared of my part in it. Because I don't know what that is.

Right on cue, a rollerblader hurtles down the lane beside

us, swooping past our bench, before wheeling along the promenade, her hair flailing. "Jeez, she scared me!" I say, clutching my heart.

Jam glances at me. "What's got into you? Come on—eat your doughnut. Sugar's good for nerves."

I'm not sure that that's a fact. But I nibble it, licking sugar from my lips. "It'll sound crazy."

"Try me," Jam says, reaching into a paper bag, pulling out two Styrofoam cups, handing one to me.

I pry off the lid, puckering my lips to drink the foamy coffee. "I don't know what I'd do without you."

"Yeah, you do."

We don't speak for a while, Jam's hand on my knee, sugar all over the bench. "Okay, time's up. You have to tell me now or I'm leaving."

I turn to look at her, wondering how much I can say. I can trust her with my life. It's just that I don't trust myself—what I said or did that night that caused Ellis to play some kind of sick game.

She sighs heavily. "Look, if it's Fred, then bring it on. Let him do his worst."

"You mean, risk losing the house?"

She nods, running her tongue over the front of her teeth. "It's just a house. It didn't bring you much luck, when you think about it. It's not worth making yourself ill over."

I give a little sniff, staring out to sea.

It's not just a house though. She knows that.

"Have you thought any more about contacting a lawyer? That one in town's supposed to be good—great at getting a fair deal for women. Gina at work used her and got the dog too."

"Maybe," I reply, pushing my free hand into my pocket to keep warm. "But not yet."

"Because…?" Her eyebrows zigzag in concern. "You're not

backing down, are you? I thought this is what you wanted and—"

"No, it isn't. I wanted to take my time and think about how it would affect Alice and Will, and Monique and—"

"And what, the kitchen sink?" She frowns more deeply, pointing her coffee at me. "This is about you—what you want. Because while it's nice to consider the kids—" she holds her hands out on either side of her "—I don't see them here right now. You're alone, in your marriage alone, and it's about what you alone want. Get it?"

That sounds like a lot of *alone* to me.

"So what's the plan?" she asks, swinging her foot up and down.

"I don't know yet."

"Well, you need to get on that!" She shivers, doing up the zip on her jacket, slipping her arm in mine. "Look, what's going on, hey? Why did you text me last night?"

I gaze at her, at her soft brown eyes. I want to tell her so badly. Pulling up the string of messages on my phone, I hand it to her.

"What am I looking at?" she asks.

"Anonymous texts...threats."

"They don't seem all that threatening to me. Is this why—?"

"I think I'm being followed."

"What?" She hands me back my phone, brushing sugar from her coat. "Who by?"

"Some young woman...I met her after you left Rumors last week. She came up to me, started talking and I don't know if my drinks were spiked or if the Viagras were too strong, but I ended up saying some stuff..."

She gazes at me, eyes large, unblinking. Will used to look like that when I read him adventure stories at bedtime. "What stuff?"

"I don't know, but I think I said I'd be better off if Fred were..." I look out to sea.

"What?"

I can barely say it.

"Dead."

There's a pause and then she laughs, throwing back her head. "So? You don't think I've planned Nate's death before? It's a running joke at work."

"Really?" I say, looking at her doubtfully. "That's pretty twisted."

"No, it's called a sense of humor in a long-term marriage."

"Well, this didn't feel jokey. It felt...dangerous."

Her eyes narrow, smile vanishing. "Why?"

"I'm not sure. I mean, you should have seen her, Jam. She was stunning—said she worked in fitness. But there was obviously something else going on. She offered to be a honey trap because I told her I wanted to keep the house and—"

"Wait." She jumps up, knocking over her empty coffee cup, staring down at me. "You told some little GD your husband's available and your house is worth fighting over? Are you for real?"

I look up at her, her hair glowing in the sunshine, a halo behind her head.

"Next you'll be telling me you said he's a catch and..." She trails off, stares at me. "You didn't, Gabby."

I look at my feet, old sneakers, ruined by sea and sand. "I don't remember."

She sits back down, setting her hand on my knee. "Are you running a dating app that I don't know about? Is this Tinder?"

"No. I don't think so."

"So does she know where you live? Did you give her any personal details?"

I shuffle my feet. "Not sure. But I think she's watching the house."

"So she knows where you live!" She looks at me in amazement. "This could be a scam, Gabby! You need to remember what you told her and fast!"

"You think I don't know that?" I sink my nails into the Styrofoam cup, feeling them catch, leaving spiky marks. "I'm scared, Jam. I don't know what happened that night. I'm missing bits. What if I did something terrible?"

"Like what? You've done nothing wrong. I *know* you, Gabs."

This makes me feel worse—her complete trust in me. Because I'm really not so sure.

"Look," she says, softening her voice, "I think you need to go to the police, show them those texts. They'll be able to trace them. And if she's following you, then—"

"I don't know for certain that it's her. She gave me her phone number when we met and although I deleted it, I went back through my call history and these numbers don't match."

She shakes her head. "That doesn't mean anything. It could be a burner phone—a cheapie that she's using and then she'll throw it away."

"But I don't even know if she's really following me. Everything's been so strange, I'm not sure what I'm imagining and what's real."

She picks up my phone, waves it. "This is real though. You have evidence here."

"But like you said—they might not be threats. Maybe I'm being paranoid." I take the phone, return it to my pocket. "What if I did something that night that she knows about? What if I implicate myself by going to the police?"

She laughs. "Now you're just talking rubbish. The only safe thing to do is report this."

"Well, I guess I'm going to have to take a risk then, Jam, because I'm not doing that."

"And that's your call to make. But don't come crying to me when it all goes tits up." She folds her arms, conversation closed.

We're not arguing. This is what we do. We've always told each other the truth. It's just that lately that's become impossible for me because I don't know what the truth is anymore.

I gaze at the sea, my nose running. I pull a tissue from my winter coat; it smells faintly of mints. I miss the woman who put that tissue there. Her daughter was at home, and her husband wasn't being a rat. Or if he was, she didn't know about it.

"I'm going to lose my home, aren't I?"

"Yeah, probably." She pats my arm. "But it'll be okay. And I didn't really mean that: you can come crying to me if you want."

We stay there for about an hour, talking about everything, nothing. When we're ready to leave, we collect the coffee cartons, sweep sugar from the bench.

As we leave, I try not to look over my shoulder for her, but can't help myself. "That's why you've been jumpy, isn't it?" Jam says. "Because of her."

"Yes."

"Well, that in itself should tell you everything."

I tug her arm for her to stop, gazing into her eyes. "What do you mean?"

She clutches my hand, shaking it as she speaks. "I've known you for thirty years, Gabs. And while you're homely and soft as mashed potatoes, I've never seen you scared of anyone. You're tougher than you think." She starts walking slowly, kicking the sand. "So if this woman's frightening you? Then I say you've got good reason."

We don't speak again, not until we part ways. She hugs me lightly and I know she's worried about me. The thing is I am too.

PART TWO

RUNNING SCARED

15

July 1980

"So everything here is under your command, Daddy?" I asked, looking at the diggers and bulldozers and dump trunks, all frozen mid-action as though under a spell. The piles of mud were like caramel, making me a bit hungry.

"Pretty much." He squeezed my hand. "So, what do you reckon?"

"It's fantastic." I gazed at the sea view, the surrounding hills, the spindly scaffolding protecting the glass-fronted building like a tooth brace. "But where do you go to the washroom?"

He laughed and I giggled, looking up at him to fully take in his face. I loved to make him laugh. "Honestly, the things you think of." He let go of my hand to tussle my hair. "That's what I enjoy about what I do. You bring someone here and they each see something different." He gestured to the view. "When I first saw this spot, I thought this would be a superb location for luxury apartments. And hey presto!" He slapped his hands against his legs.

"That's very clever, Daddy," I said, adjusting my sun visor. I'd just got it from tennis camp, including two sweatbands which I was using constantly, even on overcast days.

"It's about having imagination, seeing the potential in things." He took my hand again. "Someday, when you're ready, I'll teach you everything I know. And then it'll be you in command of everything and not me. Sound good, Batman?"

"Yes," I said, well pleased. Daddy never saw me as different to him and called me Batman because his real name was Robin, which meant I was the hero, not him, which suited me just fine. I was nine years old and already the fastest sprinter at school, of both the boys and the girls, and captain of the baseball and netball teams. I was going to take over the world someday and show everyone how it was done.

As soon as Daddy had shown me.

He was about to give me a tour of the portable cabins and toilets when there was the crunch of tires behind us and I looked over to see a car kicking up a lot of dust. They were going too fast and I was about to suggest that Daddy made them slow down since they were headed right toward the mud, when the car lurched to a halt and the driver got out with the engine still running, the door wide-open.

He was short, shorter than Daddy, with a bald head and clumps of hair on either side of his face that reminded me of a clown, but there was nothing remotely funny about him and he didn't look as though he was laughing either. "You stupid asshole!" he shouted, waving his fist.

Before I knew what was happening, he was lunging at Daddy—pushing him onto the mud, pummeling his face. Blood spurted from Daddy's nose and that's when I started screaming.

"Stop it! Get off him!" I jumped on the man's back, my hands around his neck, kicking his legs.

"Get the hell off me, you little shit!" he yelled.

Daddy's nose was pouring blood, but the man was still trying to punch him. So I did what I had to do and sunk my teeth into his back. There was a second before he reacted and then he stood straight, reaching for my leg with his hammy fist and swinging me round, flinging me onto the floor. "You little—"

"Arghhh!" Daddy charged at him, bowling him over. "Don't you dare touch her!"

Falling onto the mud, the man scrambled to his feet, retreating to his car, bandy-legged. "Stay the hell away from her, you hear me?" he shouted, then reversed with a whinnying noise, dust everywhere, until all was still again.

I gazed at the building site, the toothy machines looking back at me like silent witnesses. My bottom was in wet mud, which was seeping through my jeans. My throat felt dry and bulgy and although I wanted to cry, tears wouldn't come.

Besides me, crumpled, lying in the mud, was my sun visor with its tennis racket logo. There was a clump of my hair caught in the Velcro and I realized the back of my head was hurting.

It was a while before Daddy spoke. He took a bent cigar from his shirt pocket and played with it, turning it in his hands. I noticed they were trembling and I offered to light the cigar for him, but he shook his head.

The sun had gone in. I was getting cold. I tried to put my visor back on, but the plastic shield had split and was sticking out like a splinter. Daddy took it from me, tossed it into the dumpster.

He didn't touch me or speak to me as we went to the car and I started to worry that I'd done something wrong. Maybe that was a business partner of his and I shouldn't have jumped on his back.

Before Daddy started the engine, he got another cigar from the glove compartment and I found his gold Zippo from down between the seats and lit it for him. He never asked me to; I just liked doing it—the noise, the action, the smell.

I watched as he dragged on the end of the cigar and hoped he would blow rings of smoke, like he sometimes did. But he didn't. He wound down the window, turned his head to the side to exhale.

It was warm in the car; the leather seats were hot. I took my sweatbands off because they were muddy too and then Daddy spoke. "I'm sorry." His voice sounded scratchy. He was still bleeding—had blood all down his shirt, messed up in his beard.

"That's okay," I said, wanting to do something to help. "Shall I see if there's water in the trunk? I could wipe your face?"

He did something then that I'd never seen him do before. He cried. Not like I did. When I cried, I always went for it, howling. But he was sniffly, his head bent, pressing his eyes. And it was over in a second. And then he did something stranger—he started to laugh, gazing up at the ceiling, shaking his head and he said something like, *Oh, jeez, what a fool.*

"What must you think of me, eh?" he said, reaching for my hand. It was bloody, but I didn't like to reject him because he looked like he needed a friend. So I sat there and tried to smile, even though I was sad about my visor.

"I'll get you a new one." He patted my leg.

That was the thing about Daddy: he could read my mind.

After a while, we left, making our way along the bumpy track to the main road, our bodies jolting up and down. Daddy even knocked his head on the ceiling and laughed. I was glad he seemed happy again.

But near home, when we got near the crooked hill that I always went down too fast in my roller skates, he stopped the car and turned to look at me with a serious expression that he normally used when I broke something. "You know, Batman, sometimes heroes have secret missions."

I nodded. That was true.

"And even though you want to tell people who you love—people close to you—you can't because it's top secret and could ruin everything."

I fiddled with my sweatbands, unsure what he wanted me to say or do. It was getting hot again. "Could we open the—"

"Listen to me," he said, turning off the engine, staring at me. There was a drop of blood on the end of his nose that was dried, dark. I shuddered. "You can't tell Mommy about this. Not a word, okay?"

I nodded. I wasn't expecting him to say that. Surely, Mommy would want to know about this. The police would probably want to know too.

"Promise me you won't say anything."

I pointed to his nose. "But what about that? Won't she notice?"

He smiled. "Good point… Let's say that it was one of the construction workers. He showed up unexpectedly on site and demanded payment in advance—a cash injection before the end of the month to tide him over. And when I said no, he attacked me. How about that?"

I wasn't sure I could remember all that, wasn't really listening. I was watching a ladybug making its way along my leg and was thinking how much easier it was dealing with insects. They always stayed the same, aside from caterpillars, and you knew what you were getting. But with adults, you thought you were getting one thing and always got another.

And then the ladybug opened its wings and flew over to my dad and before I could do anything, he had squashed it. I don't think he meant to though.

As we turned into our road, I asked him the question I was dying to ask. "Who was that man?"

"No one," he said.

Our driveway had big electric gates. I didn't like them very much because I had to press a code just to get in and out of the house.

"Come on then," he said, putting his arm around me as we

went up the steps to the front door. “And don’t forget to stick to the plan.”

I smiled up at him. I loved him so much. We were best friends, Batman and Robin. I wasn’t going to tell on him. But if Mommy asked me where my visor was, I didn’t know what I was going to say. Because I loved her very much too, even though we weren’t superheroes.

“Okay, here goes,” he said, as he opened the door. “Alice?” he called out. “You home?”

16

I head out later than usual this morning, mostly because I couldn't sleep last night—checking my phone every half hour, imagining it was ringing when it wasn't—but also because I'm hoping to avoid the runner. If I continue along our road to the end, then dip down, I should be able to cut out the section of the beach where I'd have met him, like chopping off a dead tree branch.

As I start to run, I fret that perhaps I should have left at the same time because now he could be anywhere along the route. Then again, he might have set out later too because of me. Impossible to judge. And I'm tying myself in knots trying to.

At some point over the past week, my life changed from autopilot to survival mode. I feel like one of Will's Xbox characters, running, jumping, high on adrenaline. With every corner I turn, every new stretch of road I enter, I look about me, convinced there's a danger I can't see.

What would I do if I came face-to-face with her? She would be stronger, faster than me. I wouldn't stand a chance. Maybe I should start running with pepper spray. But surely nothing would happen to me here, in broad daylight? And yet there are those shocking news stories—assaults in parks, shopping malls…

It's colder again today, fine rain in the air that's sharp on my face. Zipping up my jacket, my mind turns to fretting about Fred. I haven't spoken to him or so much as glimpsed him since Saturday, when we walked home from his parents' in silence.

I turn down the alley that leads to the seafront. I don't like this one—it's dingy, overgrown; I can't always see where I'm putting my feet. I'm only five steps along when I spot a dark shape at the end, blocking the light. It's him. He's come this way to avoid me.

Instantly, I shrink, recoil, considering retreating around the corner, but I can't do that. I've every right to be here, so I force myself to press on, grateful for the distraction of my headphones. And then, as we get nearer to each other, I try to make light of it. It's clear we're going to have to stop because it's too narrow. "Well, this is awkward," I say, laughing, pausing my music.

He doesn't acknowledge me, other than to squeeze past. I think of Fred ignoring me last week when I smiled at him. "No need to be rude," I call after him, as he pounds up the hill.

That stops him. He turns, hands on hips, catching his breath. "Your friend embarrassed me. I was with business associates."

He's so puffed up I want to pop him with my fingernail. "Well, I'm sorry if we made you look less important than you obviously are."

He flicks sweat from his brow and then to my shock puts his middle finger up, before turning away. I stare at his wet back. "You're pathetic!" I shout.

"And you're a wrinkled old hag!" he shouts back. "Much better from a distance!"

His words reach me like a body blow, stealing my breath. I don't want them to—hate myself for allowing it—but I can't stop them. They're wrapping themselves python-like around my heart, embedding there so that for the rest of the day, week, month, year, my life, they can repeat over and over, on days when I'm feeling low.

"Damn it!" I kick the wall, crying in frustration. He's carrying on with his run and his day, just like Fred. They're carrying on and it's me lugging the python around until I'm so small and weighed down I can't get up in the morning.

I have to carry on running—continue what I set out to do. I even set off down the alley a few paces, but I'm shaking and my legs feel stiff. The rain is coming down heavier. Defeated, I walk slowly back up the hill, my heart hammering as though I'm still running.

As I unlock the front door, I notice Fred's leather sneakers are gone from the shoe rack, and Alice's ballet flats are gone and Will's football boots too.

Upstairs, as I undress for the shower, I'm still shaking. Stepping under the spray, I fight the sensation, the contraction in my heart, but it comes anyway and I feel myself becoming that little bit smaller still.

You're a wrinkled old hag. Much better from a distance.

"There you go, Gabby," Claire says, handing me a coffee from her tray of mugs.

"Thanks, Claire." I smile at her as she offers a plate around. It's our monthly meeting. I've got the whiteboard set up—a few things to say; admin, reports. Otherwise, the most exciting thing happening is that we've got triple chocolate chip cookies.

Shaun enters late, taking a seat with a scrape of his chair, drumming his fingers as though bored already. He resents these meetings, where we can't get away from the fact that I'm chairing them. He'll do everything he can to undermine me, so I give him my best smile and ensure he gets extra cookies. Sometimes it helps to do with him exactly what I did with the kids when they were small.

By the end of the meeting, I feel drained from the effort of deflecting him—the way he watches me constantly, hoping I'll trip up.

Back at my desk, I stare at the screen, another headache threatening. So I decide to take an early lunch, craving fresh air, even though it's still raining outside. As I stand up, my vertigo returns, the floor wobbling, the table turning upside down. I know from experience that I'll have to wait for it to go.

When I'm convinced the world's back up the right way, I head out, my mind clouded with thoughts of Shaun.

If I gave him orders, he'd call me a bitch. But when I consider his feelings, I'm weak. It doesn't matter what I do, I'm wrong. The only thing that would make it right would be him being the boss.

I'm halfway along the street, checking all around me, scanning the horizon, when Jam rings. Sheltering from the rain underneath a bakery's canopy, I take the call, inhaling sugar, butter. Even when Jam's not with me, I can smell food that's bad for me.

"Hey you," she says. "What you up to tonight?"

"Nothing. Why?" I look up and down the road, certain that Ellis is here somewhere, watching me.

"Because, well, don't freak, but there's something I need to tell you."

Cars are driving sluggishly along the road, wheels hissing on wet tarmac. I wait for a van to pass before speaking. "Tell me now. I don't want to wait until later."

"You have to, hun. It's not the sort of thing I can say over the phone. And besides, I think Nate should be there."

I frown. "Nate? What's he got to do with it?"

She pauses. "Just come straight from work. Eat at ours. About six?"

I nod.

"Gab?"

"Yes," I reply.

We end the call and I continue along my way, not knowing where I'm going until I'm standing in there, smelling aniseed, coffee. That's all I get in the time allowed because now Paige is tilting her head at me, her nose ring catching the light. "Hey there, what can I getcha?"

I see baklava, hummus, olives and then gold boxes of pralines with red ribbons. This month's special: half price. Guilt chocolates and still Fred sold me short.

I stare at her name tag and imagine telling her who I am and what's she done and how all this has made me feel and how I'm shrinking by the hour and how would she feel if this were her mother because we must be about the same age, and then she chirrups, "Spoiled for choice?"

She seems so young it disarms me. I leave, not knowing who I feel sadder for, her or me, but when a truck thunders by and splashes a puddle up my legs, I decide it's me.

I've no idea where to go for lunch. How am I supposed to make even the most basic decisions, knowing there's something so awful awaiting me tonight that Jam—who has no boundaries—can't tell me over the phone?

17

It's later than six by the time I get to Jam's. I went home first for a shower, a thick sweater, and then to the corner shop for flowers and three bottles of wine. If it's bad news then I want to be warm, numb. I lift the knocker, rapping it twice, stepping back to admire the red Virginia creeper around the door.

When I first met Jam, I assumed she'd live in one of the glassy sea-facing buildings that she sold for a living. But she and Nate live in an old cottage. Last year, she started growing prize roses in their courtyard garden. She never stops surprising me.

Nate answers the door because, judging by the smell of cinnamon wafting from the kitchen, Jam's busy baking. "You're late," he says, kissing me, his stubble scratching my cheek.

"Sorry, but I come bearing gifts." I hold up the shopping bag, bottles clinking.

"That's my girl." He takes the bag and flowers from me, sets them down, waiting for me to unbutton my coat while he stands there, butler-like, arm extended, ready to hang it up.

He may be inert, but it strikes me then that his reluctance to leave the house means he's not trying to get away from his wife. There's a compliment in there, one that's starting to sound pretty good to me.

In the kitchen, Jam already has a bottle of wine on the go, a smudge of flour on her chin. I brush it off, kissing her hello, her sweet perfume reminding me of Alice. Before pulling away, she touches my wrist. "You okay? Any more messages?"

"No." Instinctively, I feel for my phone in my pocket. Every time it rings I jump out of my skin. "Something smells good," I deflect. "What are you making?"

"An appley thing. And Nate's ordered pizza. That all right?"

"Sounds great."

She looks at me cautiously, pouring me a wine, sliding it across the counter. "Do you still think she's following you?"

"Not sure." I don't want to talk about Ellis. I want to know what it is that Jam needs to tell me.

Sensing this, she drums her nails, checks the oven, setting the timer. "We've just got time to talk before we eat."

Nate arrives with the flowers, snipping the stems, arranging the bouquet. Not like a florist, but still…

"From Gabby," he says, setting the vase on the kitchen table. No look-what-I-did expression on his face. No fishing for praise or thanks. Not like Fred. The slightest thing he did for me and I practically had to fall to the ground and kiss his feet.

"They're gorgeous, Gabs. You shouldn't have."

I watch as Nate pours himself a glass of wine, then slips from the room. And he's almost free and clear, when Jam says, "Wait, Nate?" He halts in the doorway, freezing. "Are you joining us?" It doesn't sound like a question, even though it is.

"O…kay…"

I sense from this that it's something bad indeed and that he'd rather be anywhere but here.

"Let's go through to the lounge," she says, gesturing for me to follow her.

The room is dimly lit, the cushions freshly plumped and set

apart, as though prepared for an awkward conversation. "Sit by me, Gabs," Jam says, patting the sofa.

I obey robotically. Nate perches on the edge of an armchair, pushing the footrest away. No relaxation tonight.

"What's this about?" I clear my throat, hoping that whatever they're going to tell me I can handle it.

Jam looks at her husband appealingly. "Nate?"

"Come on." I set my wine down in case I spill. "You're scaring me." I press my damp palms together.

Nate puts his wine down also, mirroring my pressing of palms. I read once that it's calming. Maybe he read that too. "There's no easy way to tell you this, Gabby…"

"Oh, for goodness' sake!" Jam says. "Just say it."

"Okay." He looks at the carpet. "I went to golf yesterday."

"Which is shocking in itself," Jam interrupts, nudging me. "He left the house! But it's not that, Gabby." She turns back to Nate. "Carry on, babes."

He smiles uneasily. "So, I was at the club, enjoying a pint, and I overheard something Tobias Small was saying. The guy's not exactly discreet."

He waits for me to react. I don't know who that is.

"He's a massive gossip."

I nod. "Okay. So…"

He picks up his wine, takes a gulp, keeping it in his hands as though he might need it again. "He was talking loudly and I didn't want to pry, but when he mentioned Fred, I listened up."

Jam shifts along the sofa, closer to me, her shoulder brushing mine.

"And, Gabby, the thing is…" he says. "Apparently Fred's been cheating on you for some time and—"

"Oh," I say, my face flushing.

I already knew this, didn't I? Monique said as much. But the shock is still real, sitting here in my friends' living room.

"Gabby…" Jam says softly.

"Rumor has it," he says, "that he's been running all over town with some young woman, lavishing gifts on her."

I stare at him, my jaw aching where I've been clamping it so tightly. "What?"

He can't look at me. Instead, he looks to his wife. She must know what to say. I look at her too.

Young woman… How young? Is it Paige?

I press my hands to my cheeks, feeling the heat of my humiliation.

"I'm so sorry, hun," Jam says, rubbing my back.

"Who else knows?" I ask my shoeless feet. They seem such a long way away, not even connected to me.

Nate puffs out his cheeks. "Not sure. But apparently, they've been spotted out and about—flaunting it."

I look at him in shock again. "Why would they do that? Aren't affairs supposed to be secret?"

"I don't think that's how those gold diggers see it." He shrugs his shoulders. "They want everyone to see them. It's about status, showing off. The guys at the club are always joking about it—how much money and jewelry it takes to get them into bed."

"Bunch of pigs," Jam says.

"That's why I don't have anything to do with them," he replies.

A silence falls. I listen to a clock ticking from somewhere out in the hallway, reminding me that this is happening, in real time, not a nightmare that will end when I wake.

Nate sits forward in his seat. "We're not all like that, you know, Gabby." His voice catches a little, like a wisp of clothing, a trace of cotton catching on a bramble.

"I know." Squeezing the bridge of my nose, I flap my hand to stave off tears.

"You don't have to be brave with us," Jam says. "Bawl away if you want to."

"I don't want to. I just want to understand what you're saying." I look at Nate. "What sort of gifts?"

"Not sure."

"So, it's what…prostitution or something?"

"Or rinsing, more like," Jam says. "That's what they call it when girls send sexy selfies in exchange for gifts and cash."

I sit up straight, holding up my hand to stop the conversation. "Actually, you know what? I don't want to talk about this anymore." I pick up my drink. "What time's the pizza coming?"

They exchange glances. "Well, you're taking it better than I thought," Nate says. "I thought we'd have to hide the best china."

I smile, but it's an effort. "So, have you seen her, Nate?"

His smile disappears. "Who, Fred's mistress?"

Fred's mistress. I can't believe we're having this conversation. I take in the Nigella cookbooks, the framed photos, the painting above the fireplace. The things that make up a home. "Yes."

"No. Why?" he asks.

"Just wondered what she looks like—who she is."

There's a knock at the door, which Nate jumps up to see to, in relief. Beside me, Jam has grown very quiet, so still I can almost hear her thoughts.

As the front door closes, she turns to look at me, her voice a whisper. "That woman…the messages… It can't be a coincidence."

"It's not what you think," I whisper back. "It's not her. She wasn't after Fred."

"How can you say for sure?"

I can't. I just remember how dismissive she was of him—the curl of her lip when she said *bullshit name.*

Nate's head appears around the door. "Food's ready, ladies. Bring your wine."

As we stand, Jam tugs my arm, gripping it. "What the hell's going on, Gabby?"

★★★

I walk home alone, even though Nate offered to go with me. It's only ten minutes and I know these streets so well. I tell him I'll run, but I don't. I'm too shaky, numb. I wanted to be numb, but not this much. I don't even bother to look around me. Let her come and show her face. Let her tell me what she wants from me so I can put this thing to rest—end it now.

Brave words, but I don't truly want her to appear, least of all now. I'm still processing what Nate said, trying to work out why Fred would do this to me. Flaunting it? That's not who I thought he was.

The rain has stopped; the pavements are shimmering under the streetlights. Occasionally, a car appears, but otherwise it's quiet. As I pass the houses lining the streets, I gaze in at yellow windows, silhouettes of people, the blue light of screens. Normal life. People going about their business, not worrying whether their husband's exchanging gifts for sex.

I stop outside a dark shop, its metal shutters shut, graffitied. I deleted Ellis's number, but it's still in my call history.

I call it, shifting my feet anxiously.

The person you are calling is unavailable.

Then I try the number from the last message again. Once more, it disconnects.

Continuing on my way, I lower my chin into my coat, feeling chilled. From the start, the neatness of everything has troubled me, the synchronicity: her appearance exactly as Alice left; those messages beginning as things deteriorated with Fred. Why is that?

As I draw closer to home, making for the side gate, I hear wheels on gravel and catch a glimpse of Fred's car pulling out of the driveway. Seeing him so soon after Nate's revelation makes my heart heavy. I can't believe this is happening to me. What happened to the man I married? Where's he going this late at night?

Entering our lonely house, it occurs to me that the only good thing about any of this is that I have the place to myself and can explore it unchallenged.

Upstairs in the spare room, Fred's new base, I start opening drawers, searching the wardrobe. And then I sit down on the bed, looking around me, thinking.

His bedside table. It's locked. Lifting it upside down, I kick the drawer until I hear it give. Then I kneel down, pulling open the unhinged drawer. It comes out askew, dangling, a tooth hanging by a thread.

Inside, there's only one item. An initialized toiletries wallet I bought him years ago. I unzip it, feeling inside, removing the object. It's a packet of condoms.

My periods stopped two years ago; last year I officially entered menopause. Even so, we never used condoms.

I think about whether to fix the drawer and set the room straight. Yes, but not yet. There's something else I must do first. Downstairs, I double-bolt the front door, ensuring that Fred can't return even with a key, and then I go through to the kitchen to get my laptop.

18

9 months earlier

Under the harsh lighting of the bathroom mirror, she smacked her lips together to distribute the nude gloss. Then she picked up her clutch and returned to the bar, sliding back onto the stool.

He had ordered another Flirtini in her absence, which she pretended to be thrilled about. She hadn't even finished the last one, wanted to stay sharp, yet he was starting to look bleary-eyed and she was certain he wouldn't notice her leaving it.

The barman would be calling last orders soon. The place had that feeling as though any second now he would shake the carpet and they'd go tumbling out into the gutter. She had to make her move.

"So…" She set her hand on his thigh, leaning toward him, chain dangling over her breasts. He seemed mesmerized by the diamanté pendant. "…Shall we go somewhere quieter?"

He knocked back his Scotch, wiped his mouth, staring at her in elation, disbelief. "What, you want to…?" He didn't complete the sentence. She was glad about that.

"Yes." She smiled, reaching her hand farther up his thigh.

He placed his left hand on hers. His wedding band was silver—

probably white gold; battered by design, rustic-looking. He followed her gaze.

"You're married?" she said, withdrawing her hand. "I didn't—"

"It's not what you think," he said, standing up, leaning in on her. He stooped to speak close to her ear. "It's over."

The smell of whiskey turned her stomach. She flinched inwardly, taking a silent deep breath. "Does your wife know you're here?"

He was still close to her, breathing into her hair, swaying on his feet. "Yes. I swear. She's fine with it."

"Are you sure? This is on the up-and-up? Because…" She cradled her arms around her, her breasts bunching. It was a clever move on two counts: little girl lost, with amazing tits. "…I've been hurt before." She didn't go as far as crying, but pouted a little, reaching for her drink.

Why wasn't he saying anything? He rocked on his feet, looking perturbed.

Maybe she'd gone too far, had made it too complicated, playing the wife card. She wasn't sure that it was even a card. It didn't have any strength. If anything, it was the Joker.

She waited, and then she got a lucky break. A young good-looking guy with a gym bag sat down at the bar, glancing sideways at her with an appreciative look.

Well, if you don't want her…

She pretended not to notice, watching her intended target out of the corner of her eye. He was somewhere else, looking into space, thinking about the Joker at home, or whether he needed to empty his bladder. And then he looked at her. "Let's go."

Gym-boy turned to watch them with his legs splayed and a smile on his face, as she slipped into her coat and they left. At the door, she glanced back at him, thinking that his buffness didn't make him any less disgusting.

"Where do you want to go?" he said, turning up the collar on his coat, taking her hand as though they were a couple.

"There's a place just behind the seafront. They do rooms."

He stopped, gazed down at her. He was tall. "You mean, a hotel?"

She smiled bashfully, pivoting on his arm. "Well, yes… You didn't think we were going to hang out in an alley, did you?"

"I…" He scratched his head. "I hadn't thought that far."

She bet he hadn't. Even the buttons on his coat were done up wrong.

"Well, I thought it might be nice, but if you'd rather not…" Her coat fell open. His eyes floated down to her cleavage, to her legs and back up again. It was like being scanned at the airport.

"No, I want to," he said, clasping her hand decisively and walking her up the road.

"It's this way then." She led him the other way.

"Oh." He laughed, then stopped underneath a lamppost, pulling her toward him, trying to kiss her. Deftly, she directed him to her neck instead. Then she moved them along, continuing on their way, sludgy snow lining the rooftops and curbs.

Outside the Neptune Hotel, she hesitated, fiddling with her bag. "What's wrong?" he asked.

"I just…" She shifted her weight as though uncertain. "Oh, it's nothing."

Pressing the small of her back, he steered her toward the revolving doors. It looked fancy, exactly what she had intended. The receptionist was wearing a pussy bow blouse, with a tired smile.

"Good evening," he said, using a posh voice as though he weren't strapped to a woman half his age. "Do you have any rooms available just for tonight?"

"One minute, sir," the receptionist said, tapping her keyboard. "Yes, we have a double luxury en suite or a—"

"Perfect." He reached into his jacket for his wallet. "Can I pay now?"

"Absolutely. Could I take your name, please?"

He hesitated, laughed quietly in embarrassment, pulling out a credit card and handing it to her.

She bet it didn't mention anything about Nigel.

The receptionist examined it, typing, the printer whirring. "Take the elevator, sir, and it's on the third floor, second on the left," she said, handing him a key card.

The elevator smelled of stale hot air. He tried to kiss her again. She pretended to have something in her eye that needed tending to in the elevator mirror. He hovered, asking if she needed help.

She didn't.

The room didn't smell much better. He opened a window, checked the mini bar, opening a bottle, taking a swig. "I needed that." And then he turned to her with a shy smile. "I'm not really called Nigel."

She tried to look as surprised as she could. "Really, then what's your name?"

"Fred." He ran his fingers through his hair, sitting down on the bed with a puffy sigh. "I don't know why I lied."

"That's disappointing," she said, sitting in the chair by the window, touching the curtain distractedly.

"I'd like it if we could start over—be fully honest with each other."

Fully honest. She smiled.

"I'd like that too." She let her heel dangle from her bare foot, his eyes tracking her every move. Then she stood up slowly in front of him, allowing him to drink her in.

"You're the most beautiful woman I've ever seen," he said, gazing up at her.

She beamed as though grateful, then allowed her face to cloud over. "Seeing as you mentioned full honesty…I think there's something I should tell you."

He frowned. It was encouraging—the level of concern, so soon. "What is it?"

"I don't know how to say it…"

He patted the bed beside him. "Come here." He handed her the miniature bottle. "This might help." She acted as though she were taking a swig, shuddering even, not a single drop entering her mouth. "So, what is it?"

"Well, it's about who I am…"

He smiled warily, squeezing her shoulder, rolling her toward him, her legs tipping. She didn't like that—set herself straight again. "What do you mean, who you are? You're you." He tapped her leg. So simple, so deluded. "Nothing you could say could put me off. I mean, look at you."

That's how deep it was, the level of conviction between them—all based on her tits and arse. She took a deep breath, placing her hands flat on her sculpted legs.

She could have said she was an alien, or Cleopatra. He wasn't interested. He would be thinking about her underwear, whether she was wearing any. Stroking her thigh as she started to speak, he was still in his work clothes, hadn't gone home yet from work. She knew where he worked, what time he left the office, which nights he stayed out late.

She thought about the blade in her bag, inches from her hand. Razor sharp, in a pink case as though it contained something girly, sweet. So easy to conceal a lethal weapon as a harmless trinket by making it feminine.

"This is really difficult," she said, starting to cry.

Disturbed by her tears, he removed his hand from her thigh, his Adam's apple wobbling, protruding like a target. She imagined an *X* written on it in marker pen, the way surgeons did before operating. Right in the middle of the carotid artery and jugular vein—one of the deadliest places to strike with a knife. He wouldn't know what had hit him.

"It's okay, Ellis," he said. "You can trust me."

19

September 1981

The sun was up bright and early. I stood by the birdbath, kicking a pine cone, squinting. I'd just learned how to squint—had seen a boy doing it at school, screwing up his face in the sunshine and I thought it looked cool so had tried it, liked it.

Daddy had left the car running in the driveway, the smell of gasoline in the air. I wished he would hurry up. I only had on my stripy top and corduroy trousers. Daddy said it would be warm out, but he didn't say anything about me standing outside here for half an hour.

Squinting up at the house, I strained my ears above the noise of the engine to hear what they were saying. Mommy was yelling, again. Daddy didn't seem to be saying anything much.

I waited, kicking the pine cone all the way to the hedge and back, and by the time I was near the car, there was Daddy, grinning at me as he darted to the car. "Come on! Get in the Batmobile!"

I ran to my side of the car, tugging the seat belt. "If I'm Batman, shouldn't I be driving?"

He slapped my leg as we took off up the leafy lane. "All in

good time. One day, you'll have everything. The Batmobile and all of Gotham City."

Daddy said that a lot. It made me smile, but afterward I always felt a bit funny because I knew he meant that one day I would have everything because he wouldn't be here.

"Where are we going?" I asked, the trees flashing past the window, branches lashing the glass.

"Wait and see. But I think you're gonna like it."

I pressed the buttons on the radio. "Tainted Love" was playing. Daddy loved this song, turned it up so loudly it felt daring. I tapped my foot to the beat, squinting out the window.

When the song ended, I turned down the volume, looked at him. He hadn't shaved yet today—had dark shadows over his chin that made him look like a criminal, a good one. "Is Mommy okay?"

"'Course. Why wouldn't she be?" And he turned the radio up again.

We drove for six songs and a newsreel and then we were going along a road that smelled expensive. Daddy had taught me how to get a nose for these things. I was worried it would mean my nose would grow too big, but he said I was being a silly Billy. I was keeping an eye on my nose though, just in case.

"Here we are," he said, pulling up alongside the curb, stopping the engine. "Ocean View Road." He got out of the car; I did the same, excitement fizzing in my tummy. No matter what we did, it was always exciting. "So, what do you think?"

I couldn't see anything at the moment—was too small. There were tall walls everywhere. But I liked the cherry blossoms growing at the side of the road, even though they were thin and had straps to hold them up.

"Thought you'd like them," he said. "Someday, they'll be big and strong, just like you." He directed me across the road, stopping at the entrance of a building site that said DANGER DO NOT ENTER.

Even though it was early, I could hear voices. Sure enough, the cement mixer was turning. Beside it, a large man in a checked shirt was lifting shovels from the back of his van. "Morning, boss," he shouted, tipping his helmet.

"All right, mate?" Daddy raised his hand in greeting and then ran up the steps to the portable cabin, which creaked and wobbled. "Follow me, kiddo."

I was kiddo here in front of the men, never Batman. But that was okay. I'd already learned that adults had names that no one else used, faces no one else saw.

Inside the portable cabin, it smelled of old coffee. I wrinkled my nose as Daddy put a helmet on my head, adjusting the chin strap. It had never fit, but I was used to holding my head a certain way so that it wouldn't fall off.

Then we stood looking at the site, his hand on my shoulder. "Number twenty-three. What a beaut."

I knew he was talking about the potential—the future, what it might look like sometime soon. So I told him I loved it, even though it was mostly rubble. But beyond the piles of dirt was the sea. And the air was so fresh I could fry it for breakfast. I could imagine a family here—laundry, the smell of suds, a football lying in the leaves.

"We're going to do something special today," he said, taking my hand, leading me toward the foundations.

"Are we?" My heart fluttered. I wondered what it could be. We'd done a lot of things over the years. I had seen every house he had ever developed. He had included me in everything and one day I would run his company. What could top that?

At the verge of the stumpy brick wall, we watched three men on their knees, cementing the ground with tools like huge cake slices. It always made me hungry. Daddy picked up a tool and joined in. I sat cross-legged on the floor for a while, listening to the men talking about things I wasn't very interested in. There was a caterpillar on my shoe, which I took over to the hedge; otherwise not much happened.

Then he told the men to take a break and beckoned me over. “Time to leave our mark,” he said.

I wasn’t sure what he meant so I copied what he was doing, leaning on the edge, pressing his hand onto the cement.

As I held my hand on the cold gloopy mixture, the sun came out, hitting our hair, our skin.

“There you go. Now there’ll always be a part of us here, you and me.”

We had left two perfect imprints, his hand next to mine. He stood up, pulling me up so I could stand without putting my hand on my clothes. “Now let’s get this washed off.”

I skipped happily alongside him, looking over my shoulder. “Will it always be there, Daddy?”

“Yep,” he replied, stopping to kiss the top of my forehead. “Always.”

Inside the portable cabin, there was someone there now. A woman with bright rusty hair and a blouse that was unbuttoned too much or too tight. I didn’t want to stare so I couldn’t tell which. “Hello there,” she said, jumping up the moment she saw me and squeezing my cheek.

I was ten years old, not three. I put my hands on my hips, squinted.

“You must be Gabriella.”

“It’s Gabrielle,” Daddy said, ruffling my hair.

I don’t know if it was my property developer nose or my imagination, but something felt wrong. I couldn’t say what. I picked up Daddy’s rubber band ball that he had grown for years, holding it in my hand. “Do you work here?” I asked.

“Well, no, not really!” She laughed, fixing her handbag on her shoulder. It was one of those leopard skin ones. I couldn’t see Mommy ever having one like that.

“Then what—?”

"Why don't you go on outside and wait for me?" Daddy said, opening the door. I felt the breeze touch my shirt, fluttering the paperwork on his desk.

"Okay." I shrugged, did as I was told.

Outside, I sat on the steps, realizing that I was still holding the rubber band ball. I bounced it on the step a few times, noticing that it was covered in chalky gray dust. It was from my hand: I forgot to wash it. I could get cement burns! Once, one of the workmen had to go to the hospital.

Running back up the steps, I burst in. "Daddy, I—"

The rusty woman had her hand on his jeans. She jumped away at the sight of me, as did Daddy, bumping into his desk, knocking over a cup of tea. "Damn it!" he yelled, as it poured all over his paperwork, dripping onto the floor. "What the hell are you doing in here?"

"It's okay, Robin... Don't shout at her." Rusty grabbed a roll of tissue paper, unraveling a chunk of it, dropping it onto the carpet, rubbing at it with her heel. She was wearing stilettos that ripped at the paper. Anyone could see that it wasn't working.

I ran forward to help. "I can fix that."

To my surprise, Daddy pushed me away. "You've already done enough!"

I lost my balance, falling backward onto the floor with a bump. Gazing up at him, I waited for him to ask if I was hurt, to say sorry, but he was too busy saving his paperwork.

I began to cry, still holding the rubber band ball, the cement so stiff on my hand now it was starting to ache. "I just wanted to wash my hand, Daddy."

He stared at me with a funny expression. Dropping the handful of tissue, he came to me, falling to his knees, drawing me into his arms. "I'm sorry, kiddo," he said, wiping my tears.

I was pleased, confused. I didn't know what he'd really done that was all that wrong, other than pushing me away, but it was my fault that I'd caught my leg on the chair, not his. "It's all right. I know you didn't mean it."

"Let me see your hand," he said, prying the ball from my fist, inspecting my palm. It was starting to burn, tingle. He hurried me to the sink, standing me on a crate so I could reach the tap.

He worked on my hand for a long time, using cold water that made me shiver, and then he poured white vinegar on it that reminded me of fish-and-chips, and used a toothbrush to go along the lines in my hand. I never knew there were so many of them. I could smell his sweat, mixed with deodorant.

"What about you, Daddy?" I asked, when he was patting my hand with a towel.

"Don't you worry about me." But I made him wash his hand too.

When we were done, all clean, I noticed that Rusty had gone. He didn't seem all that fussed about it.

As we were leaving the site, I wanted to go over to the foundations again and see our handprints, which cheered me up. One of the workmen gave me half a Kit Kat too, even better. "One day, all this will be yours, Batman," Daddy said, as we got back into the car.

There was a blister in the middle of my palm, but I didn't say anything about it. We stopped for ice creams on the way home, even though it was breakfast time. As I pulled a chocolate flake from the top of my soft-serve cone, Daddy unwrapped a cigar, tapping the end.

I had listened to everything he had ever told me, learned every trick, so that one day I could be just like him. So I could read his mind now, just like he could read mine. He didn't have to tell me what he was about to say. I would show him how smart I was and beat him to it. "It's okay, Daddy," I said. "I promise I won't say anything."

To my surprise, he didn't look all that pleased. He lit his cigar, gazed up at the sky as though looking for someone up there. I didn't ask why. The sun was coming out strong and my ice cream was beginning to drip. Maybe he was worried about that. So I carried on licking my ice cream, kicking my feet against the wall, while Daddy puffed on his cigar. And then, he blew smoke rings up into the bright blue sky, just for me.

20

The fridge starts to hum soothingly as I open the laptop, checking my emails first in case there's something from Will or Alice. Unfortunately, the only message is from Fred.

There's no greeting, no sign-off. It was sent at seven o'clock tonight, as I was sitting down with Jam and Nate.

I'm waiting to hear about your instructions re DJ Crawley & Associates. I thought you wanted a divorce as quickly as possible? Please let me know whether we're going to file a joint petition, or whether I should apply on my own. Even jointly, there will probably be delays. So it makes sense that we get the ball rolling.

If I don't hear from you by this time next week, I'll go ahead as a sole applicant. If we can't agree on the house, then I suggest we see a mediator.

Please don't just delete this.

I delete it, but then undo it, creating a folder called Fred, storing it there like nuclear waste. Jam told me to keep everything.

He's right. We should apply jointly and consult a mediator.

That's what normal people would do, in normal circumstances. But there's nothing normal about this. If he's buying gifts for a gold digger, using funds that are there to support his children through university, then I need to know more about that before pressing Go. It feels as though he's holding all the cards, mostly because I'm completely in the dark.

Taking a fortifying sip of tea, I type in the last words I ever thought I'd be searching for online.

Private investigator, Shelby, Dorset.

I go for the first company in the search results. The website is clinical, functional. They do fast same-day consultations. I complete the inquiry form, giving as little information as possible.

Before pressing BOOK A CALL, I gaze around the kitchen, my eye falling on the picture of Fred on the fridge that Alice drew years ago: curly hair, long legs, circular glasses; hearts all around him on spindly stems like strange flowers. I don't know why she drew them like that, but she was the sort of child who liked everything tied down, attached. Apron strings. She didn't want to start school. Not like Will. He raced in, storming the castle.

Yet, look at her now, all grown up, living away from home. Nothing I do must jeopardize that for her. I didn't get to finish my time away from home—my great escape. I barely even started. History won't repeat itself. I click the button.

It's the most beautiful day, an ironic touch from the universe. As I slip out of the side gate and take off along Ocean View Road, I smile briefly at the sunshine dappling through the cherry blossom trees, even though I'm feeling jittery, overwhelmed.

I didn't have the nerve to run along the beach, couldn't face being a wrinkled old hag. Instead, I'm sticking to the roads. His words are still with me—the way he said it as though it were fact, the same way that a boy at school once called me a dog, the worst possible insult back then. It never occurred to me that he might be wrong.

There's so much hurt in my chest today I don't know where to begin. If I had been setting a trap for Fred last night, trying to provoke a reaction by drawing the bolts over the door, it didn't work. He never came home.

I slept fitfully again, my face turned toward the window, listening for the sound of tires, the angry door-knocking, my phone beside me. I even had my words ready.

We can't go on like this, Fred. You need to find somewhere else to stay.

It's not like he'd be sleeping rough; he could go to his parents'. Which is more than I could do.

This morning I got up to the certain knowledge that the house was empty, the door to the spare room still wide-open from where I ransacked it. It felt like a hole had opened up in the middle of our home and I was standing on the ledge, staring down into a pit of unanswered questions.

And now I'm resorting to hiring a private investigator. It feels seedy, extreme. A business that exists solely because people can't be honest.

As I turn onto the next road, there's no breeze, the air thick with lethargy. I'm already too hot, from the inside out, molten fear bubbling. What if the truth is too ugly, too cataclysmic, for me to handle?

I go down a narrow lane, jumping over a smashed bottle, the smell of urine meeting my nose. It's possible that the runner could be making his way up here, doing the same thing as me. I increase my speed, my spine juddering with the impact of the downward slope as I dart past nettles, a bramble ripping at my skin, and then I'm on High Street.

It's deathly quiet. I turn off my music to listen for cars. Shelby has a problem of boy racers, speeding along the backstreets, backfiring through the exhaust to scare pedestrians. I'd never walk around here wearing headphones—am always telling Will and Alice the same thing.

I run past the shuttered shops, making mental lists of things to do, buy. Grapes. Socks.

My footsteps feel labored as I turn onto a road behind the seafront that I don't often venture along because it's mostly hotels, tourist shops selling souvenirs. This means I'm on my way home though and the thought lifts me. I pick up the pace. I can turn my music back on now and I'm fiddling with my phone armband, not looking where I'm going, when two figures step out in front of me from nowhere.

Thinking I'm about to be mugged, I'm raising my arms and knee in defense, when he shouts, "Gabby!"

I stop, nearly tripping over my feet, music playing, blocking my thoughts. I rip the buds from my ears and they dangle against my legs as I absorb the simple details, like one of Alice's sketches.

Fred. Jacket, polo shirt, glasses.

"What…?" I say, dazed, moving my gaze from him to the person beside him, reading her details too, except that it's a lot slower. I don't know her as well, but I do know her.

Sunkissed limbs, bleached teeth.

Above us, seagulls screech.

"What are you doing here?" He looks horrified. Subtly, he moves away from her, setting distance between them as though they're colleagues. But it's too late. He had his hand on her back. I saw it.

I stare at her, willing her to look at me, but she can't. She's wearing the same gold dress she had on the night we met.

It's Ellis. He's with Ellis.

My heart is hammering so much, I can't hear myself think—can't get anything straight in my mind. I glance at the doorway they appeared from. The Neptune Hotel, revolving doors, a lit chandelier. From within, there's the gentle sound of cutlery, breakfast.

I place my hand to my head, rubbing my damp hairline, earbuds still dangling, tinny music playing. My back's wet from running. There's a leaf stuck to my trainer.

"I don't understand..." My arm's bleeding, ripped by the bramble, a trail of blood spots on my skin. I wipe it clean, pressing it as though keeping everything inside of me from spilling out. "Why are you—?"

"I can explain everything," Fred says. He doesn't have any luggage, is wearing his wax jacket, brown leather shoes. "It's not what it looks like."

"What does it look like?" I ask, my voice faint.

"It's..." He stops as a dog-walker approaches, pulling Ellis back with him into the entrance to the hotel. I imagine them going in there last night. Gazing up at the hotel's windows, I swallow painfully, emotion swelling in my windpipe, threatening to cut me off entirely.

And then she does something which changes everything. She reaches for his hand, looking me in the eye like a challenge.

I waver and then I'm pitching forward, screaming, "Get off him!" I'm all fists, pummeling. I barely reach her before Fred is pinning me against the hotel's railings.

"That's enough! Keep it together! You're not an animal!"

"Oh, you want to talk to me about animals?" I scream up at him, trying to wrestle free, kicking his shins.

"Stop it!" he shouts, shaking my shoulders, bumping my back against the metal bars. "Stop it!"

He's never hurt me before. He doesn't now, not really. Yet, the intention brings tears to my eyes and all of a sudden my limbs sag. He feels it too, letting go of me, straightening his jacket.

I slide down the railings, squatting, hugging my legs, pressing my palms against my eyes. I'm not crying. I'm too far gone. I'm dead. I think I'm dead.

Neither of them says, does anything. And then she speaks demurely, like a wife consulting with her husband about whether to call their broker. "We should go, Fred."

I remove my hands from my eyes, leaning my weight against the railings to get to my feet. I probably wouldn't have made it otherwise. I'm muddy, wet, bleeding, but I want to face her, look her in the eye.

Neither of them react. Humans can sense when someone is about to lose and they already know I've done that.

"He's right," I say, extending my hand to her. "We can be civilized."

She has the grace, or the sense, to hesitate. "Hi," she says.

We shake hands ever so lightly, Fred's mouth a circle of anxiety.

Her hand is so cold it makes me shudder. She's every bit as perfect as I remembered. Every bit as strange, magnetic. Her eyes flood mine.

"People don't often surprise me, not anymore." My voice is quiet, yet clear. "You get to a certain age and you've seen enough, have experienced enough, to be able to make a reasonable assessment. But this…" I look her up and down "…this game of yours, whatever it is, it's one of the most twisted things I've seen. Because I…"

My throat feels blocked again. I swallow, compose myself. She waits, a flicker of a frown on her forehead, her lips parting.

"…I actually believed you, Ellis. I actually thought you could help me. Can you imagine ever being that desperate?" I laugh softly. "But then of course you can. Why else would you be doing this?"

A look flashes over her face then. I'm sure I'm not imagining it, but I can't decipher it in time because Fred is catching up. "Wait, what, you know each other?" he says, looking from me to her and back again.

I keep my gaze fixed on her. "So, what was I? An introduction? Did I cue him up for you?" I catch a glimpse of something then—a sparkle on her chest, just above her cleavage. I don't take it in properly because she's turning away from me, touching Fred's arm.

"I have to go," she says. I could swear her voice was lower, older, that night at Rumors.

"I'm confused," he says. "Have you two met before?"

I straighten my back, smoothing strands of hair away from my eyes. "Whatever you think this is, I'd think again." I point at him, stabbing the air between us. "In fact, I'd be very careful if I were you. I'd watch my back and sleep with one eye open."

"What the hell are you talking about?" he says, as I turn away, setting off.

I make it to the end of the road before stumbling into the pathway where I stop, bending over, gasping for breath. I don't have my earbuds, must have dropped them outside the hotel.

Peeking around the wall, I watch them making their way along the road in the opposite direction. They stop, Fred with his hands on her shoulders, saying something to her. I wait, expecting them to kiss, but they don't. And then they're on their way again, turning the corner, out of sight.

I think of what Fred said. It's not what it looks like.

That's the one thing we can agree on.

My limbs feel so wobbly, I can't run home, nor do I have the will to look for my buds. I hover for a moment in the pathway, dread creeping up my spine. I knew she was involved in some way, that our conversation that night wasn't random. She's been under my skin since the moment we met, as though just having contact with her was enough to get her into my system, like asbestos.

I make my way up the path, forcing myself to move, my head so full of fears that they're bumping into each other.

At the top, on the flat open road, I can think, see clearly. She played me, and it worked. She got Fred.

21

I'm taking a walk along the seafront in my lunch hour, about to get a coffee from one of the kiosks, when my phone rings, my stomach churning.

I don't recognize the number, don't grasp who it is until he speaks. "Good afternoon, is that Gabby O'Neal? This is Michael Quinn from A Plus Investigations. Are you okay to talk?"

It's a windy day, my hair running wild. "Yes, go ahead." Holding my hair away from my face, I look out to sea, fixing my gaze at a point on the horizon, like dancers do to stop themselves spinning.

"Fantastic. I'd like to run through a few details, if I may?" He sounds Irish. I imagine dark hair, blue eyes.

Behind me, a child shrieks, demanding ice cream. I move away from the kiosk, descending the steps to the beach. It's typically quiet for a school day in September; a few moms with toddlers, a couple of silver-haired swimmers. I stand by the wall, sheltering from the wind, the seaweed at my feet wafting a salty smell.

Michael Quinn checks my address, my understanding of their fees, their privacy policy, my preferred mode of contact.

And then says, "So you want me to confirm whether your husband's having an affair?"

The words catch my breath. I shift my feet, startling the clouds of flies on the seaweed. "No. I already know he is."

"Good. Because I should tell you that divorce laws have changed and apportioning blame isn't relevant in court anymore."

"I'm aware of that."

"Okay...so..."

I know what he's asking, even though he isn't asking anything. He wants me to tell him what I'm hoping to achieve. And if I'm going to get anywhere, then I will have to try to put it in words.

I fix my eye out to sea again, leaning against the wall for support. "He's cheating on me with a younger woman—maybe sleeping with her in return for gifts or cash. I don't know for sure. But I need all the facts before starting divorce proceedings, in case it impacts the division of assets. There's a lot at stake." I hold myself tense as I wait for him to answer.

I don't know what he thinks of me, but when he speaks, his voice is full of warmth. "I understand."

Does he? Because I'm not sure that I do.

"She's called Ellis." As I say her name, I realize that her betrayal of me feels worse than Fred's.

I've never heard anything so messed up in all my life.

"Well, first things first, I think we should meet. I find it best to talk in person, to make sure we're on the same page. There's a pub in the Westgate area that's discreet."

I nod, kicking a bit of seaweed, startling more flies. Westgate is on the outskirts of town, near our old house.

"Hello?" he prompts.

"Yes. That's fine."

"Can you make tonight, six o'clock? The King's Arms?"

I smile sadly. Of all the places. Fred and I went there on our first date.

"I'll be there," I say.

★★★

I'm going back to work, abandoning the idea of a coffee in the sunshine, when I become aware that someone's approaching along the promenade, waving enthusiastically at me, and that it's Monique.

She's wearing one of her home-knitted sweaters, a floral scarf around her hair, and the sight of her unsettles me so much I debate whether there's time for me to dart into one of the restaurants.

"Yoo-hoo!" she calls so loudly that I'm given no choice but to hear her. "Gabby!"

We meet, the wind tearing at our clothes, Monique's eyes watering. "How lovely to see you!" she says, reaching into her sweater for a tissue, dabbing her eyes. "How are you?"

I can't say great. We both know that's not true. Instead, I glance at my phone, gesturing ahead of me—trying to make it clear that I'm due back at the office. "I was just—"

"Come," she says, pulling me toward a bench set underneath a shelter. "Just for five minutes."

I hesitate, glance at my phone again. "Okay."

"I'm just about to meet my friend at the scallop restaurant," she says cheerfully. "But I'm a bit early." She slips her hand through my arm. "So, how did it go?"

How did what go? "I'm not sure…"

She laughs shrilly, a strand of hair escaping from her scarf, flapping across her face. She lifts it away, frowning at me. "You know: the talk."

"What talk?"

She recoils, disentangling herself from me, a space opening between us. "The one with Fred?" she says, smile disappearing.

"Monique, I don't know—"

"You mean to say that you haven't spoken to him yet? I thought he emailed you, put it in writing? That's what we advised him to do."

My spirits sink. He's getting advice from them; of course he is. I'd do the same thing for Will and Alice. Only, if they're advising him, then they can't advise me. From here on, our interests will be conflicting.

"Well, I only just got the email last night. I haven't had a chance to speak to him yet."

"Really? I'd have thought—"

"He didn't come home, Monique," I say, speaking over her.

Her face stiffens, taking on an expression I've never seen before, except that I have. It reminds me of something, someone.

I shift position, feeling uncomfortable, gazing at the sand on the tips of my boots. "We shouldn't be talking about this," I say, trying not to sound emotional. "It's more complicated than you think."

"No, it isn't," she says, smiling, but her eyes are panicky.

And I know then what she's frightened of: that her son is going to lose out somewhere along the line, cheated by his conniving money-grabbing wife.

That's me—how she sees me now.

She dabs her eyes again. "Have you had a change of heart, Gabby? Is that it?"

"No. I'm just taking my time, trying to work out what's best. Besides, I thought you cared about me too—like a daughter."

"Of course," she replies, adjusting her headscarf, tucking her stray hairs beneath it. "But I'm worried about Fred. He's put himself in a vulnerable spot because of...well...how he feels."

I turn to face her. "About whom?"

I know as soon as she stalls, breaks eye contact, that it's not about his feelings for me, even though I've known this for some time.

But that little moment of breakage hits me hard, as though she were cutting an invisible cord between us. I feel weightless, restrained only by the shelter's roof from drifting away—a helium balloon no one wanted.

"Gabby..." She softens her voice. "...This woman he's involved with... I think he has real feelings for her."

"Real feelings?" I echo, slightly incredulous. "And does she have a name?"

"Yes..."

I hear it before she says it. It's the only name it could have been. The name that's been on my mind from the moment I first heard it.

"...It's Ellis."

A shriveling feeling comes over me, a tightening of my scalp and skin. How can it be her? The night I met her she didn't even know who Fred was, did she? This can't be right.

"How long ago did they meet?" I ask, my voice clipped. I hope she doesn't notice.

Yet, she does—is looking at me funnily, askance. "Why do you ask?"

There will be no innocent conversation from now on, no casual chat. It's like we're playing with loaded guns.

"Just that you said before she'd been around for some time. So, is this the same person, this Alicia? The same person that he met some time ago?"

I deliberately get the name wrong, as though I'm not logging every detail, and also to see whether she corrects me—how invested she is in Ellis, whether she's met her, is protective of her, the way she once was with me. About ten days ago.

She doesn't correct me.

Clever Fred.

"This isn't about her, Gabby. It's about Fred. I just want him to be happy. That's all I want for him...and for you," she adds quickly. "I can't tell you what to do, but trying to keep things as amicable as possible for the sake of the children is probably for the best."

I'm the last person in the world who needs to be told that. But out of respect, kindness, I nod as though this is a revelation.

She relaxes her stance, releasing her breath, all done.

I want to tell her how skewed her viewpoint is—to set her straight. I want to tell her that Fred's running all over town with a girl young enough to be his daughter. Yet, I take in the purple tint to her nostrils, the lipstick bleeding around her lips, the paper thinness of her hands, and I can't do it. I can't do it to her. I've no idea how Fred could either.

I shift my feet, pick up my bag. "I need to get back to work."

"Gabby, I—"

"I'm so sorry, Monique, but I really feel that I have to focus on my needs. And if you don't think you can get on board with that, then, well..." I don't finish the sentence. Just in case.

But I've lost her anyway.

She frowns in frustration and it finally dawns on me where I've seen it before. The same firmness, the same microaggression around the mouth that Fred had when we were arguing about the house.

"He's not going to let you walk away with everything, you know. You won't keep your precious home. I can guarantee that."

I'm so shocked at her tone—that it's come to this so soon—that I don't know what to say, all my potential replies forming into an ugly fireball. But her thin hair and papery skin have driven any anger from me. So I don't light any matches.

"I'm sorry it came to this," I say, standing up. "I really am. I thought we'd last a little longer."

"You know, the problem with you, Gabby, is..." She hesitates.

I get the feeling she's not playing with matches so much as a flamethrower. I brace myself, gripping my bag.

"...You never learned to love anyone. They never stayed around long enough." Her voice is strained, as though from years of trying to hold back this irrepressible truth. "And I'm sorry about that. But I won't let you take my son to the cleaners, just because you're all bitter inside."

Standing up, she gazes at me, no trace of regret, her chin raised determinedly. She has chosen her side, like I knew she would. Our relationship was superficial, after all. I'd have walked on hot coals for her, and all along she was waiting for the day to make me eat them.

"There's a very dark place inside you, Gabby," she says, raising her voice so I don't miss a breath. "And it scares me. It really does." And then she turns away.

It scares me too. Yet, nothing inside me is as scary as Ellis. That's what I should tell her. I should warn her to keep a close eye on her son. But I don't, and won't. He has enough people protecting him. And besides, it's not him who I'm worried about getting hurt.

I take a deep breath, making my way back to work.

The night Ellis and I met at Rumors, she knew exactly who I was, what our house was worth, that our marriage was in shreds. She was checking out the opposition. I wouldn't have posed much of a threat, slumped in a deckchair—couldn't have been frailer the day Alice left. What a time to strike.

I step out of the way of a speeding cyclist, my pulse quickening as I process what this means.

It wasn't a coincidence, bumping into me. She targeted me—was already sleeping with Fred.

Somehow, she knows everything about me, every detail of my life. The messages, the sense of being followed are part of a plan to scare me, or worse.

She's after the house and if I'm dead…? She'll get it.

I stop walking, pulling my phone from my pocket.

Jam, what's the name of that lawyer?

I wait for her to reply, gazing at a ring pull or shiny stone on the promenade, glinting in the sunshine. And I remember something then from that night.

This morning, outside the hotel, she was wearing a sparkly

pendant, an *E* above her cleavage. But the night I met her, it wasn't an *E*. I'm sure of it. It was a *B*.

Who is she?

My phone vibrates as a message appears.

Maria Kane. 64 High Street. They call her the Rottweiler.

22

May 1982

I watched as Mommy sank the knife into the chocolate cake, some of the icing lifting up, like the way our new lawn had curled as Daddy laid the squares of grass down like carpet. I had helped him, only yesterday.

"Shouldn't we wait?" I asked, going over to the sink again, pushing up on my hands to look out the window.

She gazed at the clock, her face all scrunched. "We've waited long enough. I don't want you eating too much chocolate right before bed. You've got school in the morning."

"But it's only seven o'clock."

She pushed one of her curls away from her eyes. "No buts," she said, removing the candles one by one. I gazed at the little holes they'd left in the top of the cake.

"He said he'd be here."

"He says a lot of things he doesn't mean." She set the cake slice before me.

I ate it slowly, looking at the image on the plate, a Batman and Robin one that Daddy had got me from a vintage shop. It was rare; we only used it on special occasions. Robin in yellow and green, running, and beside him, also running, was Batman in lilac and purple, his cape spread out behind him, so much bigger than Robin's.

Since getting the plate, lilac and purple had become my favorite colors. I had my room painted the same shades, even though Mommy wanted me to have peach.

"I think we should have waited," I said.

"Don't speak with your mouth full," she replied, picking up her cup of tea, slipping an arm around her waist. She often had a bad tummy, said it was her nerves, but I didn't know what she had to be nervous about. Maybe we should have found a role for her in Gotham City. I'd thought of that before and asked her, but she didn't seem keen on the idea. So I didn't think it was that.

I finished eating, eyed the cake, hoping for more, but she was gazing into space.

"Don't worry. I know he'll be here," I said, looking at the *11 Today!* banner that he'd hung up this morning. Why would he put that there if he was going to miss my birthday tea? "He never lets me down. He's a superhero."

I knew as soon as I'd said it that it was wrong.

She glared at me as though I had sworn. And then she raised her hand and slammed it down on the table, rattling the cutlery. "He's not coming! Do you hear me?"

"Yes, he is!" I shouted. "He's going to be here!"

She reached forward, gripped my arm, staring at me so hard I thought my eyeballs would pop. "This has to stop. You're a big girl now, old enough to know the truth. He's not a superhero and this isn't a game. Do you understand?"

"Yes," I said. "Because he's only Robin. *I'm* Batman."

"Oh, for goodness' sake!" She clenched my arm so tightly I whimpered. And then she recoiled, covered her face and began to cry, shoulders shaking.

I didn't know what to do. She was wearing a poofy dress and

had done her hair and makeup especially and all I could think was that Daddy was missing it, and my birthday.

I climbed down from my stool, went to her side, rubbing her back the way I saw Daddy do when Grandpa died, and then the doorbell rang. "He's here!" I clapped my hands, jumped up and down.

She lifted her head in astonishment and then her expression changed and she looked worried, but I wasn't waiting—I was running out of the room, hurtling down the hallway. She was calling after me, but I was running so fast, legs like lightning, imagining my cape behind me.

Flinging open the door, I prepared for Daddy to lift me off my feet and throw me into the air.

I stopped. It wasn't him. It was a lady with a mop of frizzy blond hair, wearing a black-and-white stripy sweater that went all the way down almost to her knees. "Hello," she said, looking past me as though I wasn't there. "Is your mom home?"

I didn't answer, closed the door a little bit. I was looking at her earrings—big silver crosses. I wondered if she was scared of vampires. She was definitely scared of something. She was very twitchy.

"Hello?" she said, going on tiptoes to see over me. "Did you hear what I said?"

I nodded. "Moh-om?" I called over my shoulder, but she was already there, had come up quietly behind me, her makeup all streaky. I didn't want anyone to see her like that, so I swung around, blocking the frizzy woman, reaching up to wipe Mommy's face.

To my surprise, she looked so upset by my doing this I thought she was going to cry even more, but she didn't. She did something even stranger. She got down on her knees, gazed up at me, straightening my sweater, holding my arms. "You're my everything," she whispered. "Whatever happens, never forget that."

She was scaring me. "What's wrong?" I whispered.

But she just stood up, brushed off her knees, smoothed her dress, then opened the door fully. "Can I help you?"

The frizzy woman linked her hands together, shifting her weight from one foot to another, the way the school dinner ladies did when they were waiting for us to hurry up and choose sprouts or leeks. "I'm Sara," she said.

"I see. And you're here because…?"

She didn't have time to reply because suddenly there was a screech of tires and Daddy was bombing up the driveway, wheels spinning, gravel flying. I knew he would come!

I pushed past Mommy, past Frizzy and ran toward him. But he didn't seem to notice me. He'd even left the engine running, the car door open, in his hurry. "Alice!" he was shouting, his face all crinkly. "Alice, don't listen. There's nothing to worry about. It's nothing!"

What was nothing? It wasn't nothing. My chocolate cake was waiting. My sausages had gone cold. We had waited and waited. "Daddy?" I felt all hot and itchy.

Mommy was wringing her hands, as though she didn't know what to do. I stood in the middle of the driveway, watching as Daddy tried to calm Frizzy down, who was wriggling, screaming. "That's not true, Robin! Tell her! Tell her!"

"Stop it!" he shouted, trying to pull her away from the door.

"What's going on, Robin?" Mommy was saying. "Who is this woman?"

I wanted to tell him to come inside and eat tea with us, but I couldn't move or speak. Frizzy was still screaming, her voice piercing the sky.

"Tell her! Or I will!" And then she started pounding him with her fists.

I wasn't going to have that. I sprung forward as fast as I could, about to cannonball her, when Daddy swiped at me, flicking me away as though I were a wasp. I started to cry.

"You're a disgrace!" Mommy shouted. "How dare you?" And then she held her hand out for me and I ran to her and she pulled me inside the house, slamming the door.

There was a second of silence when I thought the house might crack in two and then Mommy started crying, pacing the floor. I didn't know what to do, except crumple to the floor, howling. That seemed to activate something in her and she lifted me up, carrying me upstairs to the quiet of my room, setting me down on the bed, the sheets cool against my legs. "I'll be right back," she said, crossing the landing to the bathroom.

The pipes began to screech as she ran the bath. I could hear Frizzy still screaming, Daddy's growly voice. And then the sound of tires, a car driving away.

I went to the window in disbelief. He was leaving? I could see a puff of blond hair in the seat beside him. What about my birthday? What about my tea? "Mommy?" I called, my voice breaking.

She returned, joining me at the window, reaching for my hand, clasping it. I bit my lip, my skin feeling all itchy again, heat rising up my neck the way it did when I was about to hit the baseball hard. And then I turned and ran from the room, taking the stairs so fast I nearly stumbled.

I was in the kitchen before she could stop me, before I could stop myself. My plate was still there, full of crumbs, smeared with icing. I lifted it as high as I could and let it drop onto the stone tile floor. It cracked in two, but that wasn't enough for me. I picked the pieces up and dropped them again, watching them split into shards. And then I burst into tears. What had I done?

Batman and Robin were in pieces: green, yellow, lilac, purple. I fell to my knees, clutching the biggest piece, the one where our hands were almost touching. We wouldn't be able to fix it. It was ruined.

There was a movement behind me as Mommy knelt down

with the dustpan and brush, sweeping up the mess. "It's okay," she said. "We can find you another one."

I sat on the floor, hugging my knees, my face hidden. "I don't want another one."

She cleared everything up. We had some more cake, watched TV. She ran me a bubble bath, got my nightie out of the cupboard—the one that crackled with static. She kept everything normal, to our routine, even though everything was off, like our house had been propped up on a brick.

When she turned out the light, I stared into the darkness, straining for the sound of Daddy's car returning, until I couldn't stay awake anymore. And I knew then, as I was crossing over into sleep, leaving my birthday behind, that I wasn't ever going to be Batman again.

23

I haven't been to the King's Arms for at least ten years, maybe more. We used to come here when we first met, Fred and I, but it was pricey and the more we settled into our relationship, the less we went.

As I approach the pub, a drop of water lands down the back of my coat from a hanging basket of flowers and I shiver as I pull open the door, glancing behind me. I don't seem to be able to walk five paces now without checking if I'm being followed, about to be grabbed, dragged into an alley, strangled. Stabbed. Suffocated.

My thoughts have turned more violent since seeing her with Fred. I'm worried that she's biding her time, waiting for the right time to attack me, kill me. She seems more than capable of it. Maybe Fred hasn't seen that side of her and she's manipulating him with her physical assets. But she wasn't wearing a mask for me. At least, I don't think she was. I looked into those scary eyes and while I can't remember everything that happened, I remember what I saw there—how dangerous she felt.

Like Jam said: I could go to the police. Yet, tell them what?

I don't know for sure that she's following me, or that she sent those messages. All she's done is steal my husband, in response to my telling her that I wanted him gone.

More than gone: *dead*.

I'm not sure how that would play out in a police station. For now, I'm going to have to rely on Michael Quinn.

I don't know what he looks like, aside from my mental picture of black hair, blue eyes. Yet, when I spot a blond man in the corner typing on a laptop, I know it's him.

He jumps up to greet me. "Gabby O'Neal? Michael Quinn. So, are you Irish too?" he jokes, eyes creasing.

He's young, far younger than I expected. His eyelashes are very blond. I think of Will, his white-blond baby curls, my heart bouncing sadly.

The kids… Every time I think of them, I feel sick with betrayal, guilt. If they knew I was here, doing this.

He's waiting for a reply.

"No, I don't think so. Although I've never done the family tree." Because there's no tree to speak of.

"Can I get you a drink?" he asks.

"Maybe a small glass of white wine, please?"

"Coming right up," he says, clapping his hands, springing to the bar. He moves quickly. I don't imagine that he takes a long time to make decisions, which is fine by me.

I take a seat, glancing around the room. It's quiet at this time of night, a few diners and tourists, none of whom are interested in me. My eye falls on the corner table where Fred and I sat on our first date. I can still remember what he wore: a The Who T-shirt, and a necklace which I wanted to examine—mostly as an excuse to sit closer to him. It was a St. Christopher, a gift from his parents to keep him safe. I remember being impressed by that, as well as saddened.

Michael sets the wine before me, then sits opposite, eyes

bright and alert. “Thanks for meeting me. Are you comfortable with getting straight to it? Only, I’ve got a six thirty.”

“Oh. Yes. Of course.” This is going to be less painful and more efficient than I thought. “Well, I’m here because…my husband’s cheating on me.” I glance around again, lowering my voice. “With a young woman, called Ellis. I’m not sure how long it’s been going on. I thought it was recent, but maybe not. Either way, there’s a chance he’s paying for sexual favors with gifts. And I need to know if there have been others too—other…women like her.” I wipe perspiration from my top lip, taking a sip of wine to cool me.

All this time, he’s been watching me, blond eyelashes blinking like the white pampas grasses growing in our garden. He doesn’t seem fazed by what I’m saying. I suppose that’s what he’s here for. People don’t investigate nice things.

“There’s every possibility that this Ellis is a gold digger, in which case I need to secure my assets. I want to know exactly what he’s up to, how much money he’s given her and for how long. Can you do all that?”

“Absolutely.” He removes an iPad from his backpack, propping it on the table, typing. I watch him, drinking my wine, quelling my nerves.

After a few minutes, he puts it away again, zipping his bag up in a way that feels like meeting adjourned. “I’ve just sent you a form, which I need you to fill out with all the details about your husband, including an up-to-date photo for ID purposes. If you could make sure everything’s as accurate as possible, so there’s no mistakes.”

“Okay,” I reply, smiling tensely.

“And that’s all there is to it. Although…” He gazes at me, a deep indentation forming between his eyes. There’s a ruthlessness there which is disarming, as well as reassuring. “…I do need to know the ultimate goal, Gabby. What is it that you’re really after?”

I hesitate, looking at the table where Fred and I sat, thinking of his St. Christopher. It wasn't just a chain; it was a blessing of protection over his life. He had guardian angels on his side, still does.

I think of the day we moved into Ocean View Road, the palm trees I planted, the baby oaks Will and Alice planted under my instruction, the pool I oversaw the installation of, the meals I prepared in the kitchen, the hours I spent at the dining room table helping with homework, the years I spent going up and down the stairs with laundry baskets, school uniforms, football and hockey kits.

"The house," I say. "I want the house."

I'm so exhausted when I get home I don't notice that the lounge light is on. I'm going along the hallway, my socks cold and damp underfoot, every muscle in my body aching, when Fred calls out, "Gabby?"

I stop, my hand on the banister. "What is it?"

He appears in the doorway, looking the way I feel. He rubs his hands on his face and then gestures into the room. "Can you spare me a moment?"

I think about it. "That's probably not such a good idea."

"Please? I think we should have a civil conversation. We owe it to each other."

"I don't owe you anything."

He raises his hand as though in surrender. "Please, Gabby, just five minutes." His eyes look like ghoulish holes from this angle—deep dark crevices.

"Just five minutes then."

He steps aside as I enter the room. The gas fire is lit, softly buffeting. There are two glasses of whiskey on the coffee table, the crystal decanter glowing. "I don't—"

"Just take it," he says, handing me a glass, sitting down in his chair near the fire. "I thought you might be hungry, so I made a few nibbles." Torn off pieces of baguette dipped in olive oil and sea salt, roasted. We lived on this when we first met.

It feels manipulative, yet I'm starving. I take a piece, sitting down stiffly, glass balanced on my knee. "What do you want, Fred?"

"Mostly to apologize for this morning. I'm sorry you had to go through that, but it's not what you're thinking."

My cheeks burn with the sting of this lie. "Oh, so now you know what I'm thinking?"

He sets his drink down, hands clasped before him. "Yes. That I'm sleeping with a girl half my age."

"A gold digger," I correct.

He gazes at me in surprise. "Why would you say that?"

"Because it's true. You know as well as I do how many of them there are around here." I take a gulp of whiskey—too much—feeling it burn my throat, my insides.

"I wanted to ask you: have you met her before? Because it seemed as though you knew her." He sits forward in his seat, trying to look sincere. "Please, Gabby, tell me the truth. It's important."

"The truth..." I nibble a piece of baguette, crumbs falling. "I don't think you're in a position to ask for that. Besides, surely she told you herself?"

"No. She said you'd never met—that she had no idea what you were talking about."

"Well, that must be the truth then. I'm sure she has no reason to lie to you."

I think of how stonily silent and poised she was this morning, how careful not to react in any way. The way she spoke to Fred as though completely in control, within her rights, heir to the throne.

Again, my flesh creeps with the fear that she's watching me, even though the curtains are pulled and the doors are locked, bolts drawn.

"You scared her, Gabby," he says.

"I did?" I can't help but laugh at this, taking another drink of whiskey. So, I'm the aggressor, the unhinged middle-ager coated in sweaty hormones.

Discreetly, I wipe the fine layer of moisture around my hairline.

"Yes. She didn't know who you were, but she put two and two together when you started screaming in her face."

"I don't recall doing that."

He shakes his head. "No, I don't suppose you do. It's like you weren't even Gabby. I've never seen you like that before."

It strikes me then that he is making this about me—about my bad behavior, and not his. I could argue the point, but I sense that he would never get it. He's too far gone for that, too entrenched in his own stories.

"Please tell me how you know her, Gabby."

"Why don't you tell me how *you* know her? Because that seems far more important." I set my drink down on the table, sitting upright. "Did you know that your mom accosted me down on the seafront today when I was on my lunch hour? She said you have real feelings for this woman, as though I should be setting you free to be happy. You're such a cliché, Fred—a huge bloody cliché!"

I'm shouting now, my hands angry fists. And he's just sitting there placidly, letting me get my blood pressure up.

"Do you have any idea what this is doing to me?" I spring to my feet. "None of you care about me."

He stands up, towering over me. "That's not true. Mom was saying only yesterday how much she loves you."

"Bullshit!" I'm overheating, my insides boiling and I feel strangely floaty too, as though trapped in a wet cloud. This can't be good for me. I sit back down, head spinning.

"I'm at that age, Fred… My symptoms may sound flaky to you and I know you're not interested. But it's real and you wouldn't be able to handle it, the way I feel most days. You wouldn't be able to hold down a job, let alone show up day in and day out, doing what I do." I rub my hands on my legs, trying to unreel my stress, smooth it out. "The small health decisions I make—the ones I'm making now, every day—will decide how my later years play out. So, I have to look after myself. Because it matters—I matter."

"Of course," he says, as though he wrote the book on menopause.

He doesn't know how it feels. He'll never know how it feels, because he's not listening and he's not interested. He's not going to hold my hand and age gracefully with me. Far from it.

I feel the heat leaving me, my anger dissipating. "Look, I'll let you get out fast, if that's what you want. But..."

He looks at me cautiously, shoulders raised.

"...The house, Fred. I can't part with it. It's my St. Christopher."

"I don't understand." He frowns. "You can't afford to buy me out. We have to sell it, right?"

Wrong. "I can't do that."

He opens his mouth, looking obtuse. "Then what are you asking? What do you want?"

"For you to be fair. I mean, one day you'll inherit your parents' place and I won't see any of that money if we're divorced. Surely, you don't need half of this house too?"

"But that's not the point. How am I supposed to live until then? Mom and Dad could live another twenty-five years!"

"To a hundred and five?"

He scowls. "Let's just see a mediator and get this resolved. I'll make an appointment first thing in the morning."

I'm too tired to argue. All I want is a bowl of soup and bed.

As I leave the room, he's fiddling with something and I realize he's dipping down inside his shirt, feeling for his lucky talisman, checking the universe still has his back.

At the door, I turn, my conscience nagging me to at least tell him to watch himself, but he speaks first. "I feel sorry for you, Gabby. You're going to be alone, bitter and dried up, rattling around this place by yourself if you get your way. Is that what you want?"

"See you at mediation," I reply.

In the kitchen, I keep the lights low, moody, as I set about the sorry business of reheating leftover soup to eat alone. And I'm carrying it to the stove, when the security light flicks on outside and I'm so startled I drop the bowl.

It's just the neighbor's cat, blinking at me, licking its paws.

Somehow, the bowl didn't shatter, but the soup's gone, ruined. For a moment, I'm tempted to spoon it up. That's how broken down I am. But some of it has seeped under the kitchen units. I draw the line at chasing it there.

I clean up the mess, pity tears amassing. Maybe Fred's right; I'm bitter, screwed up. I'm going to end up here all alone. The security light clicks off, plunging me back into darkness. Outside, there's a movement as the wind rustles the oaks and I twitch my head that way, seeing nothing but my own reflection. Yet, I picture her there, watching me in her gold dress, that intense look in her eyes. Someone like her could have anyone she wants. There must be plenty of men around here worth ten times more than Fred.

Why him?

There's a noise, footsteps, keys jangling. I hold myself stiff, listening, as the front door opens, then slams shut, the walls jumping in shock as he disappears off into the night.

24

9 months earlier

The hotel was morbidly quiet, as though they were the only guests here. She waited for him to stop thinking they were going to have sex, to let his brain clear. Yet, he was going to the mini bar again, going to the bathroom for a cup, filling it with orange juice, adding vodka, stirring it by swishing it round, a drop spilling on the carpet.

She was sitting very still, her dress hitched high. She had removed her heels, toenails sparkling—mulberry—setting off her tan, even in December.

"Would you like some?" he said, handing her the cup.

She pretended to drink it. He sat down beside her, the bed dipping, daring to touch her bare leg. Moving away, she reached for her bag.

"Sorry, I need to turn my phone off," she said, remaining in the chair by the window, where he could see her fully, stay hungry. Yet, enough distance between them for him to actually hear her, listen.

"So..." he said. "What awful secret do you need to tell me? What could possibly put me off you?"

She'd already had a little cry; just a flurry. More than that and she would be deemed hysterical, needy. This was delicate, a dance. "I don't want to burden you with my problems. We've only just met."

"So? If someone was about to jump off a building, I wouldn't ignore them because I didn't know them."

She nodded. "True."

Although he might, from what she knew of him.

"What is it then?" he prompted.

He was very awake, even though it was past midnight. Outside, the town would be frosty, the sludge forming icy crystals as the temperature fell. Yet, in here, they were sealed in an airless time capsule that the seasons didn't affect.

"I'm not who I said I was. I mean, I'm Ellis, obviously. But this isn't me." She gazed down at herself. "Picking up guys, wearing this dress..." She tugged carelessly at the velvet material. "It's because I..." She allowed her mouth to quiver, the sort of pathetic gesture that actresses did years ago, violins playing. But he would accept it without question: that she was weak.

"Because you what?" he asked, easing toward her, completely captivated. She'd never seen anyone hypnotized before, but thought it would look something like this.

She ran her finger along the pattern of the chair, a wild floral pattern with tendrils, moths. "I...I got you here just to use you."

He stared at her, holding the plastic cup so tightly it buckled. "Use me? How?"

"It was a setup," she said, unable to meet his eye. "I was looking for someone who could help me."

"Help you do what?" He stood up, pacing the floor as though suddenly sober and wondering what the hell he was doing here. "I don't understand. What are you talking about?"

"I wasn't going to say anything." She fiddled anxiously with her hands. "But then you had to go and say that thing about being fully honest with each other." She placed her hands against her heart. "I mean, I used to be a straight-up person. That's what drew me to you, because I could tell you're the same."

He liked that, puffed his chest a little. She was skilled at masking sarcasm.

"I want to be honest with you. I don't want you to think I'm some kind of hooker, what with us meeting in that sleazy singles' bar..."

He frowned at her. "Sleazy? It's perfectly respectable! I've been going there for years and haven't met any hookers!"

"That you know of. But if you're out late at night in a harbor town, hanging around singles' bars, you're probably going to meet one sooner or later."

"Well, not me. I'm a married man!" He gazed around the room, looking for his self-respect and his wallet. The first thing he would want to do was check it, because whores were thieves. That's what his face was saying. "Anyway, if you thought it was so sleazy, what were you doing in there? And what do you mean about a setup? Why come on to me, if you're not interested?"

When she didn't answer any of the questions, he tutted, grabbing his jacket. He was heading out, his long legs striding toward the door. So she emitted a sob, a manufactured hiccup. "I didn't say I wasn't interested."

He paused, turned. "Look, what's going on, hey?" He was clutching his jacket, tension conquering his expression. The look of a man whose guarantee of sex had fallen through.

She shook her head, another tear escaping.

"Are you in some kind of trouble?"

She didn't reply, bit her lip. He waited several beats, then tossed his jacket onto the bed, picking up the vodka, knocking it back. "If you don't tell me what's going on in the next ten seconds, I'm going to walk out of here and you'll never see me again."

She slipped off the chair, gliding noiselessly through to the bathroom where she plucked up a tissue, returning with it to her seat, dabbing her face. He was watching her the whole time. She added a flash of knickers—Christmas red—before settling again, folding her arms so her breasts were ample, impossible to ignore. "I'm so sorry. But I can't sleep with you," she said.

"What?" He wanted her so badly his confusion was palpable. Desire, lust, sinner, whore. It was all there. "Why not?"

"Because it would be wrong."

"How so?" His face tightened. "Wait, you're not—?"

"Underage? No."

"Well, that's a relief."

She played with the chain on her clutch, slipping her fingers into the loops. "I know that's the only reason you're here. Men never want to get to know me. All they see when they look at me is the promise of a mind-blowing screw."

He could put his tongue away. And his hard-on. This talk was actually turning him on.

"But then when I saw you, I thought you were different." She shivered, despite the heat in the room. "But I can see now that I had you wrong because you're just the same as all the rest. And I'm very sorry about that."

He opened his mouth, closed it, frowning.

She saw her chance to continue. "Some men will never get past the way I look."

He gazed at her legs, her body, so obviously perfect even in loose velvet. He looked hungry and thirsty, as though using all his energy not to pull up her dress, thrust himself into her. He ran his hands through his hair, over his mouth, thinking.

She waited.

"So are you saying nothing's happening tonight, but could in the future?" he said, his expression brightening.

"Yes. But I shouldn't have come here with you. I'm sorry..."

She played a risky move then. She picked up her bag, made as though she was about to put on her shoes and leave.

"I think I could work with that," he said. She reached for her coat, but he blocked her from collecting it, hand on her arm. "We don't have to rush anything."

"Please, I need to go. This wasn't fair on you. I'm so sorry, but..." He reached down, drawing her chin toward him as he stooped to kiss her, barely connecting. She shivered again, this time for real because it was a long time since she'd let someone do this. It wasn't supposed to happen, but had to. Even she could see that.

Against her body, he was aroused again, yet his kiss didn't become sloppy, urgent. "You're so beautiful," he said, breaking away. "I'd love to get to know you."

She gazed up at him, then sat down on the bed, still holding the tissue. She stretched it between her hands, seeing how strong it was.

"I think we could have something here," he said, joining her. "We could take it slowly, if that's what you want."

"Maybe?" she said coyly.

"But you need to tell me why this was a setup," he said, squeezing her leg gently, his wedding band gleaming.

"Well...it's to do with my home, or lack of." She closed her eyes briefly. "I lost all my possessions—everything—in a house fire because my roommate left a joint on the sofa and I wasn't insured. It was a dump anyway, with a coked up landlord who treated us like dirt." Her voice broke.

He reached for her hand. "I'm sorry. That sounds bad."

"My roommate did a runner. So then the landlord turned on me, said I owed him for the damages. Thousands of pounds. So I ran away too, right after he threatened me with a baseball bat—said he'd beat me to a pulp, let me bleed to death. He said no one cared about scum like me."

"Where was this? Not somewhere round here, surely?" Outside in the corridor, there was a sudden noise, a door opening and closing. He gave a start as though displaced, his face colorless. He rubbed it, getting the blood going. "Can't you report him?"

"I don't think so. Besides, I think he might be right—I owe him money. But I don't have any."

"What about your family?"

"Don't have that either. Foster kid."

He squeezed her hand tighter, his palm sweaty. "What about your friends? Surely there's someone who can put you up until you get on your feet?"

"I left them all behind, haven't had a chance to meet anyone new yet." She dropped the tissue onto the floor. "That's what I was doing in that bar. I got desperate, was hoping to meet someone rich who might...help me out or something."

"I see," he murmured, pulling his hand away. Nothing severed a connection like a freeloader. "So you were fishing for a sugar daddy?"

"No. I dunno. Maybe. I thought it was worth a shot. This area's famous for them, isn't it? But I can see now that it was stupid... *I'm* stupid."

The corners of his mouth turned down sulkily. "I hate the idea of one of those disgusting baldies groping you."

She nodded. "Same."

"So that's why I'm here?" He dropped his hands onto his knees. "A meal ticket?"

"At first." She shrugged despondently. "But then I realized I could actually see myself with you."

He gazed into the air, mouth open, seeing himself with her too.

"But I'm going to have to go back where I came from. Someone will be able to help me scrounge a bed for a week or so."

"I don't think that's an option. That guy sounds dangerous. He could do you some serious harm." He stood up, going to the curtain, lifting the dense material as though there might be someone standing there about to blow his brains out.

Then he turned to look at her, arms folded. "I might be able to help, but I need to think about it. You've definitely got no family or friends?"

"Like I said: foster kid. And when you move around as much as I did, you don't tend to pick up many friends. Not decent ones anyway." She waited, trying not to look as though she was watching him closely.

He gazed at the ceiling, then at her. "Don't leave," he said. "And don't pick up any flabby old guys." He smiled. "Other than me."

"I'll try not to," she said, giving him another flash of her underwear, as though completely unaware.

"The thing is, I don't have cash hanging around the house—not the sort you would need to get started. It's not exactly cheap around here."

"Which is why I'm going to have to leave."

"No. Don't do that," he said, sounding desperate, then checking himself, standing tall. "It's just that it feels as though you've come into my life for a reason. I think we should at least explore that for a while, see where it leads?"

"I can explore." She smiled flirtatiously.

"How about we get a few hours of sleep and think about it some more?" he suggested. "Don't know about you, but I'm shattered."

"Me too," she said, feigning a yawn. She was a light sleeper, didn't need much. She stretched out on the bed, resting her head on the pillow, hair draped around her. He kicked off his shoes, lay beside her, not touching her. She could tell he was thinking in the darkness. Out somewhere in the real world, an engine rasped, and then all was still.

When she woke, there was an envelope beside her. It was no surprise. She'd heard him moving around the room at dawn, tracking his motion through to the bathroom and out of the main door, listening to the sound of the elevator rumbling.

On his return, she acted asleep, mumbling slightly, frowning as though her worries were disturbing her dreams. He bent over her perhaps to kiss her, then changed his mind, withdrew.

His shadowy form went to the door, looked back at her and then there was a click, a sigh as the door closed and he was gone.

She didn't move for several minutes. And then she rolled onto her hip, picked up the envelope, taking it over to the curtains, pulling them aside to let the light stream in.

> I know we've only just met but I can't lose you yet, not without knowing what this is.
>
> Here's £500 to tide you over. Meet me Friday night and I'll see if I can rustle up some more. Here's my number. Call me x

In the bathroom, she pinched her cheeks, smoothing her dress. Then she left the hotel, stepping out into the early morning. The pavements were shimmering with frost underneath the streetlights, the buildings standing to attention, her heeled footsteps ricocheting up and around the rooftops like applause.

25

Maria Kane, the Rottweiler, couldn't see me until Friday, offering me a late lunch, her only available window for the next four weeks. I took it.

Her office is based at the other end of High Street from work. It's cold out, almost the end of September. I draw the belt of my trench coat tighter around me, checking my appearance in the reflection of the betting shop. I'm not a gambler, but I would bet that Ellis is watching me now. I'm on my way to get help from the toughest lawyer in the area. If I were her, I'd be watching me.

The thought of Ellis makes me overheat. I stop outside the florists, inhaling the calming aroma, fixing my hair up before continuing along my way, only to stop four steps later to remove my coat. I carry it on my arm, ignoring the familiar prickly heat spreading over my limbs. And then I'm there.

Maria Kane is a lot shorter than me, than most people. She's wearing shiny patent heels and is at the water cooler, filling a bottle, water glugging. There are peace lily plants everywhere and on her desk there's a tiny gold Buddha.

"You must be Gabby O'Neal?" she says, setting her bottle down to shake my hand.

"Yes. Thank you for seeing me." I wait for her to go behind her desk, but she doesn't. Instead, she sits on a dusky blue sofa, gesturing for me to join her. So far I'm struggling to get even a whiff of Rottweiler.

"Can I get you something to drink?" she asks.

"No, thanks."

"Then we'll get straight to it," she says, picking up a notepad and pen. "So…your husband is waiting for a decision from you on a sole or joint application, is that correct?"

"Yes." I'm squeezing my right hand. I try to unclench it, but it coils back up.

"And with both children at university, there are no dependents under the age of eighteen living at home?"

"Correct."

She tucks her hair behind her ear, revealing a sparkling crucifix on her lobe. She has neat features—smooth skin, short hair, the whites of her eyes very bright as though she takes everything off at night and washes it.

"The main sticking point, as I understand, is the house." She looks at me with the whisper of a frown. I wouldn't put her much past thirty—no wrinkles or grays. "Do you have a mortgage?"

"No."

She jots this down. "And when did you last have it valued?"

"The house?" I ask, stalling. Talking about this is always awkward. "Two years ago."

"And?" she says, pen poised.

I shuffle my feet. "It was valued at six million."

I wait for her to give a little whistle, raise an eyebrow, but she doesn't even blink. And it's then that I see the Rottweiler. She writes six million on her pad, underlining it. To be fair, there are many houses in this area worth double that. This won't be her biggest case, not by a long way. But it will be of interest, her hackles raised.

She sets her pen down. "Firstly, you should know that disputes of this nature are very common. It can feel as though whoever gets the house has won."

I nod, wanting to tell her that it's not about the money, nor a bitter struggle for territory or revenge. Doesn't everyone say that though?

"At the risk of patronizing you, I'll run through your options." She holds up her index finger, striking it off, a bracelet tinkling daintily. "One: you sell the house and buy two homes, which in your case sounds feasible."

Two homes. I smile pleasantly.

"Secondly—" she strikes off her next finger "—you buy him out."

Again, I smile. Even though that one's impossible.

"Thirdly, you postpone making any decisions until later—when your children leave university, for example."

This one gets a genuine nod.

"And finally...you transfer a portion of the value from one of you to the other as part of the settlement. So your husband might give up a share of the ownership rights, while retaining a stake in it. Hence, if it were sold at any point, he'd then receive that share."

"Okay." I'm getting a bit tangled mentally. All I want is for her to tell me what to do—how I can keep the house. "I think the last one sounds the best?"

She picks up her water bottle, taking a sip. "This house is an emotive subject for you, isn't it? I mean—" she smiles fleetingly "—it always is, but in your case it seems more so. Am I right?"

"Yes." My throat constricts, and I tighten my fist again.

"May I ask why?"

Beyond her, the phone rings, her assistant answering it. I become aware of the traffic passing the front windows, shoppers going by with carrier bags.

"It was…a gift…for me," I reply. "But I changed the deeds so my husband was co-owner, just to keep things fair."

We both hear the regret in my voice.

"I see." She doesn't probe any further, sits back in her seat, receding.

"All our assets are tied up in the house," I continue. "I can't afford to mortgage it or buy him out. We do have some savings, but…"

She touches my arm lightly. "It's okay. We don't need to get into the financial nitty-gritty today. Yet, I did want to ask you about mediation."

Something about the way she says this troubles me. "What about it?"

"Well, when you made this appointment my assistant mentioned that you seemed keen on it." She pauses. "Is it you who's keen, or your husband?"

"My husband."

"Only, I'd think about that if I were you." She sits up straight, picking up her pen. "If you wanted me to represent you, we could go ahead and apply to the court for a financial order. The main issue, however, will be whether your husband can afford to live without the sale of the house?"

I feel everything drop inside and out, my shoulders flagging. "He can't. At least, I don't think he can."

"Well, that's going to be the biggest problem, although ultimately it'll be up to the court. With the children still at university, there's a chance you could be permitted to stay, with the house still in his name and in the event of you selling, he'd then get half. Would you be okay with that?"

"Yes. I think so."

"Where there's a will, there's a way."

I wish I shared her faith.

"At the end of the day," she says, standing up, straightening her blouse, "the most important thing is ensuring that there are no power imbalances between spouses."

She gazes at me, the word *power* hanging between us. And then she reaches for a divorce pamphlet and her business card, handing them to me. It feels very much as though it's over to me now, to decide whether to hire this friendly Rottweiler.

"Can I ask what you meant about mediation?" I say, as we walk to the door. "Why did you say to think about it?"

"Oh, it's normally not the first thing that anyone rushes to do, that's all. It struck me as unusual."

I'm standing near the front desk, her assistant typing rapidly. "He's taking advice from his parents and they're quite traditional. Plus, they're keen to protect the children. So that might be it."

"I see." But I can tell from her tone that she doesn't think that's it at all.

"Is there something else to be aware of?" I ask, holding my coat in my arms like a security blanket.

"Not at this stage." She surveys the street, her eyes moving with the traffic, flitting left to right. "But if you work with me, I'll tell you."

I stare at her, my cheeks reddening. And then she laughs. "I'm kidding!"

Is she though? I don't take the chance. "I'd like to work with you."

She smiles, shaking my hand, her grip surprisingly firm. "Good. Let's fix up a meeting as soon as my diary becomes available."

I wait, eyeing her. "So…you were going to tell me?"

"Ah. Yes." She watches the traffic again, lips parted in contemplation. "Sometimes one of the parties will rush the other into mediation to prevent certain details from being disclosed."

"Details?"

She gazes up at me. "Yes. If there's something he'd want to hide."

My heart feels as though she's tightening it in her hand, one end of it bulging like a deflated balloon.

She can see the terror on my face. "Let's bring that meeting forward," she says, turning to her assistant.

I leave Maria Kane's premises like a fragile butterfly heading into a storm. It's starting to rain, the sunshine still strong, illuminating the splinters of moisture. I stop at the florists again, standing among buckets of sunflowers and calla lilies, typing on my phone.

Fred, please cancel the mediation appointment. I'm not ready yet.

I read it through twice, press Send.

Fridays are always quiet, with many of the staff working from home. A few years ago, I instated Dress Down Fridays and asked one of the young administrators to make an office playlist to liven things up. In the spirit of this, on my way back from Maria Kane's, I pick up a box of doughnuts and coffees and as I set them on my desk, a couple of people cheer. I feel temporarily soothed, happy to be here, with my team, in the rhythm of normal life, if only for a few more hours.

Shaun isn't back yet from lunch. I went late, and he went early. It's been over two hours. I try to be tolerant, flexible, but he's been doing this more and more, seeing how far he can push me. Again, it reminds me of the children when they were little—the first time Alice looked me in the eye and said *no!*

As I start work, he enters the room, looking straight at me, making sure I clock his return time. "There's a doughnut there for you, Shaun," I call out cheerfully. That was the tact I took with the kids: cheerfulness, even though I'm sure there was a bit of shrill in there, like there is now.

He's not too proud for a doughnut, takes one, biting it before he's even seated.

I think then of Maria Kane, of what she said about imbalances of power, and I realize that if Shaun is testing me then I have to have a more effective strategy than appeasement. Because he's not one of my kids and he's paid to show up at work within the conditions of his contract like everyone else. None of which I feel able to tell him.

Which is why I think I have to. Approaching his desk, I smile, not able to throw all my softening tactics away. "Shaun… could we have a quick word, please?" I don't wait for him to reply, but head to the conference room.

Naturally, he takes his time. I'm standing at the window, looking over the rooftops to the gray sea, gathering my words several times over, when he finally joins me.

"What's this about?" he asks gruffly, hands in pockets.

"Nothing too serious," I reply. "I just wanted to ask you about your working hours, whether you need a longer lunch. Because we could rethink your hours? It's not a problem." I mean this—I'm flexible.

He doesn't reply, looks past me, out the window.

"I… Well, there are some newer members of our team who might think that it's okay to choose the length of their lunch hour. Obviously, we have to be fair to everyone and keep things consistent. Because they look up to you." I add this last bit, even though it's not true, to my knowledge.

He folds his arms, lifts his chin.

"Come on, Shaun. Work with me here."

He looks at me then, in a way that's not all that nice. "I have nothing to say to you, except good luck."

"I'm sorry, but I'm not sure that I follow…" I swallow nervously, watching as a smirk forms on his lips. He's enjoying this, whatever it is.

"Funny you're in here lecturing me about fairness and consistency," he says, playing with the chain on the window blinds, twisting it in his hands, "when your husband's out there whoring."

Everything seems to lurch—my stomach, the room. Outside, the music swells, as someone turns up the volume, the bassline matching my pounding heart. "What did you just say?"

"You heard."

I stare at him. "What do you know about Fred? Why—?"

"That's gotta hurt, eh?" He drops the chain and it rattles against the glass. "What is she, like, twenty years younger than you?"

My face burns as though he slapped it. "What are you talking about?"

He looks pleased with himself, rocking on his toes. "I saw him coming out of an expensive jeweler's with some gold digger in a stripper dress. I tried not to stare, but it was difficult not to, to be honest, and I wasn't the only one." He checks his watch, taps it. "Anyhow, I'd best get back to work—be fair to everyone on the team, right?"

He leaves the room with a bit more swagger than he had five minutes ago, as though this is karma, as though my getting this job, outflanking him, meant I was due a good outflanking myself—the mother of all outflanks.

At the door, he stops, his head rolling slyly in my direction. "I'd check my bank balance if I were you, Gabby."

26

October 1982

"So, what are your thoughts, huh?" He put his arm around me. I wriggled free, stepped back.

"It's okay," I said, putting my hands in my pockets. I was wearing new jeans with cherry motifs on the pockets. It was a shame they were on my backside because I would have liked to have seen them more often.

"Okay? Are you kidding? It's magnificent!" He threw his arms up, like ta-da!

I shrugged, stood on a crunchy leaf, found another one to stand on. "Why did it take so long?"

He creased his nose, scratched it. "Well, these things don't happen overnight, for starters. We had some financing issues and construction problems, but it's here now and that's what counts. And it's more beautiful than I even imagined it."

"That's not true. It's exactly the way you imagined it. You said so yourself."

He crouched down, clasping my arms. "Now what's got into you, hey? I thought you loved this place?"

I looked up at the roof of the house, right into the sunshine, forgetting to squint. I wasn't into squinting anymore, wasn't into anything that I used to be into. Everything had changed: I was eleven, at senior school now, didn't say Mommy and Daddy, didn't pretend I lived in Gotham City. I did like the roof tiles though—the redness, how many of them there were, magically prevented from slipping off.

He led me forward. "There's the lamppost you wanted," he said, as we passed it, "like the one in *The Lion, the Witch and the*…uh…"

"Wardrobe," I said.

"Yep, that's the one. And…close your eyes a sec."

I didn't, so he did it for me, wrapping his fingers over my eyes. They smelled of cigars, even though he told Mom he'd stopped smoking. He walked me to the door. "Steady. There's a little step…" He removed his hand. "What do you reckon?"

"What?" I said blankly.

He tutted. "The knocker." He stepped back to admire it. "Like it?"

It was a brass lion, reminded me of Aslan. He knew I liked it; I'd chosen it. "S'okay," I said, pushing my hands in my pockets.

"Honestly, there's no pleasing you," he said, jokingly, but sounded hurt. "Come on, there's something else I want to show you… Shoes off." He tapped my legs.

I sat down cross-legged, slowly untying my laces. He waited patiently, pretending to examine the skirting but I could tell he was trying not to let me get to him.

We went into the room on the left, which was called the reception room on the plans. "Where's all the furniture?" I asked, my feet bouncing on the springy carpet.

"Not here yet. It's coming tomorrow, in time for the new occupants to pick up their keys and then it'll be theirs."

"I thought it was mine," I said.

He tucked his shirt into his trousers, tightening his belt. "Well, it is. The new people are only renting it. It'll stay in my name, and then someday it'll be in yours. Because what's yours is mine, eh?" He ruffled my hair as though I were six.

I twisted away, going to the window, looking out at the lawn. It all looked neat and tidy, the same way my uniform and books felt on the first day at school. The windows had metal lines on them, as though very old, and everything—the front door, staircase, window frames, some of the walls even—were made of shiny oak that had a reddish tint to it.

"Look," he said, going over to the windows. "See those squares?" He pointed to the metal frames. "That's solid lead, that is. That'll always be there, so long as the house is." He motioned for me to join him. I walked forward as slowly as I could.

"What's your birthday?" he asked, as though I was stupid. When I didn't answer, he took a deep breath. "Seventh of May. So that's seventh day, fifth month, seven five." He touched the lead, tracing it. "This is like a Battleship grid."

I gave him my full attention then—still liked Battleship. We played it sometimes, when he was home.

"If you count down seven squares from the top, see... And then five along from the right, you come to this square here at the bottom."

He turned to look at me, checking I was listening. "And that's how you'll always remember where our handprints are." He knelt down, showed me the bottom square window, traced with his finger down to the floor. "Me and you. A little piece of us here that no one can ever take away."

I stared at him, at the exact point he was showing me, thinking of our handprints in the cement; his big, mine little.

"So what do you think? Clever, hey?"

He was always asking what I thought. And it was becoming harder to know how to answer.

My throat was starting to hurt. My ears were hot. I swallowed hard and then turned on my heel and ran across that spongy carpet as though on a bouncy castle. "Where you going?"

Out in the hallway, I grabbed my shoes, thrusting my feet into them, not bothering to do up the laces. Running out to the car, I jumped inside, the leather interior warm against my back.

I sat with my feet on the seat, my arms around me, feeling my heart race. Dad was locking up the house, pushing the key into his back pocket with a scowl.

Getting into the car, he sat facing the house, not looking at me. We stayed like that for a while, my heart going back to normal.

"What's wrong?" he asked. "Is it Mom?"

She had been funny lately, spending a lot of time in bed. Back when I was still Batman, I might have answered that it was her who was wrong, yes. But things were different now, even though I didn't know how or why. "Can we go home?" I asked.

He sighed, shaking his head, starting the engine.

As we went down the driveway, I turned to look at the house right before it disappeared from view. I faced forward, my throat hurting again. "Thank you for the lamppost and the door knocker and the handprints, Daddy."

He reached for my hand, held it all the way home. "That's okay, Batman."

At home, I kicked off my sneakers and was about to run upstairs when I caught sight of something in the lounge that ripped my breath from my body.

On the sofa near the door was a mountain of frizzy blond hair, underneath which was a black-and-white sweater that I recognized from nearly six months ago when she came to our house and was screaming. She hadn't been back since, but I could tell there was a good reason why she was here now—or a bad one.

I tiptoed closer, listening, but then Dad came in, slamming the front door behind him and Frizzy jumped to attention, her eyes saucepan lids.

"Robin?" Mom called, her voice all tight.

I shrank back into the darkness underneath the stairs, squatting, knowing they would forget about me here.

He stopped in the lounge doorway. "What are you doing here? I told you not to interfere."

I couldn't see Frizzy or Mom; Dad was blocking them. He was still wearing his boots, had tracked mud down the hallway. There was a big red leaf on his heel, all the way from Ocean View Road.

"I'm sorry," Frizzy said, "but I didn't know what else to do. We can't carry on like this. It's not fair on anyone."

Mom spoke then. "Sara tells me that you're leaving."

Leaving.

The word squashed my tummy. I clasped my hands to my face, pressing my skin.

"Alice..." Dad said, moving into the room. "It wasn't supposed to happen like this." He raised his voice. "You had no right to come here, Sara!"

Frizzy started to cry. Beyond her, Mom was still sitting down, wearing a flowery shirt and jeans. I thought she looked pretty. Why was Dad doing this?

"Don't take it out on her," Mom said. "This is your doing, Robin. You're the married man. You're the father. This is all you!" She screeched the last word and I stared at her through my fingers, too scared to look without a shield.

"Oh and you think it's been a picnic living here with you?" Dad snapped back.

Mom took a moment to inhale, as though pumping herself up with air, then stood up. "Don't you dare put this on me!" she yelled. "This is nothing about me or what I could have done or didn't do or could have been better at and you damn well know it!"

"Please don't shout," Frizzy said, crying harder. "I didn't mean for this to happen. This is all my fault."

"No, it isn't," Mom said, waving her hands. "Don't flatter

yourself! If it weren't you, it would be some other young trollop. You're just some young twenty—" She broke off. "How old are you?"

"Don't answer that," Dad said.

But it was too late: Frizzy already had. "Twenty-three."

Mum rolled back her head and laughed, but it was too high-pitched and jerky to be the sort of laugh that made everyone else join in. "Oh, Robin." She folded her arms. "You've outdone yourself. What did you do? Hang around outside the playground with a packet of—"

"That's enough!" he shouted. "I will not tolerate this in my own home!"

"Then go!" Mom yelled. And then she was charging at him, hitting him with her fists. "Get out! Just go! Just get out!"

I closed my eyes, held my hands over my ears, rocking on my feet.

Don't go, Daddy. Don't go, Daddy. Don't—

The front door slammed so loudly, the walls vibrated. Everything fell quiet and then Frizzy spoke. She was standing so close I could see the details of her shoes. I recoiled farther into the shadows, my foot against the vacuum cleaner. Her sandals were red with black lace, a big bow at the front, a strap around the back.

"I'm so sorry, Mrs. Burton. I didn't mean any of this to happen, but I thought it only fair that you should know that we're in love."

I held my breath, waited.

Mom wailed and then pounced. "Get out!" she screamed. "Get out of my house!" There was a scuffling of feet, the sound of the door opening and slamming again and then Mom fell down against the door, cradling her head to her knees, sobbing.

I was about to go to her, when she sprang up and ran upstairs into her bedroom. There was a lot of clattering and bashing and then there was a clunking sound outside. I ran through to the lounge and saw Dad's shirts falling into the fishpond, a suitcase smashing in two, a pair of trousers landing in the trees. It was like carnival night, when the town was decorated with ribbons and banners.

Upstairs, she was starting to smash things now. China. Glass. I was halfway up the stairs when I realized something. This whole time, she hadn't asked where I was. She hadn't noticed whether or not I'd come home, didn't even know whether I was here.

Anger frothed up in me so quickly, I ran down the hallway, grabbed my coat from the peg, and slipped out the front door, looking for Dad.

His car was still there! I ran toward him, but he was driving away. I lurched at the boot, banging my hands on it and he braked suddenly, looking at me in alarm through the rear-view mirror.

I raced around to his side. The window was open. "Just keep driving," Frizzy said.

"No, Dad!" I said, gripping the side of the car.

"Let go," he said, prying my fingers from the window. "Let go, kiddo."

"I'm not kiddo. I'm Batman! Please, Daddy. Don't go. Please don't go. Please—"

"For Pete's sake, just accelerate," Frizzy said.

"I'm sorry, Gabrielle," he said. He started to wind up the window. I was still gripping it. "Let go!" he shouted. But I couldn't. He was about to notch the window right to the top, but stopped because he would have sliced my fingers off.

Instead, he gazed at me for a second and I saw myself in his eyes, saw everything that we'd done together, every trip we'd taken in the Batmobile, every site we'd visited, every brick we'd laid.

"Let go," he said again, even though he was beginning to

cry. I couldn't do that to him. I couldn't let him go. He didn't really want me to, or he wouldn't have been crying.

And then he hit the accelerator. I ran as fast as I could to keep up and then he turned into the road and the motion sent me flying.

I lost my balance, regained it, started running after him. He stopped again and my heart lurched because he was waiting for me, but then just as I was about to catch up, he set off again, faster now. I couldn't catch him. I screamed after him as loudly as I could, my voice lost among the houses and trees and lawnmowers and traffic.

The whole world seemed to grow silent, my ears closing over, a dullness forming. I sat on the edge of the curb and poked at the dirt with a stick. I kicked an ants' nest. I found a large pine cone. I watched two magpies pecking at berries.

Round about teatime, when it was dark, and the smell of sausages and onions was wafting along the street, Mom came looking for me. She didn't say a word, just took my elbow, led me up the front path, past all the clothes strewn on the bushes as though our laundry had had a hissy fit.

"What would you like for tea?" she asked, smashed plates all over the floor. "Would you like a milk?" she said, as though every glass in the cabinet weren't broken.

I soon caught on.

"Macaroni and cheese. And yes please to milk," I said.

"Go and put the TV on then and wait for tea."

On my way down the hallway, I spotted something red near the doormat. I picked it up, twirling it in my hand. It was the leaf from Dad's boot. I would press it, hide it in a book as a secret treasure.

I set it on my knee as I watched TV and was so lost in the program that I didn't notice when Mom came in to check on me. Before I knew it, she'd whipped the leaf away. I wanted to protest, but something had happened to my legs and mouth and I couldn't say or do anything.

I didn't have the strength to chase after her, just like I couldn't run fast enough to catch him. And so it came to be that I lost my leaf treasure from Ocean View Road and my dad, all in one day.

27

My phone pings as I'm spooning ground coffee into the machine and I jump so much I spill it everywhere. I've blocked Ellis's numbers, but she could be using yet another burner phone, like Jam said.

It's Alice. Relief loosens my shoulders.

Are you free for a call at 10?

I press the button on the coffee machine, water starting to gurgle.

Yes! xox

The dots oscillate as she replies.

Dad too?

I don't have a clue where he is. I drum my nails, thinking how to respond.

Hopefully xxx

I have two hours to find him. Phoning him, it goes straight to voicemail. I don't leave a message. Clearing the spilled coffee granules off the counter, I get my mental house in order, thinking how quiet everything is now, compared to what Saturday mornings used to be like. It's the last day of the month; somehow I've made it to the end of September without getting too scratched by my empty nest, probably because there's so much else competing for my attention.

As much as I didn't want to take advice from Shaun, I did as he said and checked my bank balance on my phone. Four times already this morning, twice in the middle of the night. But it looks fine. No strange transactions from jewelers.

I should be seething, but I'm too upset. My self-esteem has shrunk to a speck, barely visible. Somehow, I'm going to have to stop myself from disappearing all together.

One thing's for sure: Fred must be getting money from somewhere other than our joint bank account.

There's only one way to find out.

I creep downstairs to his basement, thinking of bunkers, how they're supposed to keep soldiers and civilians safe but how they're often somewhere where nasty crimes are committed. It occurs to me that if someone—Ellis—were to kill me, down here would make an ideal setting. The smack of a spade on my head, then using it to bury me deep, underneath the floorboards.

My blood running cold, I turn every light on, propping the door open with one of Fred's design books. There's no way I'm dying down here, among all this metal and wire.

Shuddering, I sit down at his desk, the seat giving, bouncing. Stuck around his screen are curly Post-Its, the ink faded. None of them make any sense. *Emptiness is dynamic*; *Alphonse Mucha Job 1898!* But there's one that does.

I peel it off, gazing at his handwriting. *AP North*, our investment broker. I didn't realize he took that keen an interest in them? Trying to stick it back in place, it flutters onto the keyboard. I debate whether to leave it, decide I shouldn't, so I tape it into place, returning upstairs.

Opening my laptop, I go to our joint bank account where I can look at it properly, on a bigger screen. I'm not great at monitoring our finances; Fred isn't either, that I know of. The passwords and security checks always bug me.

By the time I've remembered my password and entered security codes, I'm on my second cup of coffee. And then I'm in, scrolling down slowly. Money arriving from our salaries at the end of each month, then going to AP North. An electronic relay.

I click on the payments to AP North, sitting forward to read them. One was set up a year or so ago, a thousand pounds a month. And then last Christmas, as a gift to Will and Alice, five hundred each a month to their investment funds, to be continued as long as we could afford it.

Two thousand pounds is leaving our account every month, going to AP North.

I go to their website. More security checks. More coffee. Finally, I'm able to access the inquiry form, where I write:

Please could you confirm to me in writing the details of my monthly transactions?

As I press Send, Alice messages again.

Can we make it 10:30?

I'd make it on the moon if she asked.

Yes xox

I try Fred again, but this time I leave a voicemail, telling him his daughter wants to see us both, that it's important or she wouldn't be asking.

I hope he doesn't show up, but if he does, then I hope he

doesn't look like a dirty stop-out. Or maybe he should. I'm not going to cover for him anymore. If he looks bad, that's on him.

"So how's it going?" I ask.

"Fab," Alice says. She looks so well. My hands ache with the longing to reach forward and touch her—smooth her hair, press a kiss onto her nose.

I distract myself with practical matters. "Are you eating well?"

"Yep. All good. The cafeteria food's a bit nah. But it's edible." She frowns, looks to the side of me. "Dad not there?"

"Sorry. He's at work."

"Really?" she says, hurt registering on her face. "Again? Is he always there or something?"

Or something.

"Sorry, sweetheart."

"That's okay." She turns sideways, laughing, tugging at someone. And then a face appears beside her. "Mom, this is Josh."

I'm taken aback, only because I wasn't expecting him. But there's something else too, which I don't have time to process because she's expecting me to say something—anything. "Hello, Josh."

He smiles. "Hello, Mrs. O'Neal."

"Oh, please—call me Gabby."

Out in the hallway, a door slams; Fred's back.

He breezes into the kitchen, sitting down next to me, completely ignoring me. "Hi, honey," he says to the screen. "How's it…? Oh, hello!" He clocks Josh, laughs in embarrassment, ruffling his hair, glancing at me then.

I keep my eyes on the screen. "This is Josh," Alice explains, looping her arm in his. "He's on my course."

"Hello," Fred says, his voice slightly flat.

"We met on our first day." And then she turns to smile at

him and I realize: she's in love. I well up again, looking down at my lap.

"How is the course?" Fred asks, steering the subject back to something he can handle.

"It's great," they both reply at the same time and then look at each other and burst out laughing. It's adorable and tragic because she's truly gone, someone else's now more than she's ours. I can't look at Fred, but I know he's thinking the same thing. We're both very still, quiet.

The call doesn't last for much longer. Alice has laundry. She says goodbye and it's only as Josh goofily says what an honor it was to meet us that I realize what it was that struck me about him.

He looks like Fred. Whether or not she knows it, she's chosen someone who resembles her father. But then she would; she thinks he's wonderful.

As the screen goes blank, I want to turn into pixels, dive into the screen, join her there. Fred opens a cupboard, removes an energy bar, slipping from the room.

I call after him. "That's it? You have nothing to say? So this is, what, a hotel now?"

In the doorway, he stops, hanging his head like a guilty man, except it's not guilt but intolerance. I'm making him suffer unnecessarily. "No," he says, his voice waspish, "because a hotel's a pleasurable experience."

"Well, you would know."

He tuts, smiles, as though I'm the most tedious person in the world. He hasn't shaved for days, looks jaded, gray. There's a stoop to his shoulders that isn't usually there and he's still wearing his work chinos. I worry momentarily about his mental health, but then he says, "I knew you'd get like this. I don't even want to look at you right now." And all sympathy for him fades away.

"Well, that suits me just fine."

"And yet you just said you wanted to talk to me. Yet another example of your impossible demands. You're up and down, all over the place. You really should get some help with that."

I'm not taking the bait, even though my inner voice is screaming at me to take it, run with it and drag him into the pool. He's going to do everything he can to make me look irrational, difficult. His parents and his lawyer will be advising him to do this.

"I'm just thinking of the kids, Fred, even though that must be a stretch for you because you've clearly got other things on your mind. But they're still your responsibility." I set my hand on the cool marble counter. The meals I've prepared here, no matter how tired, ill, frazzled. "I think we need a plan regarding how we're going to tell them."

He laughs. "A plan? We could always roll in the whiteboard, get out the marker pens, brainstorm it."

My cheeks flush. "And what's that supposed to mean?"

"Well, isn't that how you treat everything, like a work project?"

"That's not true!" I push back my barstool, standing up. "Is that what this is about—the fact that I earn more than you? Or is it because the house's mine? Is that why you cheated, Fred, to prove you're still the man around here?"

"Don't be so stupid! Anyway, the house isn't yours. It's mine too, remember?"

"And there's not a day I don't regret doing that! Because now whoever you shack up with can run off with half of what's mine!"

"So you *do* think it's yours, no matter what that piece of paper says!" he shoots back, his jaw tightening.

I sit back down. I'm still in my pajamas—didn't know I was going to be seeing anyone but Alice. "Why are you doing this, Fred?"

"You know why."

I wait, my stomach doing an unhappy dance. He sets his eyes on me and for a moment I see the man I once loved—the man in a The Who T-shirt who bought me half a lager and lime at the King's Arms a million years ago.

"Because we turned fifty and realized we hated each other."

The air in the room is so sharp I feel it stabbing my temples. He hated me too? Somehow that hadn't occurred to me before.

His posture loosens, one leg set against the wall. This is his resting pose. He's done fighting for now. "Why aren't you ready for mediation?" he asks quietly.

"I will be. I need a little more time."

"For what?"

"Nothing. I just don't see why there's a rush."

"And what about a decision on a sole or joint application?"

"Oh, yes. Go for sole."

He frowns suspiciously. "What are you up to?"

"Nothing. I'm up to nothing, Fred." I wipe crumbs from the countertop, gathering them in my hand, getting up to brush them into the sink. Alice's cereal bowl is still there. I'll remove it soon, but not yet. "You still haven't answered my question about the kids. I want to know when we're telling them. I won't let anything derail Alice." I gaze out the window at the cedar trees lining the side of the house.

"This isn't the same as what happened to you, Gabby. Nothing will derail her."

I can remember those trees being planted—ten feet apart, the trenches eighty centimeters wide, forty centimeters deep. Some people remember facts like that; I'm one of them.

"Do you really think I'm all whiteboards and marker pens?" I can hear the victim in my voice, the neediness, but can't stop it.

"Not really."

I want to sob, but somehow manage to keep a hold of myself.

"This thing with Ellis..." he says.

I hold up my hand. "I don't want to know, not now. I can't—"

"It's not what you think. I care about her. And she cares about me."

"I hope for your sake that's true," I reply softly, "but that plays differently to me, Fred—sounds different to my ear...as an older woman..." I trail off, unable to explain—unwilling to confide how my poor tired heart is interpreting his sexual preferences.

I open the fridge, even though I couldn't think about eating. I don't even know what I'm looking for. The Stilton must be bad by now; that cheesecake's surely off. There's one small piece gone which Alice cut the night before she left. I stare at that missing portion, a neat triangle, my eyes filling with tears.

"How many others have there been?" I say, closing the door. "Besides her and Daisy?"

"Just a couple," he says with enough shame to lower his voice.

"Do your parents know?"

He shifts his feet, checking his watch. "Actually, I'm due there now."

"For lunch?"

"No. I'm staying with them awhile. I'm finding it...difficult being here."

Something about this reassures me. At least he's with family, not roaming the streets. "What about the kids? Should we schedule a conversation?"

"I'll be happy with whatever you decide, Gabby. Just let me know."

I nod, watching him leave the room, anxiety tugging at me, urging me to say something—to tell him I'm scared of Ellis, scared that she's following me, going to do something terrible to me.

He's halfway down the hallway when I run after him. "Fred?" He stops, turns, one foot on the stairs. "How much do you know about her?"

My heart is doing all kinds of funny things, none of them natural.

"Ellis?" He shrugs with his mouth. I used to like that mannerism. Thought it made him look suave. I don't think people even say suave anymore. Everything about our relationship is out-of-date.

"I know enough," he says. "It's all good."

"Are you sure?"

He smiles. "One hundred percent."

"How long have you known her, exactly?"

He wavers, just like I do now before answering any questions. "We met just before Christmas."

"Christmas?"

This fits what I'd already deduced and yet bowls me over just the same. I wrap my arms around me, trying to make sense of the facts without looking as though I'm doing that.

How can this be?

The night Ellis approached me, she'd known Fred for…eight months? Yet, she offered to help me. Why?

I retreat to the kitchen, needing to get away from him. He can't find out about that night at Rumors. There's too much that I can't remember.

"Why do you ask?" he calls, but I'm already closing the door, standing with my back against it.

What if they planned this together, to get the house? What if they're trying to get rid of me?

Staring fearfully around the room, I take in the knife block, wondering if I'd be capable of defending myself—if I'm even capable of getting out of my pajamas today. Upstairs, Fred's opening and closing doors loudly, slamming them.

And then my laptop trills the arrival of an email, cutting through my mental noise. Grabbing my reading glasses, I peer at the screen. It's from AP North.

28

My face feels like a stretched canvas as I read the email. Outside, there's the sound of muted beeping as the garage doors open, Fred's silver BMW glinting like a slippery fish. I can barely take in the words, am struggling to process them.

Dear Mrs. O'Neal,
The last payment into your account was on 30th November 2022. No further payments have been received since that time.

In addition, the two accounts in the name of MR. W. O'NEAL and MISS A. O'NEAL have not received any payments since being set up on 8th December 2022.

Nothing has been going to our investment funds for almost a year. And the children's accounts are empty.

He met Ellis in December.

At the window, I watch him reversing out of the driveway. The trees are shaking in the wind, a storm brewing. In the sky, two birds are trying to make progress, being pushed backward.

Suddenly wanting to confront him, I hurry from the room,

down the hallway and out the front door. I'm shouting, but the wind carries my voice away, his car disappearing around the corner. Stopping, I scrape my hand against the pebble dash wall of the porch, crying out in pain.

Why is he doing this? We had our problems, but nothing could have prepared me for this level of deceit. I don't even know who he is anymore.

Back in the kitchen, I lick my bleeding knuckle, tasting iron. Then I log into our bank account again, looking at the payments to AP North, noticing something I didn't notice before.

They're not automated standing orders, like they should be. They're ordinary ad hoc payments. Fred's been taking money out of the account on the same day each month, making them look like the auto payments to our investment funds. He's even called them AP North to fool me.

Two thousand pounds a month from December to September... That's twenty thousand pounds.

I feel faint, my mouth drying. Going to the fridge, I pour a glass of orange juice, drinking it slowly, wondering what to do. The only thing I can think of is to tell Michael Quinn and Maria Kane.

Neither of them answer. I leave messages, asking them to call me back. Hanging up, I feel out of my depth, outmaneuvered. Even Shaun knew what to do. If it weren't for him, I wouldn't even have checked my bank details.

I know exactly who to take my inadequacies out on. Monique should know what Fred's been doing with her grandchildren's investment funds.

I'm trembling so much as I ring her landline, I know this is a very bad thing to be doing. On the second ring, I come to my senses, disconnecting the call. No matter the high ground, I can't divulge this. I'd lose the one bargaining tool I have, the one chance I have of getting the house.

I have to be smarter than that. But I've never been a strategist—was rubbish at chess.

Sliding my phone along the breakfast bar, out of harm's reach, I think of what Monique said about me being bitter—how Fred said I was going to end up here alone, dried up. The house couldn't be quieter; even the fridge has stopped humming.

The panic builds in me so rapidly I grip the counter to stay upright, a hot flash flooding me, a wave of dread dilating outward.

I wait for it to pass, because it always does.

And then it's just me again.

The sun shifts, resting on something vaguely white, catching my attention. My running shoes, left by the patio windows to dry in the sun. I gaze at them, a flicker of hope igniting.

I get changed quickly, pulling on Lycra, and then I'm off down the driveway. Without music, I listen to my breathing, my footsteps on the tarmac, the birds calling, leaves rustling underfoot. The storm will hit late afternoon. The buildup has already begun, the wind whipping at my clothes, urging me to get on with whatever I need to do before it's too late.

I turn onto the footpath that leads up to Len and Monique's in the other direction. It used to feel like a vein linking our families, but now I see that it was an umbilical cord just for him.

I haven't taken this route for a while, because of that runner; yet I shouldn't have given it up so easily. Some days, I've dreaded work because of Shaun; I should have done something about that sooner. And now I'm about to lose my home because of Fred's infidelity.

I've been letting everyone else dictate, following a satnav for my own life.

My breathing regulates as I meet the beach, making for the shoreline. I focus on the crop of rocks at the end of the headland, and don't look out for the runner at the usual spot where I might have seen him. Nor do I think of her as I pass Rumors. It's my retreat—my refuge with Jam. She's not going to take that too.

I'm turning around, heading back along the beach when my phone rings. It's Maria Kane. I stop, putting her on speaker, catching my breath.

"Gabby?" It sounds as though she's driving; it's very in and out. "You rang?"

It's loud at this end too, waves crashing on rocks. "Hang on a sec." I run a few yards up the beach. "Yes, it's about Fred. You know you said about him having something to hide?"

"Yes..." The line crackles, breaks, and I think I've lost her. But then she says, "Go on."

I look at the foamy sea, the bits of debris, yellow foam bobbing in a rock pool. "How does stealing from the kids' investments to pay for sex sound?"

She snorts scornfully. "Like a reason for the court to take your bid for the house extremely seriously."

"Even though they're over eighteen?"

"Yes, if they're still reliant on you for financial support, then that will be taken into consideration. Just get everything to me and I'll take it from there. And Gabby? Well done."

It doesn't feel like something I've done well.

I set off along the beach again, feeling so much heavier than five minutes ago. This time, as I pass Rumors, I think of her. I've no idea who she is, what she wants, but I'm sure it's not love that she's after.

Once again, it feels as though she's watching me. Glancing over my shoulder, I almost stumble over a rock, yet there's no one there.

Continuing along my way, an elderly man in a sporty jacket approaches along the shoreline, holding the hand of a young blonde in a bronze coat that's catching the sunlight so glaringly I have to look away. That's not the only reason though. I can't bear the sight of this anymore—the gray versus the peroxide, the crinkly skin versus the golden tan.

I'm turning off the beach early, running up the alley, when my phone beeps. I'm so certain it's Maria again that I stop to deal with it properly.

Ticktock. Not long now. 

Swiveling around, I look back down the alley to the crashing waves, my stomach shifting with them. I have to do something, say something.

Leave me alone or I'm calling the police. I mean it.

Then I block the number. Setting off again, I'm faster now, fueled by fear. I don't stop until I'm home, panting for breath, slamming the door behind me.

29

"You have to go to the police," Jam says, then drinks her margarita. It's very quiet in Rumors tonight, the atmosphere subdued, regulars and tourists alike staying home on account of the gale force wind. "It's the only way to stay safe."

"I can't, Jam. I told you before: I don't know why but I feel that she has something on me."

"Yes, your husband," she says, reaching for my hand. Her fingers are cold—have been wrapped around her iced glass. "I can't believe he's being such a twat. But you've still got me, hun. And you've got the Rottweiler."

"Yep." I glance around the room, at the same faces that I looked at three minutes ago. "I still think I shouldn't have told her about the twenty grand though."

Her mouth hardens in objection. "You had to! This is what you have to do to keep the house, Gabby. Don't go doubting yourself now."

"I know but..." I sip my drink, chewing the straw.

"But what?"

I glance around the room again, still looking for Ellis, even though I know she won't be here. That would be too easy, too obvious. "It's hard to explain, but I feel like Fred's in over his head."

"Uh, you think? And whose fault's that? If you pay for sex, you're going to get into trouble, one way or another."

I shrug, the strap of my top slipping. I made an effort, wearing a camisole, even though it's itching my skin and I feel too old for it. "It's those messages and the feeling of being followed..."

"Then go to the police," she repeats, more firmly.

I shake my head. "Something's very off with the whole thing, like I'm being played somehow. And I've got the feeling that Fred is too."

"I'm sorry—" she flashes a wry smile "—but that's just wishful thinking. Why do you think mistresses are painted as the predator, and wives get the blame when marriages break down? Maybe not right away, but eventually they do... You know the spiel: he strayed because she let herself go, or was a nagging old bag." She glowers, scrunching her lips. "And all because we don't want to believe our men would do this to us and that there has to be some evil whore pulling the strings, or some other reason we were abandoned. But I'm sorry, Gabs, he's doing this. It's all him! And you've got to accept it or you're gonna fold and give him everything..." She raises her voice. "Is that what you want—to be living in a cardboard box down on the seafront?"

"Shush! It's bad enough without everyone in here knowing my business." I frown at her. "Are you done?"

She thinks about it. "Yeah, I reckon so."

Something in her expression crushes my fear, making me laugh. It feels good, a momentary respite, and I reach for her hand, cupping it. "I love you, Jam. Thanks for being such a good friend."

"My pleasure." She smiles. "Love you too. Except that I'd prefer you living and breathing, and not in some body bag."

At that, the fear returns to my veins and I shudder, watching the barman out of the corner of my eye. He's very focused on us, but only because Jam told him to keep 'em coming.

I lick my finger, tap it on the rim of my glass, tasting a crystal of salt. It tingles on my tongue. I'll have an ulcer by bedtime tonight. "I know you don't understand, but that night when I met her…it was like she was on some kind of mission."

"'Course she was on a mission. She's a GD. That's the whole point of her! She doesn't have magical powers though. She's not bloody Gandalf."

I blurt a laugh in response.

"I don't get why you're so obsessed with her, Gabs. She's just some stupid tart."

"Who could end up getting my house."

"Hardly!" she says, setting her glass down. "He's not going to marry her. You know that."

"Do I? Because I'm not so sure. This one's different, not that I know any others. But there's something about her… She's manipulating him in some way, extorting money."

"Oh, Gabby, Gabby," she says, rolling her eyes. "Will you listen to yourself? Extorting money? It's called prostitution!"

"Shush!" I say again, so loudly that two old seamen turn to look at us and one of them is wearing a hearing aid.

"Seriously, if this were Alice, you'd be reading her the riot act…" she says, adjusting her top, a gold tunic with slashed sleeves that looks gorgeous on her. We bought it together. I feel a pang of longing for those days—before Ellis.

"…But because it's you, you're still looking for the good in him that doesn't exist." She reaches for a handful of chips, crunching down on them, before continuing. "I mean, why do you always do that, hey, turn them into heroes? Why defend them? Why can't you just accept that some men are total bastards?"

She stares at me and then a change comes over her and her expression softens.

"Oh, I'm sorry," she says, looking down at her drink, waving the empty glass at the barman. He's there in a flash, taking them away.

We don't speak for a while. I don't have a lot to say. I don't want to talk about men and heroes and hookers. I just want to drink a margarita and look through the plastic sheets to the sea. I want to watch the lighthouse blinking. I want to forget any of this is happening to me.

When the cocktails arrive, Jam changes position, bringing her chair beside mine. We sit side by side, her hand on my lap, watching the sea.

When it's time to leave, we walk home, stopping at the point where our ways diverge. As I reach for her hand to say goodnight, I'm thinking that I envy her and Nate. I never used to—thought she deserved better, but lately I've changed my mind.

I squeeze her hand. "Look after Nate the Great. He's one of the good ones."

She pulls back slightly to assess my face underneath the streetlight. "What do you mean, Gabs? You're scaring me."

"Because I said your husband's good?"

"No, because you're acting strange, as though it's the last time I'm ever going to see you."

Her words send a shiver down my spine, even though she didn't mean them to. She's trying to look after me. I wish she could. I wish I could go home with her, but that would be running away and I could put her in danger too.

"Good night, hun," she says, pressing a kiss onto my cheek, the tip of her nose cold. "You take care and call me if you need anything, no matter what time of night." Her eyes widen. "And remember what I said about the police. Think about it, okay? Don't leave it too late. I couldn't bear that."

I know what she's saying.

"Text me when you're home," she calls, as we part ways.

"You too," I call back. I'm literally two minutes away from home. I wore canvas shoes so I could run.

As I put the key in the lock, I'm so out of breath from running on cocktails, I'm seeing stars. In the hallway, I bend over, catching my breath. Then I stand with my back against the wall, feeling its cool support.

I used to believe years ago, when we first moved in, that the house could sense my feelings. It seemed to adjust itself like a thermostat, reacting to my mood. I always knew this was daft, impossible, but now I think of it just the same. It's holding itself taut like me, fending off the storm that's jangling the awnings and howling down the chimney.

At the kitchen window, I stand in the dark to watch the oaks fighting in the garden, drawing on their deep roots to stay upright. In contrast, the palm trees bend, shaking playfully like cheerleaders' pom-poms. I'm so caught up in them that I don't notice her right away.

She's there, near the side gate. Wearing something dark on her lower half, she appears sinisterly legless, her silver bomber jacket catching the streetlight in flashes through the trees like mirror signals.

The sight of her—the thing I've dreaded—numbs me, a high-pitched sound ringing in my ear. The stars reappear in my eyes and for a moment I'm worried that I'm going unconscious.

Stepping away from the window, I smack my legs against the breakfast bar, suppressing a cry of pain.

I can sense the knife block behind me. The doors are locked. I double-bolted the front door, checked the windows, the patio doors. She can't get in.

My phone…

I tap my pockets, but I must have left it in the hallway. Creeping forward as close as I dare, I watch her. I know from the assured way she's standing there that she's done this before. Either that, or she doesn't know I'm here. She's looking to the side of me, not at me.

My stomach lurches as she gazes up at the house as though searching for me. It feels like a long time passes, her hair flailing around her in the storm, like Medusa's snakes. I daren't move, waiting to see what she's going to do, whether she's going to approach.

And then, suddenly, she turns away, vanishing through the side gate.

I sink onto the floor as though she pressed a button, releasing me, my breath juddery, the way the kids used to be after crying hard.

Several minutes pass before I'm able to muster the courage to check the window again. She's not there.

I get my phone, calling Jam. "Pick up, Jam… Pick—"

She answers. "Gabby?"

"She was here!" I blurt. "She was in our garden, just standing there, watching me! I don't know what to do, Jam! I don't know…" I trail off, clenching my teeth, trying to contain myself. I can't freak out too much. She'll tell me to phone the police. It's the obvious thing to do.

Yet, she doesn't. "I'm on my way."

"You don't have to do that. I'm okay."

She ignores this lie, calls out to Nate. "Can you give me a lift to Gabs's?" Then she speaks into the phone. "You just hang on, hun. I'll be right there."

I wait by the front door, don't move an inch, listening to the house creaking and moaning. I wish it were filled with people again—my family, children on sleepovers, couples for dinner. Instead, I'm all alone. Yet, I'm not completely powerless, defenseless, am I?

The house responds in utter silence, the awnings finally falling flat as though exhausted.

I wrestle again with the horror of being dragged to that nightmare place where I don't want to be—on that same cliff edge, someone about to fall to their death. This time, I'm not up high though, but on the beach, on solid ground. Fred's with me, beside me, except that now he's vanished and I can see someone ahead of me, out to sea, waist-high in the water.

I'm fighting to get my legs to work, the sea shifting relentlessly. They're going to drown! The waves are too high, forceful. I wrestle again to move, screaming, *Help! Someone help!*

Sitting up with a gasp, I look around me, dazed, gripping the sheets.

Getting up, I move to the edge of the bed, remembering what happened earlier. Ellis in the garden. Jam coming over. We drank tea, read through the phone messages again and I said that I think they're going to stop. What I didn't say though is that I think that's because she's going to show up in person from now on.

Jam didn't beg me to go to the police, like I thought she would. She knows me well enough that if I say I can't, then I can't. I must have good reason not to. If only I knew what it was.

She left in the early hours of the morning, Nate collecting her. I watched their car lights disappearing, thinking that there's only so much anyone can do for me now. This is my battle to face alone, my demons.

Going to the window, I pull back the curtains to look across the rooftops to the sea. I only know it's there, can't see it. The wind is still howling; I can just make out the sound of a distant bell. Then my eye falls to the side gate again, picturing her there.

Maybe if I could figure out who she is, what she wants, I'd have a chance at beating her. I have to make Michael Quinn work harder; tell Maria Kane to ensure that my assets are protected. I'll send them everything I've got on Fred, no holds barred.

I can't believe I was feeling guilty for betraying him—for telling Maria about the twenty thousand pounds. He's cheating every which way he can. And Ellis is playing some kind of dangerous game. Maybe with him, maybe alone. There's no way of saying for sure.

All that matters is that I don't lose—don't end up, like Jam said, in a body bag.

30

5 months earlier

She was already up and dressed when he woke, disoriented, even though he should have been familiar with this room by now. “What time is it?” he asked.

“Six.” Her tights had a golden shimmer, always the suggestion of summer about her body, even though it was April and there was a light frost outside.

“You’re so gorgeous,” he said, coming up behind her, pulling her hair away from her neck to kiss it. He was always gentle, but she hated being crept up on. She stiffened, tugging her dress down. It was a formfitting magenta number with a tie waist, the sort that made her breasts look as though they were meant to be unwrapped.

Rounding the bed, he cut her off on her way to the bathroom. He was aroused and wanted her to know it. She granted him one small press up against her, a brief kiss, and then said, “Sorry. I’d love to linger, but I have to get to work.”

“What time do you start today?” he said, checking his watch.

She never answered questions like this. It didn’t stop him trying though.

"Do you go home first to change?"

If he knew the answer to that, he would know where approximately she lived. As it was, he didn't know where she worked or what she did, other than that it was low-paid, cash in hand. Whereas, she knew almost everything about him. It wasn't a fair fight, but she could live with that.

She eased past him to the bathroom, removing her lip gloss from her bag, glancing at the case containing her blade. She wasn't squeamish, didn't mind blood, would have made a good doctor had she had the slightest urge to fix anyone.

"You don't have to dress like that, you know," he said, leaning against the door frame. "Not now that you're with me."

In the mirror, her face clouded. "What's wrong with the way I dress?" she asked, trying to look hurt.

"Nothing," he said, darting forward to pacify her. "It's just that I worry what people think when they see you."

"You think I look like a whore?"

His face flushed worriedly at the thought of losing sex—the promise of it. She imagined engaging her hip flexors and quads, kicking her leg straight out and upward, connecting her shin to his groin.

The shin delivered the maximum input, had a larger surface area than the foot, so it was harder to miss the target. Whenever she told her students this, they sniggered. But there was nothing funny about it in her opinion.

"No, Ellis. Not at all. I'm sorry. I didn't mean that."

She turned off the mirror light, left the bathroom. "I happen to like the way I look," she said, her voice squashed, girlish.

He followed her. "So do I, but so does everyone else. That's all I meant." He reached for her hand. "I'm just being greedy—want you for myself."

She acted as though this was the best possible thing he could have said, squirming shyly. "I really do have to go."

"You're okay?" he said, stooping to look in her eyes. "We're okay?"

"Yes. All good." She sat down on the bed to put on her heels. He still wasn't convinced that everything was all right, which was exactly where she wanted him to be. "I'll see you next week then," she said, tearing herself away, going to the door, deliberately sounding hurt, still.

"Wait. I'll walk with you."

With her back to him, she smiled. He never left with her, thought it too risky, but bit by bit his guard was dropping.

"Well, if you're quick..." She turned around, ruffling her mane of hair, her coat falling open. He stared at her, mesmerized, then recalled she was waiting for him so quickly gathered his things.

She checked the time, tapped her foot. They had five minutes to get outside, else her plan wouldn't work.

The Neptune Hotel was typically quiet as they went to the elevator, him grabbing for her hand. As it descended, she let him kiss her. He wanted her so badly, but hadn't worked out that if it hadn't happened by now, it probably wasn't going to happen at all. He was thriving on the hunt, the carrot that men like him needed in order to do the slightest thing. Anything to satisfy their ground rule that something had to be in it for them.

"I loved that photo you sent," he whispered into her hair. "Do you have any more?"

A grainy hazy shot that could have been anyone. Yet was in fact her. It was just easier, less hassle. "Absolutely," she purred. "I'll send you something tonight if you're a good boy."

"Damn, you're hot... Did you like the bracelet?"

"Oh, I loved it," she said, panting as though using all her control not to rip his clothes off. "But you shouldn't have, Fred. It must have cost a fortune."

"It did," he replied, breaking away from her at level two, so his erection could die before they got to reception. "But you're worth every penny."

"I can't keep accepting all these gifts though," she said, fidgeting coyly with her bag—one he'd bought her last month.

"It's my pleasure." He squeezed her hand as they stood side by side, rocking with the motion of the elevator.

"No one else sees what you see in me." She allowed a drop of emotion to fracture her voice. "It means a lot."

"It means a lot to me too," he said, tightening his grip. "You mean a lot."

"But what about your wife? Hasn't she noticed what you're spending? You're way too generous…" Simpering and sucking up didn't come easily to her, but she thought she'd pulled it off.

"Don't worry about her. I'm not. She's not worth it."

Outside, the morning air was crisp, salty, the sea audible behind the buildings. She glanced at her watch, but there was no need. She could already see him at the end of the road, walking two dogs.

"Shit!" Fred said, pulling her toward the road. "Let's go up—"

"What's wrong?" She held firm, betraying her strength had he been interested, but he wasn't. He was lowering his head, retreating into his coat.

"It's Tobias Small," he hissed.

"So?" She led him forward along the pavement, a reluctant horse. "Who is he?"

"A regular at the golf club." He was bending his head so far down now she could barely hear his voice. "A massive gossip. Everyone hates him."

"Wait…" She made him come to an abrupt halt. "Are you ashamed to be seen with me or something?"

He looked at her and then at Tobias, who was almost upon them, dogs' tongues wagging. "No. Absolutely not."

"Well, then…" She lifted her head high, continued to walk.

Tobias almost tripped over them, looking at his phone. "Sorry…" Recognition struck. "Oh, hello, mate!" He beamed, his breath visible in the cold air. And then he looked at her, his eye dropping to her breasts. She had kept her coat open deliberately. He moved his mouth to speak, but what could he say?

Fred was struggling too, eyes flitting around. She tugged his arm, her voice low, as though caught out. "We'd better get going."

They parted ways, the dogs pausing to examine a lamppost. After a few steps, she glanced back as though anxious, knowing he'd still be watching them.

"That was close," Fred said. "We'll have to be more careful from now on."

As they turned the corner, she let go of his arm. "Can I remind you, again, that I'm not actually a hooker?"

"Of course not. But I'm married," he said, straightening his jacket, running his hands through his hair, "and he'll tell everyone about this. My wife will find out."

"I thought you said she's a waste of space."

"She is."

Outside a real estate agency, she went on tiptoes to brush a kiss onto his cheek.

"See you next week," he said. "I'll call you."

Once he was out of sight, she set off quickly, in heels, on ice. She just made the bus on time, which was about to pull away, but the driver saw her skintight magenta dress and stopped for her.

An hour later, she was in another town, in a part that the tourists didn't come to. It stank of old fishnets, engine oil, seaweed. There was no lighting here, aside from the ones they'd rigged up, none of which were regulated, but no one seemed to notice or care. Every town the world over had a place like this: a dark hole where the crap was thrown.

She was later than usual when she opened the door at the

side of the building that was so covered with graffiti the original warehouse sign had been destroyed. Inside, it was grimy, smelled of sweat, synthetic clothing. There was no air conditioning; instead, the fire doors were kept open with bricks. As the first one in, she kicked the brick into place, thinking it was lucky they even had fire doors.

She was mistaken, wasn't the first one in. Guts, who owned the boxing ring next door—or said he did—was doing weights, forehead gleaming. On seeing her, he smiled into the mirror. "Morning, psycho."

Everyone called him Guts on account of his bloody history in the ring—she didn't know his real name, never asked. She went to her fruit crate in the corner where her gear was kept. They didn't have lockers; no one touched each other's stuff. She got changed behind the screen, wriggling into her leggings, a baggy T-shirt. Everything was different in here. Out there, they could ogle her all they liked. But no one crossed that line in the warehouse. She never gave them reason to even think about it.

In the gloom, she approached the pull-up bar—a homemade bar on two wooden legs, but it didn't matter. It didn't need to be fancy to do its job. Jumping up, she grabbed it, pulling herself up, her chin level with the bar before lowering herself until her elbows were straight.

Guts often stopped what he was doing to watch her. Sometimes, others did too. They wondered how she managed—a little shit like her—to do three sets of twenty reps. Most of them could only do fourteen. That was because they went too fast, trying to show off, their grip sloppy or too wide. They tried to cheat by doing a short range of motion, so they didn't build the strength.

They all knew she was good at it, but they were too proud to ask her why, never learned her technique. So they would stay at fourteen. What did she care?

Guts knew though. He laughed, shook his head.

She made her way past the treadmill which still wasn't working, and started rowing again, the machine making a grating noise.

"Got many classes today?" Guts called, a towel around his neck.

"A few."

"See you next door then," he said, laughing again before leaving.

In the quiet of the room, she drew herself back and forth, enjoying the momentum of the wires, the worn handles digging into her palms. There was a movement outside, a darkening at the doors as a face appeared that was never good news for anyone.

He didn't speak to her, didn't speak to anyone, ever. He always did the same thing, like her, working the room in silence. Everyone knew he was the toughest man around, even though he wasn't that big. Everyone knew he kept a gun at the bottom of his crate and a blade in his pocket—that he hadn't ever paid a gym membership in his life because no one could work up the nerve to ask him.

He was wearing a leather jacket with a tiger on the back. At least, that's what she thought it was, but over the years it had faded and peeled and now it was a mess of claws.

Grunting, he lifted the weights, watching himself in the mirror. She didn't realize she had stopped rowing until his gaze moved to her and they locked eyes. Looking away, she started to row again, cursing herself. There was a time and place, and it wasn't here and now. Not yet.

31

June 1985

"Gabrielle?" Mum's voice pierced the darkness, her footsteps weary on the stairs. The door opened. She felt about for the light, flicking it on. "Why aren't you ready yet? Your father's here."

I didn't reply, pulled the covers over my head.

Sighing, she drew the curtains, cranking open a window. "It's so stuffy in here. No wonder you're lethargic." She pulled back the sheets, gasped. "You're still in your pajamas? What are you playing at? He'll say I did this deliberately!" She hurried to the wardrobe, scraping the hangers along the rail. "What do you want to wear? Your new T-shirt?"

I stared up at the ceiling, at the dentists' poster. I used to love that poster so much when having my teeth checked that I asked if I could keep it when they were having the surgery refurbished. If anyone wondered why a fourteen-year-old kid wanted something to distract her from pain in her own home, no one said anything. It was just a tropical beach—turquoise sea, palm trees—but I liked it a lot. One day, when I had my own house, I'd plant palm trees everywhere.

"How about your cropped trousers? They look nice, hmm?"

Outside, there was an engine running and then it cut out. She went to the window, looking out. "Please, Gabrielle. Do this for me. Pull yourself together."

The warble in her voice drew my attention away from the tropical beach. I looked at the lines on her forehead, the gray patch in the middle of her hair, the way her nails were bitten and bled, the way her shoulders were like knobbly walnuts underneath her blouse. And she wanted me to pull myself together?

"He could make things very difficult for us." She exhaled, and her face looked so sharp, so thin, I could imagine her as a skull. "Financially."

"Okay. Keep your panties on," I said, sitting up.

She smiled, relieved. "Thank you."

I stared at her stonily. "Well…?"

She looked blank and then jumped up. "Oh, you want me to leave? Just don't be too long. I'll tell him five minutes, all right?"

I shrugged, picking up the clothes she had laid out for me. The T-shirt said Staying Alive in '85 across the front. Lately, I'd been wearing it ironically.

At the door, she smiled at me again and then left, barely needing to open the door more than a crack to fit through. She had lost a lot of weight, mostly because she was on her feet all day now as a waitress in one of the touristy cafés in town. Dad had sunk a lot of money into his new house and into expanding the business, she had said, and Sara was demanding. I didn't know if any of that were true, didn't think Mom would make it up, but then she wasn't exactly unbiased either. No one liked Frizzy, least of all me.

I knew something else was off too. It felt like the radio was between stations the whole time—low strange noises from Mars. I couldn't put my finger on it. I knew she was depressed—who wouldn't be in her shoes—but there was something else. If I'd had the energy, I might have tried to work it out, but I didn't. And then there was the lack of care. I didn't care about very much anymore. Not even Mom.

Downstairs, Dad was leaning against the car, enjoying a cigar, head turned up to the sky as he blew out smoke rings. As though that was going to wash with me anymore. I scowled, flapping my hand as I got in the car. "That stinks."

"Nice to see you too," he said, getting in beside me, cigar clenched between his teeth.

"I hate that smell." I wound down the window, sitting with my body turned away from him. On the seat, there was a long blond hair and another on the floor carpet. It smelled of her too. I hated everything about this car.

"You look nice," Dad said. "Is that new?"

As if he would know. As if he knew anything about me now.

"Where are we going?" I asked, playing with my necklace. Mom had made me put on this white bead necklace at the last minute that all the girls wore at school, and she'd combed my hair over on one side as though I were Lady Di.

"Where would you like to go?"

"Home."

He sighed, rubbed his beard. "You're already home."

I looked up at the front of our house as though surprised. "Oh, yeah!"

There was a silence. He turned off the engine. "Look, if you don't want to go, then..."

Just say it, Dad. Pull the plug. Put us both out of our misery.

Whatever he was going to say, he decided not to. He sighed again, started the engine. "Let's just see where we end up," he said.

I didn't speak the whole way. He didn't put the radio on either like old times. I sat stiffly in that new car that smelled of dead flowers and hairspray, and watched the summer pass me by outside. I hadn't gone farther than my room and school in ages, couldn't remember what freshly cut grass smelled like, how hot the sand got at the beach in a heat wave.

We ended up somewhere I hadn't thought of in a long while: No. 23, Ocean View Road. He stopped the car in the street, not pulling up in the driveway like we used to. I was thrown for a moment and then realized there were people living there now.

He reached for my hand as we walked toward the gates, then quickly withdrew it again. I knew he was acting out of memory, on autopilot, recalling a time when this would have been the most natural thing in the world to do.

At the gates, something happened. Everything began to shift within me like snow turning to sludge and I became liquid, my eyes filling. I gazed through the railings at the two cars in the driveway, side by side, the little bike standing by the garage door, the glimpse of a paddling pool in the back garden. And then I turned to Dad, buried my face in him as I cried.

At home, instead of just tooting the horn and driving off, he did something unusual and came inside with me. Seen through his eyes, the house seemed bare, cold. A lot of the decorative things here were his and when he had moved in with Frizzy, he'd taken most of it with him. He had offered to replace everything, but Mom hadn't been interested in ornaments and whatnots—hadn't seemed to notice they were gone.

"Why don't you go upstairs for a bit?" she asked, her face all pointy again the moment she saw Dad.

One minute they were telling me off for spending all my time in my room, and the next they were sending me up there. It suited me fine, most of the time, except today.

I pretended to stomp upstairs, slamming my door, and then crept back down, stopping halfway, ear between the bannisters.

"...It's not working," Dad was saying. They were in the kitchen. Mom was making him a cup of tea, but I knew from experience that he wouldn't be staying long enough to drink it. "She doesn't..." The kettle was too loud for me to hear.

I waited for it to click off.

"Well, what do you expect, Robin? Look what she's been through."

"But it shouldn't affect our relationship. I mean, I'm always nice to her."

"Nice?" Mom said, her voice shrill. "You just don't get it, do you?"

There was the clink of plates as she got biscuits, cake. He wouldn't be eating any of it.

"I think we should stop it," he said.

Stop our trips?

I picked at the paintwork, a flake chipping off, sticking painfully into my fingernail.

"Maybe you're right," she said. "I had to force her to go again. It's not fair on her."

I tried to pull the flake out of my nail, but it was wedged there.

There was more noise as Mom assembled cutlery he wouldn't be using. "Obviously it's not going to get any easier on her," she said, "once the baby comes."

My head jerked so fast away from the bannisters that I nearly toppled headfirst down the stairs. Grabbing at the wood, my heart started hurting. What baby?

"That's not going to be any day soon, at least," Dad said. "Sara's having trouble in that department."

What department?

"Well, poor her…" I could tell even from here that Mom didn't mean that.

"I have to get going." He rattled his car keys.

Knew it.

"Oh, don't you want fruit cake?"

"No, not today, Alice."

"But I made you a cup of tea."

"Another time, eh?"

I was so distracted by their conversation I forgot I wasn't supposed to be listening to it. There wasn't time for me to move or hide. Dad came into view, standing at the foot of the stairs, looking up at me in dismay.

I stared down at my fluffy socks. "How long have you been sitting there, young lady?" he said, his face all red, the way it used to be when he told a workman off for being slack, unsafe. "Were you listening in?"

"Oh, Gabrielle," Mom said. "How much did you hear?"

My shame turned into anger, inflaming my ears. "Go away, both of you!" I shouted. "I hate you!" And I ran upstairs, this time slamming my bedroom door for real.

I paced the floor, feeling all corkscrewed and knotted. I wanted to punch someone—Dad, Mom, Frizzy. I wanted to knock them all down like skittles. I wanted to punch a hole in the wall of this stupid empty house.

Mom would be standing at the front door, watching him leave. She watched him come, watched him go. I knew this had something to do with what that signal from Mars was trying to tell me—the thing I couldn't understand yet because I was only fourteen. But someday I would, and I would listen to every word until I knew it by heart.

Pulling the curtains, I got back into bed, staring up at the tropical beach, remembering how nice it was to be at the dentists', where everyone looked right at you, shined a light on you, told you exactly what they were going to do and when and for how long and how it was going to feel.

Outside, Dad's car was rumbling. I fought the urge to go to the window. I didn't want him to see me there if he looked up. I didn't want him to not see me there either and make him sad. I didn't want to look out and him not look up at me though. By the time I'd decided to go and see, it was too late and he was gone.

32

I spend Monday morning hopping between an admin job and my personal emails, shunting back and forth, gathering everything Maria Kane needs in order to prove that Fred's been abusing my trust and our finances.

The office feels peaceful, Claire typing softly, Shaun nowhere to be seen. I don't have the will to fight him today. But I did do something big first thing: I rinsed Alice's cereal bowl, put it in the dishwasher, pressed Go.

I didn't stand there listening to the water flowing, removing the last traces of my baby girl. I didn't go to the window and think of her in her strawberry swimsuit, wearing armbands in the pool. Instead, I got ready for work and somehow found my way forward to my desk.

I send Maria everything that I've got, and then I email Michael, asking him to find out what precisely the money is being spent on. How hard can it be, if Shaun saw them in the jeweler's?

Feeling satisfied, in a shaky way, I'm wondering what to start next when my phone vibrates with a message from Fred.

Are you free for lunch? Your choice where and when.

It takes me half an hour to respond. Everything about it feels contrived. I know he's summoning me to tell me something he can't say at home. Yet, if I can clear away Alice's cereal bowl, then I can handle this.

Lloyd's. 1pm.

He sends me a smiley face emoji; I don't reply.

Lloyd's is my territory, not his. I arrive ten minutes early so I can choose a seat near the open windows, facing the sea. It's where I sat with Jam, when we first discussed what I was going to do about Fred. It feels imbued with personal choice, empowerment, both of which I could do with now. It's October, a fresh start, a chill in the air that bites at my arms as I take a seat, dabbing my hands on the tablecloth.

It's gloriously sunny, and as I wait for Fred, the waiter hovering, bringing water and menus, asking if I'm warm enough, I take in the sight of the autumnal sea: stormier with the strong gales due to Atlantic depressions moving over the country; more fishing boats as the summer species linger on and the winter species arrive, creating a bigger haul.

It's easier for me to fill my head with work facts, rather than worrying about what fresh hell Fred's bringing. Jam says I need to focus on him, not that creepy little GD—that by taking him out, she'll fall too.

I hope she's right.

"Gabby." I look up as he arrives, hesitating about how to greet me, hands wavering before opting to do nothing except pull out his chair and sit down. "Sorry I'm late."

"You're not. I was early."

He looks around, rubbing his legs apprehensively. "So this is nice? Is this where you usually come with Jamillah?"

"Yes. The fish is very good, if you're wondering."

He picks up a menu. "I might just get a salad."

"Me too."

We both know this lunch isn't about eating. "Wine?" he asks.

I shake my head. "Better not." I'm not sure how this would pan out with alcohol in the mix.

We order water, Greek salads. And then it's just us and the sea breeze lifting the tablecloths.

"It was good to see Alice," he says. "Her boyfriend seems okay."

"Yes. But you didn't come here to talk about him." I clasp my hands on the table. "What's up?"

He picks up his water, drinking it. "I need to talk to you. It's about…Ellis. About how I feel."

I gaze at his lips, the trace of moisture there, my stomach squeezing guiltily at the thought of my emails being opened by Maria, containing information that will ruin his reputation and—

"I'm in love with her. And as soon as I can, as soon as I'm free, I intend to propose. I know it's not conventional, but you don't know her and if you did, if you got to know her like I do, I think you'd like her too. More than like her."

I stare at him as though he's just set fire to the tablecloth. "What?"

He shifts position, his eyes flitting away. "I'm sorry, Gabby. It's just the way I feel."

So he maneuvered me into instigating a divorce and now he's rushing it through. And all because he wants to be free… to propose?

My hands clench up. Everything clenches. I can feel myself tightening, spiraling, a boxing glove on a spring. "You brought me here to tell me this?"

He swallows awkwardly. "It's not that bad."

"Not that bad?" My voice rises. "Are you serious?" I look

about me blindly for something to throw at him, too angry to action the thought.

"Keep a lid on it, Gabby. We're in public."

"How dare you?" I grip my fork, holding it upright like a pitchfork, banging it down, rattling the cutlery. "You think you're so clever, bringing me here, where you think I won't scream and shout. Well, you can think again because I'm just as capable of screaming and shouting in here as I am at home!"

"Shush, you're embarrassing yourself," he says, hunching his shoulders, trying to seem inconspicuous.

"Oh, I'm embarrassing?" I say even louder. "Not as much as sleeping with a prostitute and parading her all over town!"

"She's not a prostitute. And no one's parading," he says, sinking in his seat.

"Really? Because Shaun knows! Did you know that? Shaun knows and he's using it to undermine me at work. Do you have any idea how humiliating this is?"

His face flushes, a frown flickering. "I'm sorry if this has caused you distress. It wasn't our intention."

Our intention. Does he hear it? Does he know he sounds like a politician defending a lewd act?

They're not a couple. They're not! She's a gold digger! He's a middle-aged father!

The waiter is bringing our salads, isn't so sure, hovering, plates midair, body half-turned. I motion for him to approach. Nervously, he complies, setting the plates down as fast as he can.

Before Fred can react, I'm on my feet, snatching up his salad, tipping it over his head. "I'll see you in court."

"You stupid bitch!" he shouts, jumping up, tomato sliding from his hair. "I've got to go back to work!"

I grab my bag, pointing it at him. "You should have thought about that before you slept with her! She's only doing it for the money. Why can't you see that, you moron? Stop thinking with your dick and use your brain for once! She wants the house!"

He's wiping his head and shoulders with a napkin, cucumber caught between his shirt and neck. "She loves me. Not that you'd know anything about that!"

"She doesn't love you, Fred!" I shout, waving my arms.

"Yes she does!" he shouts back, a vein bulging in his forehead. I think for one second that he's going to have a heart attack. My anger quells just like that and I take a step back, bumping into a table.

He's not having a heart attack. He's brushing feta from his sleeve.

The thought of death sobers me, calms me. I fold my coat over my arm, trying to retain some semblance of order. "You can forget about getting half the house if you marry her. I can tell you that for nothing. That'll happen over my dead body, you hear me?"

I break off, becoming aware of the room around me. The waiter is frozen behind the bar. Over in the corner, an elderly couple are cowering behind their menus; a group of tourists in anoraks is staring at us.

I pick up my bag, smiling at them on my way out. "The cod here is very good."

I don't return to work right away, go to the beach instead, sitting on the wet sand with my bag and coat on my lap, staring at the horizon. I don't have my sunglasses, the glare is fierce, but I stare anyway.

I can't believe I acted like that—let him drive me to the point where I lost control. It won't be him having the heart attack; it'll be me. Taking a tissue from my bag, I wipe the back of my neck and hairline. And then I ring him. I was going to leave an abusive message, but he picks up.

"If you don't give me the house," I say, "I'm going to tell your parents who Ellis is and what she does for a living."

He's somewhere echoey, probably in the bathroom at Lloyd's, picking cucumber from his hair. "That's not the threat that you think it is."

I watch a water-skier passing, bouncing up and down on the waves, boat engine humming. "Why not?"

There's salad dressing on my trousers—oil, herbs, feta. I take a handful of sand, rub it against the material, brush it off. It works, sort of.

"Because, contrary to what you seem to think, she's not some kind of sex worker."

"But you're—" I stop, going quiet.

"But I'm what?" he asks, voice swamped in suspicion.

You're giving her money.

The skier tumbles, submerges, pops up above water again. My focus returns to what Fred just said. "I'm sorry, but what does she do for a living then?"

"I..."

His hesitation tightens my chest. If he doesn't know the answer to this most basic of questions, then things are worse than I thought because he has no idea who she is either.

I have to stand, catch a breath, my coat tumbling onto seaweed, sand hoppers jumping all over it. "Well...?"

"It doesn't matter what she does, Gabby. I love her. And when Mom and Dad meet her, they'll love her too. So, get used to the idea because that's going to happen. So the sooner you—"

I hang up on him, immediately pulling up his parents' number. I want to tell them about the money here and now. Instead, I ring Michael Quinn, leaving him a message.

"I don't know how far you've got, Michael, but I really need you to step it up, please. I'll pay extra, but I need to know exactly who Ellis is. I'm certain that's not her real name. Can you call me when you get the chance?"

I salvage my coat, going back to work with sand in my shoes and stuck to my oily trousers.

At my desk, I read my emails, telling myself that I have to try to stay one step ahead of Fred; and that's when Shaun finally shows up. I check the absence calendar, but nothing's been authorized. He was supposed to be here this morning. It's one thing taking a two-hour lunch break, but showing up for work in the afternoon?

"Shaun, I think we need another talk," I say, stopping in front of his desk. There's a distinct whiff of alcohol. This time, I don't smile. I don't soften anything.

"Yes, ma'am!" he says, saluting me, turning to grin at the rest of the team who look awkward, averting their eyes. Going to the conference room, I hold the door open for him, waiting patiently as he clowns around, time-wasting.

We take our positions on opposite sides of the table, both standing. He's not drunk, at least. He seems perfectly lucid. But still. I'm going to have to do this.

"You've left me no choice, Shaun, but to give you a written warning. Your behavior has been…erratic lately. And I think we need to pull things back into line."

"Right you are, ma'am!" That wasn't funny a minute ago and it isn't funny now. Again, I don't smile. I wonder at my feeling the need to do so, so many times with him. The cookies and groveling, as though I owed him something—a huge apology for usurping him.

I don't have any apologies. Just a written letter for him, which will be ready by end of day.

He leaves the room, closing the door behind him, even though he knows I'm going to follow after him. He'll continue to undermine me and I'll continue to warn him, going through the procedural motions until eventually I'll have to sack him. And then I'll have one less problem to deal with, one less liability.

Back at my desk, I feel proud of myself, elated, then drained.

These things used to come naturally to me. I used to be feisty, assertive. I don't know when it changed. But it did. And one day I woke up, scared of my daughter's empty cereal bowl, scared of the empty space beside me where my husband used to be.

33

September 1989

"Are you sure you're going to be okay?" Dad asked.

"Yep." I wasn't looking at him, was looking at the students behind me in the queue as we waited to sign in at the warden's office. I didn't want him to be here, but had no choice. Mom wouldn't let me get the train with all my luggage and she didn't have a driving license. Only Dad could have taken me, even though I had asked the school principal too. Dad had hit the roof about that. I wished I'd never told him, but had wanted him to know that there were other people who cared about me, even though the principal didn't know my name and said no to the lift.

"Did you have to wear that?" Dad whispered.

"What's wrong with it?" I was in all black, like I had spent the past two years. Black eyeliner, black hair, black lipstick. Dad called me Darth Vader. I didn't care what he called me.

"Didn't you have something, I dunno…frilly?"

I didn't bother to reply to that. I was first in the queue now and a man with shiny cheeks was gazing up at me. His was the first face I ever properly took in at university. I wanted to remember every moment—the pores in the end of his nose, the sandwich on his desk. He was saying something; I wasn't listening, wasn't good at listening. I wasn't good at very much at all. It was a wonder I'd got into university, Dad had said at least five times on the journey here—that at least I had something to show for not having left my room.

I took the form the man was handing me and the keys and turned to look at my dad in surprise, wondering what he was still doing there. "Don't you want a hand with your luggage?" he said.

"S'pose."

Going down the path, luggage wheels squeaking, I held a potted plant that Mom made me take, which would be dead in two weeks, while Dad brought everything else. There was a line of sweat down his back that I liked seeing. I hadn't got a lot of sweat out of him for the past decade.

"Would it kill you to be nice, just this once?" he said, resting for breath as I grappled with the keys in the door. "You're not going to see much of me anymore."

As if I did already.

I took in the room—the large windows, sink, wooden desk, wooden bedframe.

"Well, this is all right." He rubbed his hands together. "This will do nicely, eh?"

I didn't have an opinion, not one that I was going to share with him. I sat on the edge of the bed, watching as he wheeled in my cases. "Where are you going to put that?" he asked.

I was still holding the plant. I shrugged.

"Shall we make a drink?" he suggested.

There was a kettle somewhere in my luggage—one of those small plastic ones that took half a year to boil. Mom had packed a fruit cake and skimmed milk powder and loads of other stuff, as though I'd be serving afternoon tea in here. Her face had been all shriveled and pained at the window when we left this morning and then she'd disappeared and had reappeared on the doorstep, running to the car, tears streaming down her face.

"Get a grip, Alice," Dad had muttered.

And that was all it had taken. I had jumped out, hugging her, telling her I loved her, would write every week.

I was thinking all this before he had said anything, but it took those four words from him to spur me into action. Before that, I was also thinking she needed to get a life. It was a bit harsh, but she was so thin, her shoulders at risk of snapping. He'd completely crushed her and it had become my mission in life to learn how and why he'd done this, and why she had let him, so it would never happen to me.

I hadn't liked leaving her. It had made me feel small and shrunken. But if I hadn't gone, I would have been stuck there, rotting forever. This was my one chance.

The closer we got to campus, the more I hated Dad for saying she should get a grip. He'd never had a grip. Everything slipped out of his greasy hands. Whereas at least Mom had put in the time, was always there to turn my light out at night.

Sitting there in that new room, Dad trying to think what to say, how to advise me—clean your teeth, don't walk around in the dark—all I could think was why hadn't Mom joined us? She could have seen my new home too. Maybe she hadn't wanted to, would have found it too painful. Yet, as far as I knew, no one had asked her.

"Did you ever even see her?" I asked, as he fiddled with my tap, checking it ran.

"Eh?"

"Mom. When you were married to her."

He turned off the tap. "I don't get what you mean."

I left it at that. What was the point?

He started to unpack the box Mom had carefully taped up, marked Treats in her sad wobbly handwriting, but I stopped him. "Get off," I said. "I'll do that."

He whistled softly, as though trying to keep his temper. He

didn't have to restrain himself on my account. I wanted him to explode, so that we could part on foul, honest terms.

I went to the door, held it open. "Well, thanks for everything. Safe journey back."

Out in the corridor, someone else was arriving—student, mom, dad, little brother. Dad smiled at them politely and then turned back to me. "Don't leave it like this," he said. "I know it's tough, what with the new baby on the way, but it doesn't have to change things between us, hey?"

I couldn't look at him. He was watering up and I couldn't deal with that—not with boxes to unpack and families all around and people who were going to be living here with me who would already be deciding to give me a wide berth because I was a wreck.

He tried to reach for my hand and I pulled it away with an abrupt jerk that was a bit too overplayed, smacking it against the door. I was so angry that I'd hurt myself and that my new life was starting out exactly the same as the old one that I closed the door in his face.

I stood with my head against the wood, listening for him. He didn't plead, didn't knock, didn't call my name. He jangled his car keys, left, saying hello to someone on his way out as though he were father of the year.

The moment he'd gone, I did what I always did: panicked. I shouldn't have left it like that. Running over to the window, I strained to look out, hoping for a glimpse of him, but he was nowhere to be seen.

I gazed at Mom's handwriting on the box and I knew then that this was exactly what had happened to her too, this panic. It was something to do with this and I had to work it out, if there was going to be any hope for me at all, about anything.

It took two weeks at university to discover what I needed to know. Here, on campus, the signal to the radio station was clear—the one I'd thought was on Mars. It wasn't on Mars. It was far closer to home, in the people around me, the ones I met during the first few days, the friends I made. Normal life, normal people with families that were just like mine, except they weren't.

Slowly through the fog, through those late-night conversations during those intense few weeks of information and oversharing and outpouring of secrets, politics, and preferences, I discovered something that had been missing all along. And it was simple.

Dad had all the power. Mom had none. Therefore, I, by default, had none also.

One evening, in the rain, I ran all the way to the telephone box to talk to her, to tell her I loved her. We talked until the time ran out, until we were cut off. She sounded happy. I told her that when I got home at Christmas we'd do things together. We would go shopping, make trifle, go for walks, talk. I wanted to tell her everything I had learned, about how she needed to have power somehow, become powerful.

I didn't say that to her though. It would have sounded weird over the phone. I didn't try to put it in a letter either. I wasn't clear enough in my own mind about what to do, how it might work for either of us. I didn't have all the answers, was only eighteen, but it was a start.

A knocking on the door woke me. This wasn't unusual. People knocked all the time, lost keys, threw shoes at windows. I barely moved.

The knock came louder. "Gabrielle? You in there?"

Dad.

I sat up, dragging the sheets with me. What was he doing here? I reached for my alarm clock, looking at the illuminated hands: three o'clock in the morning.

"Gabrielle?" The banging was loud—a fist on the door.

What the hell was wrong with him? Everyone would hear.

I opened the door, checking my pajamas were buttoned up at the front. "What?"

He looked horrendous, hair stuck on end, shirt half-tucked. He didn't wait to be asked to come in, pushed past me, sinking into my chair, not removing the clothes that were there. I tried to get my sweater out from underneath him, but it wouldn't budge. He wasn't registering it, was staring into space, gripping his keys.

Was it about the baby? The baby was born early this morning. Yesterday morning, now. I'd missed his call, was at lectures, but had found a note under my door: *the baby was born.* I didn't need any more information than that, didn't care. It had nothing to do with me.

But I was starting to get a nasty feeling, a shiver creeping through me. I eyed my dressing gown on the door peg. "What is it?" I said.

He looked at me then as though having forgotten where he was, who I was. "I don't know how to…" His voice was hoarse.

"How to what?"

I started to shiver properly then, making a move for my gown, but the look on his face stopped me. He was staring up at me as though his soul had fallen right out of him.

"Gabrielle…it's your mom."

"Mom? What do you mean?"

He stood up, set his hands on my shoulders, looking down at me. I could see right into his eyes, red blood vessels, murky irises. "She's gone. She…" He swallowed, removed his hands.

"Tell me," I said, raising my voice.

The red blood vessels again, a net of tiny lifelines. "She… she's dead. She walked into the sea. She drowned herself."

He crumpled onto my disheveled bed, holding his head. "Oh…Alice… Alice. What have you done?"

I stared at the top of his head, at the patch of scalp that was beginning to show through his hair. I'd never noticed it before.

It was new. I thought of the new baby born this morning, yesterday morning, its tiny crinkly skin. I didn't know if it was a boy or girl. It was related to me, a half brother or sister, but I didn't know the basic details. I didn't know anything.

I didn't understand why he was here, telling me this, with that patch of scalp on his head. It didn't feel like it had anything to do with me. I went to the door, opened it. "You can go now."

He looked at me as though I had turned the entire room upside down. "You what?"

I didn't know what I was doing either. I only knew that if he was going to fall apart, then I wasn't going to, because there was a distance between us that had been put there by myself to protect me. We shared nothing now.

"What the hell is wrong with you?" he shouted. "Your mother's dead, did you hear me?"

Out in the corridor, lights came on, spilling into the darkness. "You're waking everyone up. We have lectures in the morning."

His mouth coiled in disgust. "I can't believe this, Gabrielle. I'm ashamed of you."

I waited for him to leave. For the first time, I didn't panic. I sat up quietly all night, thinking about what to do.

The next morning, I took the train home. What I couldn't carry I left in that room with the wooden desk and the wooden bedframe. I didn't say goodbye to anyone, couldn't face it.

I lasted four minutes inside the house, and then the grief set in.

34

2 weeks earlier

The radiators began to creak as though waking up. He unscrewed a bottle of wine, pouring it into two plastic cups from the bathroom. The routine was so mechanical, predictable, she used it to get to sleep at night.

But everything—the routine, this hotel, this warped dance—was about to change, the way things often did in September. He just didn't know it yet, even though he thought he did.

"Here's to being free," he said, touching his cup to hers. "My wife's finally asked for a divorce."

"That's so sad. But if that's what you wanted, then I'm pleased for you."

"And for you."

How? So much delusion, denial. They hadn't even slept together. Nine months of teasing, sexy pics, and in return he'd emptied his savings accounts, buying her gifts, giving her cash handouts when she said she was short.

It was so easy to resell the stuff. He never even had the sense to ask where the jewelry was, or the handbags, lingerie.

It didn't seem to occur to him that she was still wearing charity shop castoffs.

He never saw the details, didn't want to see them. To him, she was an orgasm he'd willingly anticipate for the rest of his life. She knew there were rich men out there who mailed gifts to girls in exchange for photos, not even pornographic ones—tasteful, stockings and suspenders. A virtual girlfriend who would never hold them accountable, ask questions. A blow-up doll, with her own postal address.

He was one of these fantasists, inventing stories in his own mind. Yet, now he was getting ahead of himself, as though they actually had a future. It almost made her feel sorry for him. He was way more lost than he looked.

"I'm going to tell her about us soon." He kissed her forehead in a way that felt surprisingly affectionate. "I just have to time it right. But she's suspicious, knows I'm seeing someone."

You don't say.

"I hope she won't be too upset," she said.

"Nah. She'll be fine. Tough as old boots."

She hoped no one described her like that one day. Yet, in some ways it was a compliment. Better that than fragile.

"So, now you're on your feet, you're definitely going to stay in the area, yes?" he asked, sitting on the bed beside her, pillows propped behind them. The headboard was lumpy; she shifted position, hoping he wouldn't touch her. She was wearing a long dress with a side slit like a banana being peeled. He liked that slit, kept eyeing it.

She wasn't going to answer that question.

"Is your apartment somewhere local?"

Nor that one.

"Maybe near the harbor?"

Same.

"I've got one for you," she said, rolling onto one arm to look at him. "Why do all this?"

"What, help you out, keep you safe?" he said. "I suppose because you didn't have anyone else to turn to. I wasn't going to let you fall on the mercy of those disgusting flabby rich men. You're too good for that."

She smiled; he was a real hero.

"Plus, I enjoy your company," he said, running his hand up her leg, tracing the slit in her dress. "Even though you're mysterious…but maybe that's part of the appeal." He kissed her shoulder, lifted her hair to nuzzle her neck.

She wriggled away, picking up her wine. "But everything you've been spending… It's such a lot."

"It's only money. It doesn't mean anything. Gabby wanted it for the kids' investments, but—"

"Gabby?" She turned to look at him. "She's called Gabby?"

He frowned. "Yes. Why?"

"You haven't mentioned her name before, that's all."

"Well, I wouldn't, would I."

She sipped her wine, drawing her knees to her chest. "So, what's she like, aside from tough as boots?"

That wasn't how Gabby had come across three nights ago at the bar—so miserable about her daughter leaving. There hadn't been anything tough about her at all. It had been sad to see.

"My wife?" He looked taken aback.

"Well, yeah, she's a person, isn't she?"

"Yes, but I don't want to discuss her here, with you."

"Why not?"

"Because…she's…" Irritated, he picked up his wine. "Let's just change the subject. How's work going?"

"Not too bad."

"Well, just say the word if you need anything."

"It's okay," she said, using her best purry voice. "You've done more than enough, Freddy."

He so wasn't a Freddy. But he seemed to like it.

"And I'll do more still, if it means keeping you here with me."

She tried to look pleased about that. "So the money…it's from your kids' investments?"

He played with the strap on her dress, slipping his finger underneath it. "They'll be fine, Ellis, if that's what you're getting at. The house is worth six million and that was two years ago. How much more of an investment do they need?"

She looked shocked, lifting her eyebrows. "Six mill? I had no idea!"

"That's nothing around here. Trust me, we're the poor ones along our street."

She played with her necklace, biting the cheap metal. "Still, that's a lot of money. So…when you split up, who'll get the house?"

"Well, that's the big question." He smiled, edging closer. "Why, are you saying you'd like to live there with me?" he murmured, tickling her ribs.

"Oh, my gosh, no!" she said, giggling, something she never did.

"Seriously though, why not? You'd love the pool. I can see you there, sunning yourself… Let's buy you a sexy bikini, a gold string…"

"But your wife wants the house. She'll never let it go."

She watched his reaction, the hardening of his expression, the recoiling motion. "How do you know that?"

She shrugged, her strap falling from her shoulder. She let it dangle, an invitation. "It's obvious. Women always fight for their homes, especially ones worth six million."

He was looking at her skeptically, wavering, and then decided with a grunt that she was right.

"Were you ever happy there?" she asked, running her hand across his chest.

"For a while…" he said.

"So, what happened?"

"Oh, just life… Kids… Aging…"

"So, you looked for happiness elsewhere?"

He loosened his tie. "I guess."

"With younger women? I mean, they do it for you then?"

"Not in a pervy way." He traced the rim of his cup round and round with his finger. "But it happens to everyone in midlife—the siren call of youth."

"Siren call?" she echoed, acting thick.

He looked at her. "It means wanting something, being pulled toward it."

"Oh."

"You'll understand some day." He pursed his lips in contemplation. "Death looks a lot closer after fifty. Suddenly you start backpedaling away from old age. Women do it through their kids, oversharing, meddling. And men… Well…" He turned to her, raised his glass. "Case in point."

"So you cheat because you don't want to get old? You don't want to die?"

"Does anyone?"

She looked away, up at the decorative plasterwork on the ceiling—leaves, flowers, circles. She thought of the neck ache, craftsmanship, hours spent; how thousands of people came and went without even looking up at it. "So why doesn't every man go off with a young woman?"

She already knew the answer—knew it was the same reason why one man labored on the ceiling and another lay on his back with a hooker on his balls. But she wanted to hear it anyway.

He took a long time to reply. "Some of us are braver than others."

She tried to assess whether he was being sarcastic, funny. Yet, he seemed to mean it.

He actually thought this was brave.

She woke at first light, stepping into her heels. He joined her at the window, arms draped over her front. He was so tall he could rest his chin on her head. "The offer's there," he said. "A gold bikini, the pool, a beautiful house..."

Six million.

"That would only happen if she dropped dead."

"Well, I could always ask her if she'd oblige," he replied.

She smiled to herself, swiveled on her heel to kiss his cheek. "See you soon."

"I'll call you."

"Bye, Freddy," she said, almost giving herself away by casting a glance around the room that she would never set foot in again.

Outside, she felt the first chill of autumn. Drawing her coat around her, she began to run quietly to the bus stop. She couldn't run all the way in heels, didn't want to risk injury, so stopped when she got near the cobblestones, walking fast instead.

She always smelled the old fishnets before she saw them, before the building came into sight, a poster hanging off the wall like a flopping tongue. The fire door was open, brick in place, liked she'd hoped it would be. It meant Guts was here. She didn't want to be alone for this, needed backup. He'd never indicated he would ever help or had any interest in her at all, save for the fact that she was here every day, wasn't any trouble, ran her classes in a corner of his boxing training room, giving him a cut of her takings and always on time too.

"Morning, psycho," he said.

She went to her crate, got her clothes, changed behind the screen. She felt sluggish today. The pull-up bar didn't seem appealing, but she made herself do it anyway. By the time she'd finished, she hoped he was here. But he wasn't.

The treadmill was still broken, so she made for the rowing machine, one eye on the door. As she pulled the sticky handles, the dark rope straining, she tried to ignore the irregular beat of her heart, the dizziness. It was just adrenaline, the increase of blood in her brain and muscles, sugar levels rising, preparing her for fight-or-flight.

The door darkened and there he was. He didn't speak, went to his fruit crate, which seemed demeaning for someone like him, the tiger on the back of his jacket appearing as he squatted to pick up his gear.

He wouldn't want her to talk to him while he was changing, or while lifting weights, or when he was all sweaty and done. He wouldn't want to talk to her at any point. But she'd thought of a way around that—had thought of barely anything else.

In here, she had always been the girl no one wanted to talk to because she would bite their hand. No one had seen her in any other light. It was time to give them something different.

She stopped rowing, the mechanism whirring, then flapped her baggy T-shirt. Too hot, she wrestled out of her top, flinging it down. Underneath, she was wearing a sports bra, sculpting leggings.

Slowly, she picked up her bottle, drinking from it, ribs protruding. Then she looked round the room as though coming back to her senses, glancing down at herself self-consciously, making her way to the weights.

He was watching her in the mirror as she approached, his teeth clenched as though bolted. She leaned against the wall, taking another drink of water.

Guts was watching them both, towel around his neck, ready to leave and go next door, wondering whether to do so and miss this.

"I heard you've got a gun," she said.

He carried on lifting, beads of sweat escaping, running into his eyes.

"And that you're handy with a blade?" she said. "How much to do a job for me?"

He knew what she was asking. There was a creaking as Guts moved his feet.

"Twenty K." His voice was squashed between lifts. "Never mind how."

Exactly what she'd heard. Exactly what she had.

"Cash up front," he added.

She picked up a small dumbbell, taking it to the mat in the darkest corner, starting a Russian Twist. His face was clouded, distracted by the disappointment of not being able to see her anymore.

Lifting her legs, she held the dumbbell before her, twisting from side to side.

It took him much longer than she'd thought. She had finished her mat work, was wondering what to do next, when he approached, armpits glistening. He squatted down again, like a sumo wrestler. "You good for the money?"

Guts was pretending to tidy up, pushing crates together, straightening them. There was a noise behind them as he kicked a crate into place.

"Yes," she replied, sitting cross-legged, arms behind her, body on display.

"Okay." He glanced over his shoulder. "Who?"

"I'll give you the details. But I need you to be one hundred percent accurate, no mistakes, no trace what-so-ever." She dragged out the syllables.

This angered him. He twitched his chin brusquely. "Who d'you think I am? This ain't no hobby."

"Just checking," she said.

He pulled a small book and pen from his pocket, threw them onto her mat. "Write it down." He glanced all around him. "No trace."

She propped the book on her knee, began to write, thinking of the hands that had touched this pen and pad before her. "There you go."

He read it. "Bring the cash tomorrow." The book went back

in his pocket and then he left, kicking the brick behind him so they knew he was gone, the fire door slamming shut.

Guts approached, a vein snaking across his forehead. "What the hell was that? What you playing at, eh? Eh?"

She let him cluck on as she collected her things, packing up her fruit crate.

"I hope you know what you're doing, because he doesn't mess around!" He followed her across the room, agitated, hopping from foot to foot.

"That's good," she said, pushing down on the bar to open the fire door. "Because neither do I."

Outside, it was cloudy. As Guts unlocked the training room, she surveyed the harbor, looking at the oily water, the seagulls pecking bins.

"You must have a death wish or summat, talking to him," Guts went on, feeling for the light switch. "No wonder they call you psycho."

"Yeah," she agreed, heading toward her corner to set up the mats for her class. "No wonder."

They called her that just because she was better than them at pull-ups. It made them feel better about themselves, believing she was mentally imbalanced. Whereas in actual fact they had no idea who she was, no idea at all.

35

April 1990

I started running because I was scared of sitting still any longer. One day, I got up and decided that I didn't want to wear dark colors and never see daylight and poke through Mom's old clothes and draw faces on the dusty mantelpiece. But I probably wouldn't have made those decisions if it weren't for the phone call.

One of my friends from university rang. I didn't even know we'd swapped numbers. She was a mature student, a divorcée—wanted to know how I was doing, why I'd left. I thought it was an odd thing for her to do out of the blue, but then considered that maybe something had sparked things at her end too. Something small, exactly like what was happening to me.

Before she hung up, she said don't let it define you, and I wrote that down. I didn't know what it meant exactly, but it felt like the best piece of advice anyone had ever given me. We said we would stay in touch, knew we wouldn't. We'd only known each other two weeks but that time had been so rich for me; I clung to her wise words as though they were the meaning of life.

The first thing I did after speaking to her was visit the sea, to forgive it, if I could. I didn't that first time, or the second. But one day, while trying, I noticed a woman in a yellow shirt and red shorts and realized she was a lifeguard, that it was a new service on the beach.

I was curious, asked her what the job involved, and she told me how to get fit by running and different swim training styles to try. She must have found it hilarious, looking at the state of me, but didn't say so. She talked to me like I was Cindy Crawford.

I never did become a lifeguard, but I did start running, all because she told me I looked strong, capable.

"So you're thinking about becoming a lifeguard?" Frizzy said, spooning gunk into the baby's mouth. It was a girl, Libby, shrivel-faced like a brussels sprout. There was no way we were related.

"Yeah, maybe. But I'm also applying for some other jobs." Given that I obviously wasn't going to run my Dad's company anymore.

"Well, that's great," he said, smiling tightly. Things were still off between us, probably always would be. He hadn't forgiven me for closing the door in his face and I hadn't forgiven him for killing my mom. The two things weren't equal, but somehow he couldn't see that.

"So you have to be, like, fit and everything?" Frizzy said.

"Yeah and everything," I said sarcastically, chasing a pea around my plate, floating in gravy. Dad gave me a dirty look in warning, but I was being an angel compared to what was going on inside my head. I was doing the math: Frizzy was twelve years older than me, so we could have been sisters. But no, that was the baby with orange food all over its chin, even though there were eighteen years between us. And at the head of the table, in charge of all this, was Robin Burton, Property Developer, fallen hero.

Except that he hadn't fallen; not even a little bit. It seemed to be the women in his life who were aging prematurely, whereas he was in good shape, clearly using hair dye and doing some kind of resistance training.

I wondered then, not for the first time, why he had raised me to be strong when he didn't seem to like strong women very much at all.

Maybe it was different because I was his daughter; or maybe he had liked me before I became a woman. Would the same thing apply to the little brussels sprout?

I watched as Frizzy set the spoon down for a moment as though exhausted by its weight, her arms looking scrawny, frail. I'd seen that look before. She was going the exact same way as Mom; anyone could see that. In fact, I was so wrapped up in seeing that, in being smug about how doomed they were, I didn't see the guillotine falling onto my own head.

We were standing in the hallway, the place where most of the dramas in my life had taken place, when he said, "Sara wanted me to talk to you about something."

"Oh?" I said, hoping I sounded as disinterested as I felt.

"Yep." He rocked on his heels, looking up at the ceiling as though noticing a crack. "It's…uh…about calling me Dad."

I didn't understand what he meant, but something was going on that was bigger than I was realizing. I could tell by the look on his face.

He put his hand lightly on my arm. "Sara doesn't want you to call me that anymore."

"Hey? Then what am I supposed to call you?"

He smiled, but it was tugging on his eyes. "Robin."

My heart grew heavy and light at once. I felt it swell, sink.

"I know it's difficult, what with your mom…" he said quietly, "but it's for the best. Sara thinks Libby will find it too confusing and it's best that we stamp it out now."

Stamp it out, like fire, disease.

"It doesn't change anything," he said even more quietly, glancing over his shoulder. "We'll still—"

"It changes everything. That name was all we had left to connect us—the only proof that we're actually family," I said, trying to control the emotion in my voice. "Are you just going to do whatever Frizzy says and—?"

"Frizzy?" He frowned. "Who's—?"

"So, where does this leave me?" I started crying, big bubbly tears that I was caught out by because I'd never intended to let my guard down here, ever. Frizzy had seen to it that I couldn't—was never given enough rope. Just enough to hang myself with.

"I'm sorry," he said, patting my arm. "Don't cry, Gabby. I promise I'll make this right by you. Just give me some time, eh?"

"No!" I said, pushing him away. "You have to decide now. If you do this, if you make me do this, I will never come here again. I swear I'll never see you again." I stared up at him, awaiting his reaction.

Did I mean it? I didn't know.

"You don't mean that," he decided for me.

"Yes, I do. Say I can still call you Dad. Say it!" I stamped my foot.

There was a movement in the doorway and Frizzy appeared, jigging the baby on her hip. "Everything all right?" she said, as though I were the paperboy.

I lifted my chin defiantly, still looking at Dad, waiting.

"I'm sorry," he said. "But Sara's my wife."

My throat swelled so painfully, I couldn't breathe. I blinked back my tears, too proud to cry in front of her. "Dad," I whimpered.

He bowed his head, pinching the top of his nose. I knew that sign—knew what it meant.

I let myself out, cried all the way home, walking in the rain, and then running. As I ran, gasping for breath, my unfit legs buckling, a plan formed in my mind, a scratchy patchy plan, but it made sense the more it grew, the more I wheezed.

He raised me to be strong, so that was what I'd be. I'd start with that. I wouldn't wither away, feeling sorry for myself, hiding indoors, but I'd go running and be as fit as I could manage and one day I'd rule the world, just like he said I was going to, before he betrayed me and abandoned me.

And some day, if I ever had a daughter, I would call her Alice and would never ever tell her not to call me Mom.

PART THREE

FIGHTING BACK

36

The week scrambles past. I don't so much as glimpse Fred's car, or catch sight of Ellis in the garden, despite checking incessantly. Life feels deceptively normal, but doesn't fool me. I don't allow myself to sleep deeply, or to ever be at home without the door double-bolted. I keep my phone with me at all times and I've reduced my time alone, lingering at the office, spending more time with Jam. We went for a beach walk last night, during which she asked if I'd considered the possibility that Fred has set all this up himself to get rid of me.

I have, yes.

When Friday lunchtime arrives, I'm relieved to have made it to the end of the week, slipping out of the office before anyone can ask why. Today, unlike every other day, isn't about Fred and Ellis, or even me.

I zip up my fleece and run downstairs in my Dress Down Friday shorts—still warm enough for them, but they'll be gone by the end of the month. I brought my car to work, parking it in the courtyard out back. If anyone ever noticed, they would know I do the same thing on this day every year.

It's a twenty-minute drive, the autumnal colors vibrant as they flash past. I'm glad it's sunny; small mercies.

I slow down as I approach the building with the ominous chimney, pulling into the car park. As I walk across the courtyard, I hear organ music. Coming toward me are mourners in black, heels clipping the air. I feel self-conscious in my shorts, so I dart along a path between rose bushes, going toward the magnolia trees, turning to look over my shoulder every few steps. Being killed in a crematorium's memorial garden would be crass, but I wouldn't put it past her.

There's a bench there which I'm making for, until I spot a crop of white hair that seems familiar. And then as I round the corner, the head turns my way and smiles and it's Len.

I smile back, pretending I'm pleased to see him here. I'm not put out, just surprised. I've always done this alone.

Our hands touch as he stoops to press a kiss on my cheek. I inhale his smell; nothing I could describe. Just Len. "Is it okay that I'm here?" He's still holding my hand as he looks down at me. Fred got his height from him, but nothing else that I can see.

"Yes, of course." I gaze at the brass plaques, strewn with leaves. The magnolias are ablaze with green and yellow foliage, reminding me of mango skin. I wish I were somewhere tropical; I wish I could have taken her with me.

Hers is the third along from the break in the stonework, set right between a couple, Sharon and Harry, which always feels apt to me.

"How did you know I'd be here?" I ask, as he sits down beside me with the sigh and grunt befitting his age.

"Just a good guess. Are you on your lunch hour?"

"Yes."

We fall silent and then he nudges me. "Fancy a cup of tea?"

I check my watch and then over my shoulder nervously.

I'm always nervous now. I wonder whether he notices. "Just quickly then."

"Good girl," he says, as though I've done something great.

He pours the tea into tin mugs, setting them on the bench between us, unwrapping a stack of biscuits. We clink our mugs together. "Cheers."

A robin is pecking at the soil between the plaques, near Mom's wording. It took me an age to think of what to say. I was only eighteen; what did I know about death? Quite a lot as it turned out. Losing a parent at that age taught me everything I needed to know and a bit more.

"I'm sorry about Fred," Len says. "He's a complete disgrace."

I nod politely. He's allowed to talk Fred down, but I'm not. I know how it works. I drink my tea, nibble a biscuit.

"I shouldn't say this, but I blame Monique." He shifts in his seat, stretching his right leg with a wince. "She spoiled him something rotten. I used to try to enforce discipline, but when I got home from work, she'd have undone it all." He shakes his head. "I used to say that it wasn't going to do him any good, but she wouldn't listen. She was always blind when it came to him—still is."

This much is true. But although he's reaching for a reason, an explanation for me, in truth Jam got it right the other night when she said women always get the blame. Yet, this one's all on Fred.

Behind us, a twig snaps and I jump. Len narrows his eyes at me. "You okay, love?"

I stand up, shaking my cup dry, looking at the shrubbery behind us. It must have been a bird. But still, it's enough to make me want to get going. Staying in one place for any length of time doesn't seem wise anymore. "Thanks for coming, Len. But I should get back to work."

He gazes up at me, his face creased in the sunshine, his hair cloud white. "I know things are difficult, but you're still family as far as I'm concerned."

"I really appreciate that. But I thought Monique..." I don't finish the sentence, can't think of a way to say it nicely.

Using the bench to push himself upright, he stands, swaying, getting his balance. "She'll have to lump it. I'm sorry, but I don't have a daughter, always wanted one." His voice tremors and I have to look away. I can't do this here, by Mom's plaque.

He leaves it at that. Neither of us look like we can handle a scene. He stoops to pick up his bag. "I'll walk with you," he says.

As we approach the crematorium, Latin American music is playing, a gentle samba that makes me wish I were anywhere but here. At the car, he turns to face me, taking my hands. "We're not all like him, you know, Gabby."

"I know. It's okay."

He bends his knees, his watery eyes meeting mine. "Don't let them win."

This startles me, even though I know what he means and why he's saying it. It's just that I never thought he'd be saying something like this to me, on the brink of my divorcing his son.

I know he doesn't mean the house though.

"Thanks, Len." I go on tiptoes to press a kiss onto his dry cheek. "Thanks for the tea and for thinking of me." He squeezes my hand and we part ways.

On the drive back to work, checking my rearview mirror constantly, no music playing so I can focus on where I'm going and who might be following, I think of how much easier my life might have been if I'd had a dad like Len, and how Fred might have turned out if he'd had a mom like mine. He might have learned from an early age to protect her, be there for her. As it was, he learned a very different pattern that set him up for where he is now.

My dad set me up too, but couldn't follow through. He

raised me to be strong, a match for him, but didn't know what that looked like once I reached puberty—didn't know how to take it from a childhood comic strip to an adult with a body and mind of her own.

Maybe no one set him up properly either.

As I reach the outskirts of town, I slow down, gripping the wheel, tension rising as I draw closer to home, where anything could happen.

I never saw my dad again, after he told me not to call him Dad. He phoned me a couple of times, but I didn't pick up. I moved two towns away, put physical distance between us, not thinking it would be permanent. It just happened. The space grew between us.

Then one day, eight years ago, I got a letter stating that Robin J. Burton had left me the estate of 23 Ocean View Road in his last will and testament. And my first reaction was that I didn't know what the *J* stood for—didn't know he had a middle name.

The fact that I didn't even know he was dead, that I'd missed his funeral, that no one had told me about it only occurred to me later, as though my brain were eking thoughts out to prevent me from overloading.

But I overloaded anyway. I don't remember seeing Fred much that winter, as we organized the house move, and I went through the routine of work, collecting the kids, feeding them. I know now that I was in shock, unavailable, and that Fred wasn't used to me not pivoting around him. Maybe that was the catalyst. I don't know. But if my father's death was the reason Fred cheated on his family, then that says more about him than it ever will about me.

Back in the office, I immerse myself in work, hounded by the sensation that there's something I'm supposed to be doing, or realizing. By the time I'm locking up for the night, my head is hurting from thinking, fretting.

I check my messages to see if Michael Quinn has replied, but there's nothing from him. And then I hurry to my car, locking the doors, driving home in silence, running inside the house, double-locking the front door, fending off all the possible horrors for another day, all the while knowing that the worst horrors are right here, with me.

Because there's something I'm missing—have been missing right from the start. And until I know what it is, the possibility of it is going to terrorize me. I leave another voicemail for Michael Quinn, the shadows growing around me.

37

It's a warm evening so I take my wine and pasta outside, sitting close to the open patio doors, phone on my lap, one eye on the side gate where I last saw her. I feel as though I'm living in a compound, beyond which the world is too unsafe to set foot in. I'm not sure that I'm even safe here, but I could run inside in a heartbeat, secure myself, phone for help.

The pool is covered, the palm trees very still. From several doors away, a toddler is crying, an adult voice raised in response. I fork pasta mechanically, thinking of the times my father brought me here—how this side of the house, the back, was off-limits and how intriguing that made it. Most of my time was spent hanging out on the steps of the portable cabin, playing cards. I used to wonder what the garden might look like someday, filled with family.

It didn't feel like I thought it would. The day we moved in, I felt detached, as though I'd never set eyes on the place before. And then we started to grow into it, filling the space, and the house became about Will's football kits, Alice's science experiments, Fred's cheating.

It suited me to disconnect from my early memories of Dad, to pretend there was a separate part of my life that started the day I walked away from him. I gathered the memories up, tossed them into a dark place, didn't think about them anymore.

When he died, I didn't even know the cause, had no one to ask. I wasn't going to ask his wife, Sara—that's if she was still his wife. I did work out his age though (seventy-two) and guessed cancer or heart attack.

I sip my wine. The child has stopped crying. From somewhere in the darkness, an owl hoots.

Returning indoors, I slip through to the front room, inhaling the stale air. The house feels shut up, empty already, as though it doesn't count that it's just me living here now. Over by the window, I count seven squares from the top, five along from the right, the seventh of May.

Me and you. A little piece of us here that no one can ever take away.

I kneel at the window, my hand on the parquet floor, imagining his large handprint next to my small one. And then I cry, for Batman and Robin, for my Mom.

When I'm done, I go back to the kitchen for more wine, knowing as I pour it that the answer doesn't lie in the bottle, yet I'll try to find it there anyway.

I'm closing the fridge, looking once more at that spindly drawing of Alice's that should have gone by now, when I realize something shocking, yet obvious.

I need to let go of the house.

Sitting down on the stool, I watch the moths and daddy longlegs circling the lights, bouncing off the walls because I kept the patio doors open earlier.

The handprint in cement hurt me; it was an awful day. This beautiful house was given to me in compensation for all the pain of my childhood. Yet, getting it only brought more. And clinging to it will bring even more still.

This revelation sets my teeth on edge. I drink more wine.

We have to sell the house. It's the only thing that makes sense—the only way I can see us having any kind of relationship for the sake of the kids.

I don't know if I'll still feel like this in the morning. It could be the wine. I don't know whether I can change course, unclench what I've been hanging on to for so long, whether I can cope with giving Fred what he wants—whether I can cope with giving her what she wants.

It feels so counterintuitive, to the point of self-destructiveness. And I'm wondering which instinct to listen to, when there's a crunch of tires outside and Fred's BMW appears, headlights blazing. He doesn't stop to lock the car—is running toward me, shouting. I watch anxiously, not liking the look on his face.

"What the hell did you say to her?" he says, bursting through the doors, slamming them behind him with a thump that makes them bounce open again.

I stare at him in confusion. "I don't know what—"

"Don't bullshit me!" he shouts, drawing so close I can smell his day-old aftershave. "I know this is your doing!" He prods my shoulder.

That does it. I set my glass down, glaring at him. "Who do you think you are, coming in here, yelling at me? I'm not your punching bag, you know!"

"What did you do?" he repeats, eyes boggling in rage.

I'm trying to think what might have caused this and then I've got it.

"Has she disappeared on you?"

He leans on the breakfast bar, arms outstretched, head hanging. This is a moment of triumph for me, but it's short-lived.

Because if she's not out there where he—we—can see her, then that feels more dangerous.

"How do you know for sure?" I ask gently, hoping he'll realize that I'm not going to lord it over him. To his face.

His voice sounds far away, muffled by his jacket. "She's not answering her calls or messages—hasn't for days. I've no other way of reaching her." Then he looks at me and his face is haggard, drawn, his eyes red-rimmed. Has he been crying? "Do you think it was a scam, Gabby?"

I take my time replying, filling the kettle. She's stolen twenty thousand pounds, yet has rejected a potential three million more. She could have accepted his proposal, hung in there for a year or so to get half the house if money was her sole objective, surely?

"Maybe she's just busy."

He laughs quietly. "Yeah, right."

"Fred..." I waver with the milk in my hands, holding it midair, wondering whether to proceed. If I'm not going to fight him for the house, there's no reason not to tell him. Yet, I haven't decided about that—can't decide something that big with a belly full of wine.

I sit down at the breakfast bar. "It's about Ellis... There's something you should know."

He looks at me intently. If I clicked my fingers, he'd jump. He's so obviously in love with her, my heart quiets, stills, as I absorb this. He loves someone else, no longer me. I don't know when it was me and when it wasn't, but it happened at some point and there's no undoing it now. The sad thing is: it doesn't hurt as much as it should.

"I met her before, only once, briefly, at Rumors."

"Rumors?" he says. "What—?"

"She approached me, started a conversation." I pour the milk into the mugs, my hand shaking. I don't think he notices. "I thought she was a complete stranger, didn't know me or you or anything about us. But I've since learned...well...that she already knew you."

I can't look at him. He's staring at me. "When was this?"

I get up to put the milk away, needing an excuse to move. "A couple weeks ago, last month... September."

He's thinking about this. I shut the fridge door, standing with my back to it, watching him.

"But why would she do that?" he says. "It makes no sense. What did she talk to you about?"

I busy myself wiping the sink. "About you, mainly. Our marriage—whether I was happy."

His mouth hardens. "And what did you say?"

"Well, what do you think?"

He tuts. "So you told her our personal business?"

I have to laugh at that, turning on my heel to face him. "Yes, while you were sleeping with her. Let's not forget that, Fred, before you start preaching."

"I wasn't sleeping with her." He stands up, pacing the floor. "I was helping her, which I've already tried to tell you before now, but you won't listen."

"Yes and I'm not listening now either. There's no way you can expect me to believe you were just holding hands with that girl in the Neptune Hotel!" I break off, still clutching the dishcloth, emotional heat rising through me.

We're arguing again. We'll never be able to discuss this, or her, or his affairs, without arguing. And I know for sure then that I don't want to give him what he wants—to split the house or do anything he says.

"Why didn't you tell me this before?" he asks.

Because we're at war, and information is valuable.

I throw the cloth into the sink, suddenly exhausted. "I can't keep doing this—can't do my job or function properly, not with all this going on. It's too much."

And then I do something unpredictable: I drop my only weapon, because I'm tired of carrying it.

"I know about the investments, Fred… How *could* you?"

He turns to look at me, his mouth tense. "I'll make it up to you, Gabby. I'll get that money back into the account—every penny."

"No, you won't, because you don't have it to give."

"I will if we sell this place." He glances around the room dispassionately.

I sit down at the table, cradling my mug. "Did you tell her what it's worth?"

"I'm not sure. I might have mentioned it, yes."

"Wow." I shake my head. "Then I'm sure she'll be back!"

Ludicrously, this brightens him, his eyebrows lifting. "Maybe you're right. Maybe she's just gone off the grid for a few days."

"Could be," I say, not believing it. "But don't you know anything about her? Where she lives? Where she works?"

"No. She didn't want to discuss personal details because it was complicated… But we were getting round to all that."

I know he doesn't know anything, and how stupid that makes him. He hears it too.

First thing tomorrow, I'm chasing Michael Quinn again.

"I made the application," he says, "for divorce," he adds, as though that needed clarifying. "You'll get a copy of the petition any day now."

"Fine. And I'm using Maria Kane."

I hope that name doesn't mean anything to him. He can stick with his parents' old-school legal recommendation and I'll go with Kane. She had me at power.

"You should probably also know…" I begin slowly, watching him closely, gauging his reaction "…that Ellis was here the other night, prowling about."

He works his jaw ponderously, surprised—as far as I can tell. "What do you mean, prowling? What was she doing?"

"How would I know? I was hoping you might be able to tell me." I motion in the direction of the garden. "She just stood there, staring at the house."

A look passes over his face then, a recognition of some kind.

"Does she want to move in?" I ask. "Is that what she was doing—picking her room?"

"Hardly!" He laughs. But there's that look again.

I decide to risk another piece of information for my own protection. "I'm scared of her."

"Ellis?" He smiles, going to the sink to rinse his mug. "Don't be ridiculous."

"If there's anything I should know, Fred, then now's the time..." I say, tracking his movements, noting how stilted, affected, they seem.

"Like what?" he says, blowing a fake whistle as he wipes the mug.

"I don't know. Just anything. Like... Well, you haven't discussed doing anything to me, have you? You haven't been planning to..."

He's staring at me as though I've grown wings. "If you're saying what I think you're saying, then I can't believe you're even thinking that, Gabby!" he says, his tone righteous, indignant. "You're the mother of my children! Things might be bad between us, but they're not that bad, are they?"

I don't answer.

His phone buzzes. He used to have a kooky ringtone—one that Alice picked—but now it's a covert vibration. I didn't even know he had changed it. Of all the things that have happened of late, this strikes me as one of the saddest.

He reads the message. "It's Mom, wondering whether I want supper."

"Must be nice, a home-cooked meal."

I meant it genuinely, sort of, but his mouth curdles. "Don't start, Gabby." He tucks in his shirt, sets his hand on his hips, changing the subject. "Do you remember that trouser press?"

"Yes. It's in the attic."

"I might grab it, if you don't mind." He picks up his phone, taps it.

"Be my guest."

As he leaves the room, I eye his phone, the fact that he's left it on the table. I have about two seconds to snatch it before it blacks out, locks.

Listening for him, the floorboards creaking above me, I check the text. Sure enough, it was Monique.

I go to the other latest messages, a thread from E. My pulse skipping, I scroll down, skim-reading. Standard details, meeting times. And then there's a photo.

I don't hesitate before clicking on it, don't take a moment to prepare myself. There's not enough time. Staring at it, I raise my hand to my mouth, my heart pounding.

Black lingerie, one hand down her knickers, eyelids drowsily heavy.

Prepare to bring the heat.

I drop the phone, panicking, and then grab it again before it locks. Trembling, I scroll through, looking for more. They're all the same. Ellis in creamy lace; in baby pink. Nothing explicit, all suggestive.

Her eyes meet mine as though she's laughing at me.

My blood is swishing in my ears. I can't hear Fred anymore. I pause for an instant, gazing at the ceiling. There's the bang of the attic door; he's on his way down. Quickly, I go to his stored photos. They're in files, named with letters of the alphabet. Six or seven of them. I click on *A*.

I don't hear his footsteps, the door opening, until he's standing there, just as I click on an image of a young woman with startling red hair, wearing an electric blue camisole, her body turned to reveal her rear.

"What do you think you're doing?" he says, holding the trouser press.

I ignore him, clicking on *J*. Blond hair is all I get in time. He rounds the table, grabbing the phone. "Stay away from my stuff, Gabby!"

J is still glowing, and then she's gone. He saw it though, his face blanching. He's trying to think of something to say and can't.

I can't either. The words are forming, falling over themselves. He's picking up the trouser press and is leaving.

Somehow, I find my voice, half of what it used to be. "How long has this been going on?"

At the French windows, he stops. "This isn't going to help anyone. Least of all you."

"Just tell me. I need to know."

He exhales, standing with his back to me. "A few years."

My eyes fill with tears, even though I thought I'd never cry over him again. "Why?"

He hesitates so much I know it's the truth. "I was lonely."

This is the last thing I expected him to say. How can that be? He was married to me. Why did he need a whole alphabet of women?

"How did you… How did you afford it?"

"My own money, from my salary." He shrugs defensively.

"And these girls are…what, escorts or prostitutes or…?" I trail off, something that Jam said coming to mind. "Is this rinsing?" I'm not sure what I'm talking about—if that's the right word. He doesn't reply anyway.

"Is this what you've been doing with Ellis?" I ask.

"No. It's not the same. With those other girls, I don't know who they are, haven't met them. But Ellis…" It's his turn to trail off.

"You've been sending strangers money to see them in their underwear? Is that it? Girls the same age as Alice?"

He firms his grip on the trouser press, as though that's the only thing standing between him and a complete loss of pride—the idea that tomorrow he will press his trousers and go to work. "It didn't mean anything. And I'm sure they're not as young as they look. They use filters."

Filters.

That's his explanation, his reasoning.

A silence descends, one that seems to end things between us. There's a sense of disconnection, a cord being cut, the same sensation I felt that day with Monique at the beach.

I gaze at him a while longer, and then I let go.

I pick up my glass, taking it to the sink. "Any compassion I may have had for you is gone. As of now, Fred, you're dead to me."

He looks at me in bewilderment, as though he could never imagine me thinking anything like that about him, despite everything he's said and done to push me to this point.

And then, with a surrendering sigh, he takes his leave, carrying the press in his arms the way he once held our children, night air creeping in around my ankles like the cold tide.

As he starts the car, vanishes, my words linger, buzzing in my ears, their horror coiling around my heart because I know they're true.

You're dead to me.

38

She watches as her students arrive one by one, never chatting. There's a somberness about this class which the others don't have. Zumba, her least favorite, is loud, sociable. Krav Maga is completely different.

She doesn't tend to say hello to them, aside from a nod. She lets them scrabble about in the dark corners, dropping off bags, eyeing the boxing ring anxiously, jumping every time the metal doors scrape back and some guy enters wearing a hoodie. These girls don't like boxers, but it's understandable. Most of them are here because they're scared. They have dark circles under their eyes and the jitteriness of someone who doesn't want anyone to touch them.

It would have been better teaching them somewhere smarter, cleaner, without the smell of male sweat, but it's all she can manage for now. Besides, many of the girls are students and her low prices suit them.

They come in cowering, leave glowing. Krav Maga's a violent combat style, used by the Israeli military. It's for real life, not for contrived situations in class that would never happen on the streets. It's down and dirty: groin strikes, throat punches, eye pokes. Fast, easy to learn, quick to teach. No one has time to perfect moves when under threat. They just need to know what to do, how to do it.

There's only one rule: do what it takes to survive.

Today, she's showing them how to fall if knocked to the ground. She goes over to the tarnished mirrors, motioning for the girls to follow her.

She demonstrates the back fall break—what to do if pushed backward. It will help them to fall properly, reduce injury. Twenty frightened eyes track her in silence. Then there's the side fall, backward roll, forward roll. They break off into pairs on the sticky mats, learning the moves while she circulates.

After class, they're more vocal. One of them, maybe as young as fourteen, asks where she got her leggings from. One of them, an older woman, says she doesn't trust her husband anymore.

She listens to these comments, giving one-word responses, keeping things on the dial down. She doesn't want more and they don't want to give it either. That's okay. She keeps her distance.

They pay cash, some of which she passes on to Guts for the use of his grimy room. And then, between classes, she works out again.

"Hello?" She open the door, which is off the latch. She keeps telling her mom to lock it, but always finds it undone. "Mom?"

She tiptoes forward in case her mother's asleep, even though it's midday. She doesn't want to startle her. On the hallway table, there's a bag containing wine and Marlboro Lights.

Her mother's watching TV in the lounge. It's on so softly, it's hard to hear it. "Hey, Mom. You okay?"

"Oh, hello, dear!" her mom replies, as though she's not here every single day, checking up on her. "Busy at the bank?"

That's where her mom thinks she works, even though she's always in gym wear. "Yeah. Pretty busy."

"I just saw on the television that interest rates are rising. Does that affect you?"

"Yes, Mom." Reaching between the curtains, she cranks a window, leaving the curtains slightly parted, a spear of sunshine hitting the wall. "Have you eaten yet?"

"No, not yet." There's not a bit of interest in her voice.

"Would you like me to make you a sandwich?"

Her mother flaps her hand. "No, don't you worry about that. Just see to yourself. There's ham somewhere." Hopefully in the fridge.

She goes through to the kitchen, eyeing the mess. Seriously, there's no need. She rolls up her sleeves, collecting mugs, dropping them into the washing-up bowl. Then she checks the fruit bowl, examining the contents—counting the pills.

She returns to the lounge, hands on hips. "Why aren't you taking your meds?"

"Oh, no reason." A cigarette dangles on her lip as she speaks.

"Well, that's not good enough. You know what the doctor said. You've got to keep them up, Mom. You can't just pick and choose when."

"I know, dear. But I've got these, look." She smiles, waggles her cigarette, rising to the French doors to open them, standing half in, half out like a teenager sneaking a puff.

"That's not going to do you any good though, is it? It's just killing you. Honestly..." Frustrated, she stomps to the kitchen, scrubbing mugs and plates, anger rising. If her mother doesn't take her pills, she'll start having seizures again—full-blown panic attacks.

It's like she doesn't want help. It's like she wants to spend the rest of her life here, watching daytime TV. She's sixty-four, not ninety-four. She needs fresh air, friends, hobbies—something, anything.

Slamming cupboard doors, she wipes the surfaces, checking the fridge contains the ham. It does, but little else: a lump of cheese, a random egg. She drops the cheese into the bin, sitting down at the table to make a list of basics. She can't make it to the shop and back before her next class—will have to come back again tonight.

Returning to the lounge, her mother is in her chair again, her mouth knitted with smoker's wrinkles. Everything about her is shriveling, disintegrating.

"I have to go," she says, leaning down to press a kiss onto her mother's smoky hair. "But I'll be back later with some supplies… You can't live like this, Mom. It's not…" She's about to say right, but stops herself.

Her mother already knows this. She doesn't need wise cracks, judgment. If she could get out of that chair and go running into the sunshine and live her life to the full, whatever that might look like, she'd be doing it.

"Why don't you move back home with me then, hey?"

Her mother asks this every time and she always says the same thing in response. "Because I need my own space. You know that."

"But look at all the room here! It doesn't make sense."

"Yes it does, to me."

"If you say so." Her mother's eyes return to the TV—a program about relocating to Spain. As if that's an option. "See you later then. Enjoy your afternoon."

As she opens the front door, her mother calls out, "You still there?"

She stops, listens. "Yeah?"

"Love you."

"Okay, Mom." She leaves, her shoulders high and tight. It's a twenty-minute walk to the harbor, which she has to run. Why does her mom always mention her moving back home? Living there would be regressing, depressing.

She just makes her next Krav Maga, entering the class at the same time as the students, which she hates doing. Guts is teaching in the ring, his voice down out of some sense of respect. He looks up, nods, as she starts the lesson. He said Krav Maga was too violent and brutal for women—that no one around here would want to do it.

It's her biggest class.

"Okay, listen up," she says, tossing her sweater behind her. "Today we're focusing on hand fighting and elbow strikes again."

An older woman in the front row pumps her fist and says, "Yes!"

39

Michael Quinn won't meet me on the weekend. He doesn't say so, but it becomes obvious when he doesn't return my call until Monday morning, just as I'm logging on at work.

I spent the weekend with Jam. She stayed over, we drank wine, looked up rinsing online, psychoanalyzed Fred, combed through my bank accounts noting all the blank spaces I'd failed to spot, trying to work out whether to let the house go or cling to it in compensation. For the second time in my life.

By Sunday night, I felt like I'd been vacuum-packed, compressed, everything so tight I was struggling to breathe.

I still feel like that. I'm listening to Michael's voice and it's taking a while to reach me. "…The King's Arms again, six o'clock?"

We're meeting tonight.

When I hang up, Claire touches my shoulder and I jump in my seat, clutching my heart. "Oh, you scared me! Sorry, Claire, I'm a bundle of nerves today."

She looks apologetic. "I just wanted to ask if you'd like a coffee?"

"Oh, yes, please. Thank you. You're a star." I smile, my mouth twitching with the effort. Rows of faces look up, evaluating me. I know I look dark under the eyes, edgy, wired. Shaun would be enjoying this, if he were in yet. I make a written note to start logging his hours, and a mental one to look for better concealer makeup at lunchtime and to check out herbal remedies, something to get me through the day without my skin leaving my bones.

At six o'clock I enter the King's Arms, having checked all around me first, scrutinizing the immediate area with an efficiency that would impress a hit squad. I'm not taking any chances anymore. I bought a personal alarm and self-defense spray at lunchtime; Claire told me, after my discreet inquiries, that they sell them in a tourist shop of all places and she was right.

Michael is already inside the pub, doing paperwork in the corner near the empty fireplace. There's no one else around, the barman laying out cutlery, folding napkins.

"Gabby," he says, extending his hand. He seems on edge, less poised than before, and I immediately wonder why, stomach churning. Nerves are infectious, especially with a private investigator, because if he doesn't like what he's found, then I'm sure as hell not going to.

I force a smile as I set my bag down. "So...what have you got for me?"

He glances past me to the bar. "Would you like a drink?"

"No, thanks." No need for schmoozing or placebos tonight. When I get home, I'll decompress, the way risotto rice does when I snip the packet, air escaping. But for now I'm as rock steady as the table he's leaning on. At least, I hope I am.

Clearing his throat, he pulls a piece of paper from his file, handing it to me. "That's your invoice, Gabby. I'm really sorry."

"Because it's low?" It's nothing—a pittance. I paid more to have the boiler serviced.

He shuffles his feet, sets his pen on the table, aligning it with his file. "I couldn't justify charging more. It's the minimum fee."

"But why?" I fold the paper, concealing it inside my bag.

"Well, because..." His blond eyelashes flutter rapidly and then he looks all around the room, leaning in to speak quietly. "I can't go any further with this case."

I don't understand. "Because you couldn't find anything about her? 'Cos I told you I don't think that's her real name and—"

He holds up his hand. "It's not that. It's because..." Again, he glances around, lowering his voice even more so that I have to strain to hear him. "...I can't get involved with this."

"What do you mean? Why not?"

"Because it's too dodgy. I'd lose my job." He folds his arms. "I don't know what you think private investigators do, but it's not this. At least, not our company. It's not worth it. And..." He stabs the table with his finger. "...If my boss were to find out about this?" His voice is a whisper. "I'd be sacked on the spot."

I stare at him, swallowing slowly, wishing now that I'd taken that offer of wine. "What did you find out? Tell me. Please."

He deliberates this, twisting his pen round and round on the table top like a compass, telling him which way to go. "I'll just tell you this and then I can't speak to you again about it. Okay?"

I nod, my stomach shriveling. What can be so bad that he had to drop the case?

"Like you thought—Ellis has adopted an alias and she's good at what she does. She's a shadow, doesn't leave a trail. But I managed to find her, follow her...and that's when I had to shut everything down."

"Why?" I ask, shifting to the edge of the seat, certain I'm about to fall off.

"Because she's involved with the warehouse lot in Seaport."

That means nothing to me. Seaport is two towns away along the coastline, a ratty place I've only been to once and got out again fast. I wait for more information.

"They occupy the derelict warehouses by the harbor. And I don't mean kids vaping. I mean proper criminals. Drugs, illegal arms. At least, that's what the rumors are. They're set up as small businesses, gyms, coffee bars. But they're slippery as hell. The police can't pin anything on them—have tried for years allegedly." He throws his pen down, closes his notepad. "And that's all I'm saying."

I shift uncomfortably. "But if they're pretending to be aboveboard, then why are you scared to go down there? Couldn't you be a customer?"

He looks angry for the first time, his jawline hardening. "No, Gabby, I'm not scared. But some unknown guy, sniffing around down there? They'd kill me in my sleep. And like I said: my boss would sack me if he knew I was handling this case. We don't touch serious organized crime and I'm pretty sure that's what we have here."

The pub is completely silent, the barman gazing at us.

"This isn't for me," Michael says, picking up his laptop bag, swinging it onto the table. "To be perfectly honest, you should be going to the police."

I watch as he assembles his paperwork methodically, placing it neatly inside the bag. If I was looking for a maverick, someone to bend the rules a little, I chose the wrong guy. "I'm afraid I have to go. But there's no rush for payment under the circumstances."

I stare at the colorful lit bottles behind the bar, thinking that this could not have been worse news. Because not only am I more at risk than I realized, but the person I was hoping would dig me out of the hole is bailing on me.

"It was nice meeting you, Gabby. I'm sorry I couldn't help."

"Not as sorry as I am."

His face clouds with regret. Stooping down to speak, his eyes are so serious they're scary. "Get out of this while you can. I mean it. Either go to the police or pack up and go. One or the other. Because whatever this is? It's not safe." Giving me a lingering look of warning, he leaves, the door swinging behind him.

I stay awhile, too stunned to move. I'm not going to be decompressing anytime soon, after all.

When I finally get myself together, the barman wishes me a great evening and I smile as though that's exactly what I've got lined up.

In the lobby, I notice a flyer for a local taxi service. *Be safe, not sorry*, it says. Dialing the number, I'm told it'll be half an hour. I return to the bar, ordering a glass of wine while I wait. "Did your willpower break in the end, eh?" the barman says cheerily.

"Something like that," I reply, too distracted to think of anything else. Sitting back down where I was with Michael, I gaze at the blank space where he was seated.

Drugs. Illegal arms. Get out while you can.

I'm fairly certain that Fred doesn't know who Ellis is—what he's getting into. What the hell am I going to do?

My wine is so chilled I shiver, nestling into my scarf, thinking about what Jam found online over the weekend. We were looking up rinsing and somehow she moved on to memory loss, certain that I should have remembered exactly what happened that night at Rumors by now.

She zoomed in, highlighting a sentence that went round and round in my mind, like a panicking bird trapped in a room.

> With selective memory, we conveniently forget our mistakes, allowing us not to take responsibility for our actions.

Is that me? Is that what I've been doing?

I gaze at Michael's empty place again. When he was talking about the warehouse in Seaport, I had a horrible feeling that I was guilty in some way and he could sense it. He didn't trust me and I don't blame him.

The truth is hard to admit, especially when it's appalling. But I think that all along I've been protecting myself from recalling something terrible, something which Ellis—potential psychopath, criminal—knows.

40

She's putting away the mats at the end of Krav Maga when she's aware of a noise behind her and turns to see a shape at the door, so thick it blocks the light. Guts has gone next door to the gym; through the walls comes the throb of a beat, a bass that vibrates in the brickwork and her heart.

He waits for her to notice him, go to him. When she does, a trickle of perspiration slips down her back. It's too hot in here, needs better ventilation. Flicking up the spout of her water bottle, she sips as she walks, moving slowly, as though he's no big deal.

This irritates him. He looks her up and down, dismissing her with his eyes. "Tonight."

She replies with a glare that says she came all the way over there just to hear one word, before turning away. There's nothing else to be said. The less she knows, the better. Even so, she can guess the details, has done enough background checks of her own, could probably name the time and place if she had to.

The light changes and when she turns toward the door again, he's gone. She exhales in relief, sitting down on the edge of the stack of mats, holding her shaking hands out in front of her. She traps them underneath her armpits, stilling them, and then collects her things, cramming them into her bag before leaving the warehouse.

When she's out of sight of the gym, she quickens her pace, pulling up her hood, walking with her face down. She knows what she has to do—has been through it enough times in her mind, but suddenly it feels real and acid burns in her stomach, setting fire to her lungs. There's not a soul in sight, not that anyone would want to hang around here, but it makes her feel lonely for the first time, scared. She can't dwell on that though, or she'll lose her nerve.

Turning up a dark alley, she runs up the steps, feet like pistons. There's litter, syringes everywhere, and graffiti which she doesn't understand or see the point of, and then she's standing outside her apartment building, looking over her shoulder before booting the front door twice to open it.

There's a pile of junk mail which she snatches up, dropping it onto the table. On the message board, someone's written *ET phone home.* Hilarious. Like anyone would actually be helping anyone. Upstairs, a baby's crying behind a closed door; someone's having a coughing fit; there's the theme tune of a daytime show—the same one her mom's probably watching.

Inside her apartment, it smells of yesterday's food—not hers. Smells travel here, through floorboards and walls, like the noise. She's lost count of the amount of times she's heard her neighbors orgasming while she eats noodles from a plastic pot.

Undressing, she jumps into the bathtub, attaching the rubber mouth to the tap, holding the shower head over her body. There's a splutter and then the water drizzles out, barely enough to wash with.

Satisfied that she doesn't smell like the gym anymore, she goes to the mirror, wiping off the steam, watching it steam up again. Too soon.

In the bedroom, she pulls clothes from drawers, throwing them all over the bed, trying to find her hoodie, tracksuit bottoms, wondering why she didn't have them ready. Because she hadn't known it was going to be tonight—thought she had more time.

The hoodie and bottoms are in the cardboard box that she uses for a laundry basket. Tipping it upside down, she shakes them out, sniffs them, decides they've passed.

The mirror is clear now, but her hand is shaking worse than before. She closes her eyes, steeling herself, then picks up a pair of scissors, holds her hair out straight to one side, grits her teeth, cuts.

Her feet are tickled by hair as it tumbles down. She peers forward to do the fringe, trying to get it as straight as she can, thinking that hairdressers deserve more credit.

She examines the results, turning her head from side to side, running her hand around her emancipated neck. Getting back into the tub, she holds her head under the water, hair amassing in the plug.

She gets dressed quickly, the material cloying to her wet skin. In the bedroom, she drops to the floor to pull a shoebox out from underneath the dresser. Ripping the chain from her neck in one yank, she tosses it into the corner of the room. And then she removes the necklace from inside the tissue paper, reinstating it, the diamanté *B* sitting squarely on her chest.

In the living space, there's a miniscule shelf holding a framed photo. Hitting the back off, she slides the photo out, pushing it into the pocket of her tracksuit bottoms.

Casting her eye around the room, she tries to think whether there's anything else here she'll need or miss. She doesn't think so. Her clothes are all crap. She could set fire to the whole lot and nothing would be lost.

As a last-minute precaution, she retrieves the broken necklace, brushes up her hair from the floor and unplugs the bath, taking the mess with her in a plastic bag. And then she's out of there, slamming the door behind her.

Hood up, eyes down, she runs back down the steps of the alley, nearly turning her ankle to miss an abandoned kebab. Halfway, there's a bin that's always there, always full. Slipping the bag down the side of it, she runs back up the steps, making for the corner shop.

Her heart's hammering as she buys milk, eggs, cheese, tomatoes, enough for her mother to make an omelet, trying to ignore the resentment poking her ribs. She packs the food into a cheap carrier, the sort that looks like the bottom will give way after four steps, telling herself that if that happens, she's ditching the lot and her mother will have to make do for one evening without her. As if she didn't have enough to worry about.

Fear's a funny thing. She teaches this every day—how not to freeze if jumped in the dark. Yet, her fingers and toes are tingling, her vision is starting to narrow as though she's hemmed in on either side, and the resentment is turning into something worse: guilt.

No one looks at her as she skirts puddles, twisting to avoid knocking into pedestrians. To them, she's no one—a boy figure in baggy clothing, probably up to no good because none of them ever are.

She runs all the way to her mother's house, where she rings the doorbell to give her the heads-up and then pelts down the hallway, shouting, "I've brought you some food, Mom. Make sure you eat!"

She hesitates, listens, as she shoves her backpack out of the way underneath the shoe rack in the hallway where no one will notice it.

"Okay, dear," her mom calls. "Thank—"

She doesn't hear the rest, is down the driveway, past the sun dial and the nude statue, and through the gates, her footsteps echoing around the redbrick buildings and high walls.

The bus is late. She shifts her weight, stamping her feet, trying to stop them tingling. The electronic message says it should have been here five minutes ago. Darkness is falling, the letters glowing, branding themselves on her retinas.

When the bus shows up, she barely speaks, going right to the back, hunching in the corner. The journey's an hour long, feels more, the engine straining on hills.

And then at last she's ringing the bell, darting down the aisle as it lurches to a stop, and she's standing in High Street, not far from the singles' bar where she first met him. But there's no need to think of that now. Instead, as she runs down a side road, passing the Neptune Hotel, she thinks of the thick shape at the warehouse earlier, the tiger on his back, the one word he said.

Tonight. That's here; it's now. As if in response, from somewhere above, a lonely cat mews.

Running up an alley, her tunnel vision returns and she has to stop, lean against the wall, catching her breath. Bending over, she focuses on her feet, the whiteness of her shoes hurting her eyes. She's so hot and cold; she goes to put her hair up before realizing it's all gone.

She continues on her way, slower, taking off her hoodie, tying it around her waist. At the top, she glances into a car window at her reflection, barely recognizing herself.

Things are starting to become more familiar now and she begins to feel calmer. She slows down even more, checking that the photo's still in her pocket.

Finally, she's there, on Ocean View Road, the cherry blossom trees iron-still. Wiping her hands on her trousers, she counts the houses as she passes them, to help with her nerves. She doesn't need to otherwise. She knows exactly which one it is.

41

I shouldn't have had the wine at the pub. It was too cold, leaving a gnawing chill in my bones. At the breakfast bar, I'm shivering as I force myself to eat, even though the heating's on and I'm wearing a warm cardigan.

The taxi driver told me to take care and stay safe as he dropped me outside and I nearly asked him to just keep on driving. Michael told me to leave, as though things like that are possible in this complicated day and age. But I did think about it on the way home—whether I could pack a bag and disappear for a few weeks.

Where would I go? And who's to say I'd be safer there? People like Ellis don't give up just because of a change of address. She would find me if she wanted to.

On the counter beside me, my phone beeps, flashing a message from Jam.

Did you get home okay? What did Michael say?

Before replying, I go to the fridge, wondering about more wine, coming up with reasons for and against, when something outside catches the corner of my eye and I gasp.

It's me. My own reflection.

That settles it. I pour a large glass of wine and am replacing the bottle, when the security light flicks on outside and I see Alice.

What on earth…? Is she okay? I shove the bottle back into the fridge, hurrying to the patio doors.

It's not Alice. I almost smack straight into the glass, pulling up abruptly, my chest squeezing the breath from me.

She's standing near the summerhouse, hair fixed up, out of sight; a ghost, a vision all in gray.

The security light flicks off, startling me, and then she's gone. I gulp for air, sagging in relief, until I realize that she can see everything I'm doing in here. Grappling for the lights, I turn them off. My eyes adjust to the dark and now I can see her again.

It's just me and her, face-to-face, some thirty steps between us. Somehow, I always knew it would be like this—that it was about me, not Fred.

I reach for my phone, gripping it, trying to think whom to contact. Raising my hand, I make it obvious to her that I'm about to make a call. She moves then, approaching steadily, nothing in her hands that I can see, yet the hoodie around her waist is bulky—could be concealing something.

These doors are triple-glazed. She can't get in. She'd have to smash her way in with a sledgehammer.

I'm still holding my phone in the air. "Don't do that," she shouts, her voice muffled. Stopping in front of the glass, she taps it. "Put your phone down." Like it's a gun.

I wish it were. I see now that a personal alarm and spray wouldn't have helped. They're not even within reach—are in my bag, out in the hallway. Even so, I don't think spray would stop her.

"We need to talk." She motions for me to unlock the door.

I'm not going to do that. I shake my head, heart pounding.

The security light is on again, flooding her features and I notice her hair isn't up: it's completely gone. She's rubbing her neck as though it's itching and then her arms are back by her sides, military-like.

There's no way I'm opening those doors.

"Please..." she says, frowning.

There's an earnestness about her that I haven't seen before, but it may be the hair—the way her features are laid bare, child-like. "What do you want?" I shout.

The earnest look again, hands raised in appeal. "To talk."

"No."

She waits, as though I might change my mind, and then reaches into her trouser pocket.

This is it. She's going to pull a gun, blow a hole in me, right through the glass. I'm feeling faint, dark spots appearing in my vision, when she holds something up, pressing it against the glass.

I inch forward to look at it, unable to believe what I'm seeing.

It's a photograph, of me. And Dad... It's Dad. And Frizzy. "Why do you have that? What are you doing with it?" The spots thicken in my eyes, my thoughts clotting.

"Let me in and I'll explain."

Her eyes widen and I see Alice in her again, but everything is muddled, and in my panic, I'm reaching for someone I love.

"I'm not going to hurt you, Gabby. I promise."

Indecision floods me. If I don't let her in, I'll always be in the dark. But if I do...she could kill me.

She's never going to go away. She'll stand outside here forever, following me, haunting me.

I go to the knife block, removing the largest one, the one I rarely use, blade glinting. Then I return to the doors. "I swear, I'll use it if I have to."

She nods.

I swallow dryly, my hand trembling as I reach to unlock the

door. It gives a horrible click and I immediately retreat behind the breakfast bar, holding the knife upright, my phone in my pocket.

"Thank you," she says, looking about the kitchen. "Well, this is nice… I can see why you love it so much." She unties her sweater, folds it, setting it near the door in a neat pile. She does the same with her shoes. She doesn't appear to have anything else on her, aside from the photo, which she sets on the counter between us.

The color is faded and there's a border around it as though it's been in a frame for years. I can't imagine who would have wanted to frame it. No one looks happy, aside from Dad. It was April 1990; the last time I ever saw him.

"Why do you have that?" The knife feels slippery in my hand. I tighten my grip on it.

"Because I knew you wouldn't believe me without proof."

"Of what?"

She smiles mysteriously, adjusting her top. I eye her abdomen, taut and golden like shiny leather. She's wearing a crop top, the sort dancers wear, and baggy tracksuit bottoms, the perfect outfit for freedom of movement.

"What happened to your hair?" I ask.

She rubs her neck again. "Like it?"

"Why the sudden change?"

"This is how I usually wear it." She smooths the marble work surface with her hand. "This is lovely. You have great taste."

My wine is between us on the breakfast bar, untouched. She points to it. "May I?"

I don't reply.

She takes a sip, flaps her face as though warm. "Phew! I'm boiling!" She's shivering though, her lips lined with lilac.

"If you don't tell me why you're here, I'm phoning the police."

"But you let me in," she says politely.

"Because you said you'd tell me who you are."

She sets the glass down carefully on a coaster, the most polite houseguest I've ever had. "I don't think I actually said that did I?"

"Stop playing games! And tell me your real name." My gaze drops to the *B* pendant above her cleavage; she's changed it yet again.

She glances down at it too. "Well, if you must know...I'm Be."

I frown. "Bea?"

"Without the *A*. I thought it was cool, but someday I might add the *A*. I'll see how it goes." She touches an apple in the bowl, lifts it to her nose, smells it. "Apples remind me of my old home. We had apple trees out back." She says this as though it should mean something to me.

When it doesn't, she replaces the fruit and the earnest look returns. She holds her hand against her bare chest. "I'm Elizabeth."

This doesn't mean anything either. I loosen my grip on the knife for a second, my hand aching, before tightening it again. In my pocket, my phone beeps. It'll be Jam; I didn't answer her earlier.

"Do you need to get that?" she asks.

"Just tell me who you are."

She seems disappointed, bites her lip. "You really don't know?"

"Well, you're obviously not Ellis."

"It's kind of like Elizabeth though, isn't it?" She cocks her head at me appraisingly, the way she did when we first met. "I mean, all the clues were there for you to find."

"Clues? This isn't a treasure hunt. I'm not playing games with you."

"No one was playing games," she says, standing up straight, posture perfect. I wish Alice would stand like that.

The thought of her makes me panicky. I'm a mom. Could I kill this woman, if I had to?

"There's no need to be scared of me," she says, reading my expression. "I'm not going to harm you."

"But those messages... *Ticktock*? *Not long now*?... Why were you threatening me?"

She looks surprised. "They weren't threats. Well, not aimed at you, anyway. Why would you even think that?"

I gaze at her in confusion, too many things vying for my attention.

"In fact..." She pushes down on the work surface, giving herself a little lift up, biceps bulging. "...All of this was for you." Her feet drop lightly to the floor, noiselessly, like a cat.

"What do you mean? All what?"

She gestures around the room. "This place. I know how much it means to you. Which is why I'm helping you keep it."

"I don't understand..." The knife slips, falters, my arm aching with the effort of holding it up. Bolstering my grip, I use both hands. "Why would you care?"

Her face changes, becoming intense, the way she was at Rumors. I've thought of that look so many times. But now it seems fiercer, fear prickling my skin.

"I know all about his affairs, Gabby. And I feel your pain and humiliation. So I'm improving your chances of keeping what's rightfully yours." She holds her hands out, palms upward. "The house."

She picks up the same apple, smelling it. "Everyone's seen us around town, I made sure of that: Fred, with some young ho... And using his kids' investments to pay?" She smiles. "He came up with that one all by himself, tying the noose around his own neck. I mean, it's up to the court, but there's a good chance they'll deem him financially negligent and at least allow you to stay here until you want to sell." Her smile widens. "I took legal advice, see."

I gaze at the blade before me, the overhead lighting bouncing off it, flashing in my eyes.

"You want to know the best part?" She leans across the breakfast bar toward me.

I look at her numbly.

"We didn't even sleep together. But then, who's gonna believe that, hey?" She sets the fruit down, folds her arms. "You can thank me when you're ready."

I don't know what to say, but it's not thank you.

"Why would you do this?" Setting the knife down, I feel dazed, defenseless, my feet ice blocks.

She has me now, and probably knows it.

She reaches her tanned arm forward, sliding the picture toward me until it's right under my nose, the grainy colors dancing. "Because of this."

I look at it: me, Dad, Frizzy. "But you're not..."

"There? Look again, Gabby."

Picking up the photo, I examine it, holding it to the light. I can't see details without my glasses, but am not going to admit that to her. I can see enough.

Frizzy, frail by then; Dad, faking a smile; me, several steps apart. And behind me...a tiny face in the background, wrinkled like a sprout.

There's a silence so deep, so thick, I feel entombed by it.

I lower the picture, stare at her. "You're Libby?"

She stares back at me—the first time I've seen fear on her. "Short for Elizabeth."

"How...? I—"

"Dad called me Libby, but I hated it." She shrugs, her voice breaking a fraction. "I always knew he only called me that because it sounded like Gabby." She smiles, her mouth wobbling. "It was obvious he loved you more than me. It was like he ran out of energy, couldn't be arsed the second time around."

I'm still holding the photo, my clammy fingerprints all over it. I set it down, wiping my hands on my trousers. "Sara…was your mom?"

"Is my mom. She's still alive," she says, as though that's remarkable. I don't realize why right away.

She reaches for the wine, regaining her poise, arching her back. "I didn't even know you existed until I was twenty-four."

"How old are you now?"

"Thirty-four."

She seems younger, and older, than that.

"And that was only because I found the photo. Mom said it was the last time they saw you—that she felt bad about it. But obviously not that bad because no one contacted you, right?"

"Right," I say, shifting my cold feet.

"Then when I asked Dad about it, the floodgates opened and he was all Gabby this, Gabby that. Like you were the one person he truly cared about."

I well up at that, looking away.

"So then I wanted to meet you because I didn't have any other siblings. But he wouldn't let me—said it was complicated, that you wouldn't want to see me." Her voice wavers again.

"I wouldn't have minded," I say, possibly meaning it. "I didn't have any family either."

"But your mom…" she says, watching me intently, and that's when I understand why she said what she said about her mother still being alive.

I look away, at the photo, then at Alice's painting on the fridge. Anywhere but at her. I know what's coming.

"Dad said she died the day I was born. It had to have been linked, Gabby—can't have been a coincidence."

I look at her then. "It wasn't. It was the final straw."

"My birth killed her?"

It's unfair that she thinks that, but I can't bring myself to say so. Instead, I nudge my hand closer to the knife.

"I grew up watching him cheat over and over," she says,

"treating my mom like absolute shit, watching her get weaker. And it made me harder, more determined not to end up like that myself, you know?"

I do. But again I don't say a word. My fingers are now touching the knife.

"So I started to fight back, making myself physically strong. He was good at that: took me for runs along the beach, one of the few things he ever did with me."

Something in me stirs, a recognition. He was good at that with me too. I ran because of him—with him and then from him.

"I put up with it for years, but then when I found out about you and what happened to your mom, I lost my shit. We had a huge fight and he got really angry and said you'd always be okay because of this place, that he was going to leave it to you in his will. And he told me about the handprints, Gabby… I know about that."

I wrap my fingers around the knife, feeling exposed, vulnerable. Clinging to this house, fighting for it childishly, and all for four imprints that were just limestone, shells, chalk, sand.

"Then eight years ago, I realized he was going to leave Mom," she says. "For some ho at work with big tits. Even though he'd already upgraded your mom for my mom. He was gonna do the exact same thing again, with someone even younger. So I had to do something about it. Because I couldn't just stand there and watch her…"

Fall apart? Like my mom?

Something else about what she just said is worrying me though. I gaze at the photo on the counter, Dad's face smiling up at me.

"So I took my time, planned it all out. There was no way I was going down for it, not after everything he'd put me through. I had to be smart, make it look like an accident."

Eight years ago. There's a stabbing sensation in my chest, an alarm ringing in my head.

"He was on heart meds, so I started swapping them with vitamins. And I asked him to start running with me again, like I wanted to bond. Then I waited for a heat wave, crazy hot… and on the hottest day, when he'd been off his meds for long enough, we set out for a run."

She pauses, the stabbing sensation in my chest now a clench as I watch her mouth moving, the words slowly meeting my ears.

"There was this killer hill… I told him he was as strong as any twenty-year-old—that if he could make it, he could do anything he wanted. Of course, I meant do *anyone* he wanted…" She grimaces, rubbing her arms, shivering. "He accepted the challenge, like I knew he would, arrogant bastard, and off he went."

I gaze at her, my throat burning. "You…*killed* him?"

"No. The hill did. And his out-of-control ego."

"He had a heart attack?"

"Yeah, he did," she says matter-of-factly.

I feel my blood draining through me, pooling in my feet. I can't breathe or move. I can't hear anything above the commotion of cells, tissues, organs.

"Are you okay?" She goes to round the breakfast bar to join me, before deciding not to, stepping backward. I'm holding the knife upright, didn't even realize it.

"You killed him…? Why? Why would you do that?"

She stiffens her shoulders, widening her stance. "Well, isn't it obvious?"

"No, it isn't! You're going to have to spell it out for me, Ellis, or whatever the hell you're called."

Her hands withdraw to her sides and she looks military again, the way I always think of her.

"So you'd inherit the house."

"What?" My wrist buckles with the weight of the knife, almost dropping it.

She looks confused. "I thought that's what you wanted. Isn't that what you wanted?"

"No!" I shout. "I wanted him alive! I loved him!"

"Loved him?" she shouts back. "How can you say that? He was a twat, a cheating arsehole, just like Fred!"

At the sound of his name, my skin goose bumps, my mind backtracking through her words—what she said about the messages.

They weren't threats. Not aimed at you, anyway.

"Who were you threatening?" I ask.

When she doesn't answer, I do it for her. "Fred?"

Her head jerks as she lifts her chin. Still, she doesn't answer.

"Where is he?" I say, holding the knife higher. "If you don't tell me, I swear I'll—"

"I don't know. But it's too late anyway."

"For what?" I stare at her in horror. "What have you done?"

"Gabby, I'm sorry, I..."

Dropping the knife with a clatter, I run to the hallway, pushing my feet into my sneakers, returning to the kitchen because it'll be faster leaving from there.

She's already outside, holding her shoes. I push past her. "Gabby, wait! You don't know what you're doing! It's not safe!"

I block her from my mind, focusing on getting away. The garage door takes an age to open. She's behind me, grabbing my arm. "Gabby, listen to me! Please! Don't do this!" It's the most humane she's ever sounded, the most genuine, but I'm not listening to her.

Scrambling to the car, I'm a fraction faster, reaching the doors before her, locking them before she can get inside. I don't know where she is, whether I'm going to kill her, knock her down. I don't check or care. Reversing as fast as I can, the tires screech out of the driveway. It's only as I get to the end of the road that I realize I don't know where the hell I'm going. I just have to find him.

42

It's half past eight on my dashboard clock. Fred will be at his parents'. I take the corner too fast, ripping up the hill, blood hissing in my ears.

Stopping the car, I run up their driveway, banging on the door. When there's no response, I turn the handle. It gives and then I'm pelting down the hallway, following the sound of voices to the lounge.

They're watching TV, dinner trays on their laps. "What the heck…?" Monique says.

Len sets his tray aside. "You okay, love?"

"Where's Fred?" I look around the room as though he's hiding. "Where is he?"

They exchange a wary glance. "Well, not here," Monique says. "We haven't seen him all day. He's not home from work yet… Why?"

"Because—" I stop myself just in time, instinct telling me to shut up.

"Is it about the solicitors?" Len says softly. "Did you get the petition?"

It arrived today, at least I guessed that's what it was. I haven't opened it yet. But now this will be my story—the reason I'm here. I clutch the lifeline, nodding.

"Well, barging in here is hardly going to bolster your plea."

"Shush, Monique," Len says, flapping his hand at her.

"Don't you shush me!" she snaps.

I step backward, withdrawing. "Sorry. I don't know what I was thinking. I shouldn't have come."

"That's okay," Len says.

"No, it isn't. She didn't even ring the doorbell!"

"Yes, she did."

Did I? "Sorry," I call again, leaving as unhurriedly as I can bear, my head hung as though repentant.

Pulling out of the road, panic needles my temples and I step on the accelerator. Where is he? The golf club? A bar in town?

I head to High Street, trawling it, hoping to spot him walking along the road, sitting in the window of a bar. It's a long shot though. I'm better off trying his office. He could still be there? I should have asked Len if that was likely. Sometimes he stays late if on a deadline, but I don't know whether he is because we haven't spoken about minutiae lately—have lost track of each other's routines, turning them to dust.

Pixel8D Designs is on an old trading estate on the edge of Shelby. No one lives out here anymore because the river often bursts its banks. Sometimes, it's so bad there are pools of water in the fields, dark bottomless crevices. I've always found this part of town creepy, isolated.

I pull into the car park underneath the office block, hands slipping on the steering wheel, relieved that there are a couple of vehicles here and the lights are still on upstairs. It's an ugly building, on stilts for protection from flooding. The car park lighting isn't great, the corners deep and desolate.

There are no security cameras that I know of. The perfect scene for a crime.

As I am getting out of the car, everything is so quiet, nausea rises in my stomach. I leave the keys in the ignition, the door open in case I need to get away quickly. I'm so preoccupied with the shadows all around me, I don't see right away what I need to know.

Fred's BMW is here.

Oh, thank goodness. I exhale, pulling my cardigan around me.

I'm walking toward the main entrance, thinking about what to say to Fred, when my shoe grinds on glass, the noise jarring me. There are diamonds of shattered glass everywhere, catching the light.

I notice then that there's someone over in the corner by the bicycle cage; a dark shape moving. Instinctively, I squat down behind a car, my heart hammering.

Did they see me?

I don't know that it's anything bad. It could be someone getting their bike.

And then my phone rings. Grabbing it from my pocket, I go to stop it, Jam's name flashing on the screen, but it's too late.

They're coming, feet crunching on glass. I bow my head, faint with fear, limbs melting.

He stops right in front of me. I stare at his feet. Heavy boots.

I think of Will, Alice, my mom, Dad. I think for one moment that he can't see me. He's pausing, considering something. And then he's crouching down, on my level, balancing on heels. He's wearing a mask, eyes glinting.

I swallow, unable to move. And then he stands up, pulling something from his pocket. A rope. I start to cry. "Don't. Please! Let me go. I—"

"Shut up!" He yanks me to my feet as though I'm a doll, retracts his fist and before I know what's happening, he punches my jaw. I fall backward with the impact, onto the ground.

Grunting, he drags me to my knees. I try to bite his hand as it gags me. So he punches me again and this time I'm silenced.

I taste blood as it trickles into my mouth. "Get up!" he hisses. When I can't, he wrenches my arm, shockwaves of pain rattling me.

Making a knot with the rope, he glances around him as though someone's coming. Anyone could come from upstairs. Fred. I lose consciousness for a second. Maybe more. He's holding me underneath my arms, dragging me, my feet grating on glass.

And then suddenly, he lets me go. My back meets the concrete first and then my head. And I'm gone.

43

"You weren't supposed to touch her."

I open my eyes, my left eye throbbing. The pain in my shoulder is excruciating. I know that voice.

"Then what's she doing here?" Him. I can just see his boots. The taste of blood is stronger now, warm. I put my hand slowly to my mouth, scared to move in case they see me, notice me. I'm underneath a car. I smell petrol, oil. Retching, tears sting my eyes. If they start the car, I'll die. They'll drag me along, kill me.

I try to shrink away from the metal, ease myself out from underneath, where I can breathe. My head is in something wet. A puddle. I realize then that it's my own blood.

"If this goes to shit, you're dead." Him.

"Then get the hell out of here! What are you waiting for?" Ellis.

I can't think how she's here—how she got here so fast. I left her at the house.

"Not without her." He's speaking very fast, whispering.

Someone will be here soon, surely—find them. There are people upstairs. I saw lights.

I remember then that the car park is shared with the office next door. Upstairs could be deserted.

"She's nothing to do with this. Leave her out of it."

"Oh, you think I take orders from you, skinny little bitch?"

"Don't you touch me," she snaps. "I mean it."

He laughs, a wheezy rasping laugh. He's still scared someone's coming.

They're not. No one's coming.

"Why, what you gonna do about it?"

"This," she says. There's a pause, a grinding of glass underfoot and I look up just as her hand extends like a starfish, her arm straight, and then she knocks his head so far back I see the whites of his eyes.

Shocked, I scramble upright, my shoulder numb, tingling.

"What the—?" He regains his balance, just as her elbow smacks into his jawline. But he barely flinches this time, the element of surprise gone. There's something on his back, an emblem. It moves as he reaches into his back pocket, drawing a knife.

I try to warn her, call out, but my voice is broken, gone. *Someone come. Please someone.*

Leaning backward, she lifts her leg so high, high enough to kick his jawline. There's a crunch, a snapping sound. He staggers, drawing closer to me, his heavy boot landing on my ankle. Stumbling, he lurches sideways, toward another car.

She sees me then, glances at me and for a moment I think she's doing this for me, showing me what she can do. Grabbing his knife from him, she's still looking at me as she draws it back then plunges it straight at him, into his stomach.

There's a sickening noise. His body, his skin, a snapping sucking sound as the metal meets him, lunging against his flesh. And then his pain. An animal sound. No longer scared someone's coming. Knowing now that they aren't.

I start to cry, calling her name. I don't know if I'm saying it out loud or in my head.

Don't, Ellis. Please don't. Please stop.

She's lunging again, the blade meeting his stomach, tearing his clothes. She doesn't need to. He's given up, sprawled against the side of the car, an open target. And then he buckles, falling to his knees, meeting the ground with a smack of bone that reverberates through me.

She meets my eyes, then pulls the knife from him, wiping it on her baggy trousers, looking on the floor for the sheath, snatching it, tucking the knife down the back of herself somewhere.

"Get up," she says. "Get the hell up. Now!" She's tugging at me, trying to get me to stand, but I can't. I'm in too much pain. "Gabby." She kneels down, gazing into my eyes. She smells of something. It's blood. She smells of blood. "Please. We have to get out of here. Now."

She looks around her frantically, gazing at the car I'm resting against. "Hey, this is your car! Come on. Let's go."

"I'm not going anywhere with you," I say, my voice alien to me. I start to cry again, my mouth hurting. "What have you done?"

"What I had to do." She bristles, her teeth chattering. "He was gonna kill you, okay?"

Nothing's okay. A man's dying, dead. I have to do something. My phone is here somewhere.

"Get in the car, Gabby!" She tries to take my hand. "Let's go! NOW."

"No!" I shout.

She hesitates, biting her lip, and then curses, jumping into my car, starting the engine. I left the keys in the ignition. She's leaving me here, covered in blood. With him.

The headlamps glare across the car park, lighting the bicycle cage, revealing a shape on the floor. And then she's screeching away, gone.

I gaze about me, at the empty spot where the car was. My phone is there. I make my way toward it, clutching it. Beside me, within touching distance, is the man in the heavy boots, his clothes shredded, his eyes still open.

I should check for a pulse, but I can't. I'm petrified I'll get his blood all over me. I think I already have it on my clothes. She put her hands all over me. She's wiped him all over me.

My mind returns to that shape in the dark, near the bicycle cage, and I look that way fearfully.

I push myself upright and, cradling my shoulder, I make my way to him. I know it's him, even before I see the leather of his shoes—the ones I hated.

"Fred!" I barely acknowledge the pain as I drop to my knees, taking in the deathly outline of his face. He's lying with his head against the cage, eyes closed, legs twisted. "Fred!"

Getting up, I shout into the darkness. "Help! Someone!"

I phone for help, whimpering as it starts to ring, connects. "I need an ambulance. A man's been hurt. Two men. I need help!… It's Pixel8D Designs, Oakleigh Trading Estate."

The call handler is asking a series of questions. I don't know the answers. I try to focus. My name. She wants to know my name.

"Okay, Gabby. Now, stay on the line, okay? Set the phone down somewhere to hand, where you can hear it. Put me on speaker. Can you do that for me?"

I put the phone on the floor, kneeling beside Fred.

"Is he conscious? Is he responsive?" Her voice crackles down the line.

"No," I call back. "I don't think so."

"Okay, then I need you to listen to me very carefully. Don't be scared, okay? Just do exactly what I say. You ready?"

I have to be. I have to do this for him. It's too late for the other man. I don't know what's going to happen to me, where Ellis has gone, why any of this has happened.

The phone startles me, a metallic voice. "Gabby? Are you there?"

"Yes! Is someone on their way? Please hurry!"

"Gabby, listen to me. Is he breathing?"

I'm scared to touch him. I know it's not good to move injured people. What if I do more harm than good?

"Is he breathing?" she repeats. "Lean forward, without hurting him. Lean down as close as you can and listen to his mouth. Okay?" She waits. "Are you doing that?"

I am.

I can't hear anything. What if he's dead? What if Fred's dead?

"What's happening, Gabby? Talk to me."

"He's not breathing. I don't know if he's breathing."

"Gabby, listen to me. You need to stay calm, okay? Where's he injured? Can you see where it is?"

He's wearing his polo shirt, jacket strewn to one side. Reaching forward, I touch something dark on his chest, an inky pool.

"…Chest compressions… Okay?…"

I listen to what she's telling me to do. Take something off. My cardigan. Press it to the wound, holding it as hard as I can.

"Are you doing chest compressions, Gabby? Tell me what's happening."

"Yes," I call, clasping my hands together, centering my weight over him, counting to thirty. I listen to his mouth again. Still nothing. I hope I'm doing it right. Please, let me be doing it right.

She speaks again. I don't catch it. My phone blacks out. From somewhere in the darkness, something screeches—a cat, a fox.

I hear the ambulances long before they appear, wailing through the streets. I don't move; I stay where I am, pressing Fred's wound, praying silently. The world feels numb, heavy. I'm pushed to one side where I dissolve into the shadows, my eyes fixed on Fred.

I watch them working on him, ripping clothes, finding more wounds I didn't know about.

The other man died on impact, someone says.

They lift both the living and the dead onto ambulances and then someone sees to my shoulder, my head, drapes a blanket over me, asks whether I'd like to come along with them. And then we're leaving, everything padded and quiet on the back seat. I pick at a thread on the blanket, the pain in my shoulder shaking me every time we turn a corner. Someone—a man—is asking me who I am, what my relationship is to the deceased, what I was doing there.

The deceased. Fred? Or that man? Which one of them do they mean? Is Fred dead?

I'm too horrified to ask, the outside world flashing past, white streetlights, shop fronts, finally the glaringly bright forecourt of the hospital.

And only then do I fully absorb that I'm in a police car.

They unclip their seat belts, radios crackling, solemn faces looming as they open my door, asking if I need assistance walking. When I don't reply, a police officer asks for a wheelchair, pushing me forward in it, the other officer pressing very close, shielding me or containing me. I don't know which.

As the glass doors swoosh open, I begin to panic, taking in the blood on my legs and arms. Blood that isn't mine, blood that I didn't shed.

I don't truly know anything about her. I can't prove that she did this, that she was there.

Or that she's even real.

44

They keep me in for observation, tending to my injuries. I try telling them there's nothing wrong with me, now that my shoulder's where it should be, but they insist. I think they want to keep me where they can see me.

My head is so fuzzy I feel as though I'm levitating. I gaze at a crack in the ceiling, listening to the beep of my monitor. I don't have a concussion, but they said there was a lot of blood. I don't ask whose. My arm's in a sling and it's throbbing like a heartbeat. I won't be able to drive for a while. I don't even know where my car is.

Ellis is the only one who can answer that, and she's vanished. It doesn't even feel as though what happened tonight was real.

Has she set me up?

A police officer with large freckles that make her look more innocent than she probably is, brings me a cup of tea, heaped with sugars, plumping my pillows, helping me sit up. "So..." she says. "Let's go through the details again."

I keep having the same conversation with lots of different faces. I've told them everything I can remember about how I met her. And I'm more than a little thankful that I still can't remember everything. It's more than convenient. It's saving my skin.

"So, she's called Ellis." She glances down at her notebook. "Or Elizabeth, Libby, or Bea?"

"Yes. That's what she said."

"And she's your half sister?"

"Apparently, but she could be lying. I can't vouch for anything about her."

She nods, reads through her notes.

"Am I in trouble?" I ask, moving my arm, trying not to moan or cry. I don't want more pain relief—to be groggier than I already am. I'm starting to worry they think I made up Ellis and that she's me, an alter ego I invented to exact revenge on Fred. They know we're at war, that I've hired the Rottweiler. The murky half sister tale must sound suspect to them.

She doesn't answer my question right away. I sip my tea, panic rippling through me, trembling my hands: Fred's critical, the man in the heavy boots is dead. Killed by Ellis. And almost everything can be traced back to that night at Rumors.

"I don't think you should be panicking just yet," she says, tucking her notebook into her top pocket. "You reported the crime, plus the paramedics said you were great."

I wasn't. I was petrified, hoping and praying I was doing the chest compressions properly. They found me numb with shock, unable to move my hands and release my cardigan that was stopping his blood flow. They had to pry me away.

"If you remember anything else, let me know." She smiles, like she knows there are gaps in my story. "I'll leave you in peace."

I don't think they will. Sure enough, five minutes later a man in a suit comes in and we go back through the same conversation all over again, only slower.

I shift position, pins and needles in my legs, moving my feet up and down in time to the sound of a distant beep. I've been allowed to leave my room, but am not permitted to enter the resuscitation room. Fred was admitted there earlier wearing a ventilator, still bleeding, but no one will tell me anything other than the consultant working on him is the best vascular and trauma surgeon in the area.

It's just after two o'clock in the morning. I'll sit here all night if I have to. Every so often, I allow myself to think of Will and Alice—to worry about how to tell them, when to tell them. But the worry is so huge I can't handle it, so I avoid it, playing with my sling, touching the bandage on the back of my head.

It's four o'clock when I think about phoning Len. Monique answers, her voice all wrinkled from sleep. I tell her about Fred. She starts to cry and then Len takes over and says they'll be right there.

Fred is conscious, beachy green and blue curtains separating him from the patient in the next cubicle. I've been here for four days, no longer as a patient now but as a visitor, and my skin is itching from dryness and lack of fresh air. Len keeps offering to walk me round the courtyard downstairs, to admire the roses, but I don't want to go anywhere. Guilt keeps me pressed to Fred's side, pinning me to this padded chair.

He's rallying though. The police have been in again this morning to check on him. And me. Mostly me, I feel. They're pleased; the surgeon is too. But no one is more pleased than me. I can't think about what would have happened if it had gone the other way.

"Got a moment?" the detective in the suit asks, as though I'm going somewhere.

I nod, motioning to the spare chair beside me.

"So, how are you feeling today?" he asks, tugging his trousers at the knees as he sits down.

"Not too bad. I can go home, but obviously I don't want to."

"Quite," he agrees. He hasn't looked at me yet, his eyes fixed on Fred, which I find strange because I thought their job was to watch suspects for signs of guilt. And that's when it occurs to me: maybe I'm not one.

He crosses one leg over the other, looping an arm over the back of the seat. "So, the deceased who attempted to kill your husband was a known criminal. A nasty piece of work, with priors as long as your arms."

I gaze stupidly at my arms.

"We think it's more than likely that Ellis contracted him to kill your husband. But then when you showed up, you interrupted him from finishing the job... Good timing."

Or bad. Had I got there even sooner, he wouldn't be in a hospital bed.

"As it currently stands, Gabby, we've no idea where she is. Nor do we have many solid facts about her."

Again, I get the feeling they think I'm inventing her. I pick at a loose thread on my sling.

He shifts his legs, changes position. "So, you intercept the attack and he attacks you. So, then she rescues you by killing him." He looks at me then.

"I haven't really thought of it that way, as a rescue," I begin hesitantly, cautiously. "I mean, I wouldn't have been there in the first place if it weren't for her."

"And yet she got there very fast, suggesting not only that she knew precisely where to go, but that she was hell-bent on protecting you."

"I wouldn't like to say... But she seems to be under the impression that we're family or something."

"You don't feel the same way?" he asks, eyes boring into me.

"I barely know her."

"I see." He raps his fingers on his knee. "And there's nothing you're not telling me?"

"No." I focus on my sling, still holding the thread.

"Any idea why she'd want your husband dead?"

I hope and pray for the life of me that I don't visibly jolt at that question. "No. I thought it was me she was after because of the house."

"Ah. The house." He raps his fingers again. "And yet you didn't go to the police?"

"No." I let go of my sling, gazing at him. This part is true—all true. "I didn't think I had enough to report. Just a nasty feeling. And as it turns out, I was right."

He purses his lips. I can't tell if it's an agreement or a judgment.

"One final question, Gabby..."

I brace myself. They always save the worst ones till last; everyone knows that.

"...Do you happen to know whether she's left-handed?"

I think about it. "No, I don't. Sorry."

"That's okay." And he leaves me then, casting a long look at Fred on his way out.

So she's a lefty. A small but vital blessing, moving me further along the blame chain.

She must have left her handiwork all over that man's body. Lowlife or not, the way he died was horrific. I'll never forget it—will never be able to erase it from my mind.

I slump in my chair, pressing the corners of my eyes, too dry and depleted to cry.

And then Len arrives with pasta salad, which he made himself, even though he can barely boil an egg. Monique can't bring herself to speak to me. I know she is silently blaming me. She tends to her son, pulling his covers about even though he's asleep, the purple marks on his face looking gray under the lights.

"Have you eaten?" Len asks, sitting beside me. Monique is looking at Fred's chart like she can understand it.

"Not yet. I will do."

"You need to keep your strength up."

Monique puts the chart back, folding her arms. *It's not her strength we need to be worrying about*, her expression reads.

"They'll find her, don't worry," Len says, looking at Fred, watching his monitor. "I've been following up with the police and they seem fairly confident."

I touch the back of my head, feeling the raised bump, a tender scab forming. Maybe I do it because I want to draw Monique's attention to the fact that I got hurt too. Yet, it's wasted because she still isn't looking my way.

"How did she even know Fred? A psychopath like that?" she says. "That's what I want to know."

I look up sharply at this, my eyes flitting between them.

Len stretches his legs to fish in his pocket for loose change. "Mon, you couldn't get us a cup of tea, could you?" He turns to me. "Would you like one, love?"

I decline, much to her obvious relief.

As soon as she's gone, he turns to me. "She doesn't know Fred's girlfriend and that woman are one and the same. And I'd like to keep it that way."

I remain quiet.

"The police found all those…images on his phone." He glances at me. "I take it you knew about them?"

"Yes."

"I don't want her to know about any of that either. It's too much, on top of all this."

"Okay." My shoulder aches as I shift position, reminding me of what that man did to me—the click in my shoulder as he wrenched me to my feet. Closing my eyes, fear trembles through me.

Monique returns, holding a cup of tea as though it's infectious. "I think it's disgraceful you haven't told the children," she says. "They deserve to know."

She believes that it's me who's a disgrace, not Fred.

I don't see the point in fighting her; she was always going to do this. It would be like trying to change her blood type. Yet, I can't let her completely railroad me.

"I'm sorry, Monique, but I don't want to worry them with it, not just yet. Alice has only just started uni. And I'm not prepared to let anyone spoil that, least of all Fred with his—" I'm about to say dicking around. Len's nudging me, but I would have stopped anyway. Probably.

"So when do you intend to tell them?" she asks, clipping her earrings off, rubbing the lobes.

Maybe never. Maybe I'll let Fred do it. It's his chaos, not mine. Although is that entirely true?

We all look at him then because he's stirring, opening his eyes. Monique darts to his side, hand to his forehead, telling him how pale he is—does he want water? Is he comfortable? Should she call the nurse?

"Why don't you go home, take a break?" Len suggests, patting my hand. "You've done all you can."

I gaze at Fred. He looks up at the same time, our eyes meeting, his parents vanishing, and I imagine for one moment that it's our wedding day and he's about to kiss me at the altar. And then I blink and we're on the ward again.

I'm no longer needed here, that much is clear. Standing up, I do my best to look stronger than I'm feeling. Passing Fred's bed, I'm surprised when he extends his hand toward me, reaching for me.

I stop, gazing down at him. He's smiling, but his eyes are sad. There's all kinds of things I can read there, but I don't want to. Instead, I pull away, taking my leave.

At the nurses' desk, the police officer with the large freckles grabs me, telling me that my car has been retrieved. I imagine it as a burned-out carcass, dumped over a cliff, or abandoned by an airport. But it's not.

It's in my driveway. Forensics are almost finished with it, but unfortunately it's looking pretty clean.

45

I'm back there again, ripping my legs on gorse, trying to wake up. There are two men on the cliff edge; I'm petrified one of them is Will. It was him moments ago, but now it's the man in the heavy boots. He's bleeding, staggering, clutching his chest.

Help! I scream. *Get away from the edge!*

The other man turns to look at me. It's Fred, smiling. But someone's coming up beside me, leading me forward, taking me with her. Before I can stop her, she shunts both of them forward over the edge.

I stare at my hands, covered in blood. And it's then the truth hits me: she didn't push Fred.

I did. It was me.

I sit up, drenched in sweat, my heart racing, shoulder twinging. Flicking on the light, I look at my hands. No blood. Smoothing my hair, calming myself down, I undress out of my moist pajamas, going down the silent hallway to Alice's room.

No one's been in here for a while. I unfold a T-shirt from

her chair, holding it to my nose, inhaling her sweet perfume, relieved to find a sensory trace of her, and then I slip it on.

I'm not sure if I've touched anything in her room since the day she left when I cried on her bed. I draw Big Bear to me. And then, soothed by my child, my love, my memories of her, I sleep.

The world seems asleep as I cross the garden, buttoning up my coat. The security light clicks on as I undo the side gate, my breath visible in the chilly air. It's November, almost four weeks since that horrific night, but it feels like yesterday. I walk quickly, looking all around me, my heels catching on the ground as I turn down the alley, eyes fixed on the light at the end, the shimmer of the sea.

I thought about ordering a taxi, but it's such a short distance, and I'm trying to build up my confidence. Yet, I'll never feel completely safe, not until I know where she is.

As I fix my bag on my shoulder, it aches, almost healed but not quite. I've been left with a nagging pain, not just there but everywhere in my body. I'm still struggling to sleep, missing the children more than ever, finding the house so empty and lonely on my own. Just like Fred predicted.

And Fred… I can't think about him without feeling angry, betrayed. We're in the cooling-off or reflection period, as Maria Kane calls it: twenty weeks to think about who's getting what. Yet, I don't think there's much hope of equanimity or peace. He's still living with his parents, being nursed back to health by Monique; he'll be returning to work soon.

The police haven't found Ellis. The lead has run cold and Fred isn't pushing them to do more, given his transgressions. No one seems to care about the man who died. There will be other cases out there warranting their attention—greater injustices.

It may just be me, but I care. I care that she killed him. And my father too, if that's true.

Turning the corner onto the seafront, I run the last bit, ascending the steps to Rumors. Jam is waiting for me at our usual table and I couldn't be happier to see her. She kisses me, rips open two packets of chips, piling them on top of each other, sliding a milky cocktail toward me. "Santa's Little Helper."

"Isn't it a bit early?"

"Nah. It's never too early to celebrate." She looks beautiful, in a red dress, red lipstick. We've dressed up tonight, for no reason.

"So, how's Nate?" I ask, sick of talking about Fred.

"Oh, you know…" she says, taking a mouthful of chips. I can tell she's going to criticize him and here it comes. "He wants to teach me chess, can you believe…? I'd rather masturbate with sandpaper."

I laugh, glancing around the room for a disapproving elderly woman, but there aren't any. It's all yachties and GDs, just the way it's always been.

And then the waiter leans in, placing a glass down in front of me. "One Liquid Viagra?"

"No, not for—"

"From the lady outside," he says, pointing discreetly to the doors.

I turn to look, my heart freezing at the sight of her. She's there on the decking, staring at me, completely still.

"What's wrong?" Jam swivels on her chair, her face tightening. "Is that *her*?"

I push back my chair.

"Gabby, you're not seriously going to…"

I am.

I need to hear the truth.

"Think about this," she says, gripping my wrist. "Are you sure you want to do this?"

"Yes." I smooth my blouse, tucking it into my pencil skirt. I feel like a dry branch that could snap.

She removes her phone from her bag. "Then I'm calling the police. If you keep her talking, we can trap her."

"No, don't. Not yet." I look over my shoulder again. She's still staring at me, waiting. I look back at Jam. "Don't take your eyes off me. When I nod, call them, okay?"

She nods solemnly.

Right on cue, my shoulder throbs as I go across the room, recalling pain that's locked in my body, as I squeeze between people, chairs.

And then I'm opening the door and it slams behind me and it's just her and me on the decking, as though the past three months have rewound and we're back where we started.

"Gabby," she says, extending her hand toward me like an old friend.

"You've got a lot of nerve, coming here… They're looking for you. And they'll find you."

"Maybe." As though it's no big deal. She looks different—smaller, because I'm in heels. Her shorn hair is tucked behind her ears, and she's still dressed like a dancer. But something about her has changed.

"Shall we?" She motions to the deckchairs, glancing all around her.

She's twitchy now, no longer self-assured. But then who would be, in her position?

"I'd rather stand." It's so cold out here, a lone gull flapping to make traction against the wind. I wish I'd brought my coat and glance back at Jam, who's standing at the bar watching me, but I'm careful not to nod, yet.

"Why risk coming here?" I ask. "What could be worth it?"

"You, Gabby." She smiles shyly. "You're worth it. I wanted to see you."

This seems impossible to believe. There can't be any sentiment left between us—wasn't any to begin with. But not now, after what I witnessed.

Folding my arms, I suppress a shiver. "What do you want?"

"What I've always wanted: to talk."

"Then talk."

Again, the shyness. "Not like this. Not with you so angry."

"What do you expect? You stabbed that man to death! It was horrific!"

"Shush!" she says, looking about her again.

I lower my voice, stepping toward her. "You said you killed my father?"

"Our father," she corrects.

"Well, did you?"

"Yes."

My mouth falls open, amazed by her apparent lack of remorse, her coldness. "Aren't you even a little bit sorry?"

"Well, obviously, I'd rather not have done it. But it was a case of choosing between him and my mom," she says, zipping up her bomber jacket. "And I chose her. And I'd do it all over again too… Just like I did with you."

She gazes at me and I absorb then what I hadn't noticed before: her blue eyes, wide and trusting. Like Alice.

"It was him or you, and I chose you because I love you, Gabby. You should be thanking me."

"I don't think so." I look over my shoulder again at Jam; she's still watching me. "That's the last thing I'm going to do."

She tries to reach for me, touching my sleeve, yet I recoil, stepping backward. "But don't you see?" she says. "They deserved it. Especially Dad. Look what he did to your mom!"

I look away from her, at the sea. I don't want to talk to her about this. If it weren't for her, Mom might still be here but I'm not going to lay that at her door because that's one of the few things that isn't her fault.

"I did it for you and my mom—for the women in my family." She draws closer again, the silky material of her jacket catching the light of the Chinese lanterns, illuminating her face. She's still beautiful, breathtakingly so. "We're sisters."

"No, we're not," I say. "You robbed me of my chance to spend time with my dad. Who knows what might have been, if it weren't for you?"

A look of anger passes over her face, one hand moving to her hip. "Oh, you think he'd have been hanging out with you, playing happy families? Dream on, Gabby! He was too busy screwing twenty-year-olds."

"Well, I guess we'll never know. But one thing's for sure—" I look her up and down "—we're not family. You make me sick to my stomach. We're nothing alike, you and me…"

Her bottom lip trembles, but she recovers quickly, lifting her chin. "Well, that's where you're wrong, see. Because I was just going to help you get the house. I figured Dad owed you, after what happened to your mom. But then…"

"Then what?" The way she's speaking—the expression on her face—is making me feel funny, queasy. My shoulder aches, the image of the man with the rope flashing through my mind.

She examines her fingernail, glancing past me into the bar. "Well, then I met you in person, just to make sure I was on the right track—that you really wanted the house. And that's when you said what you said about Fred."

The ground lurches beneath me. I clutch the back of the deckchair—almost in exactly the same position as when I first met her. Everything feels weighted, dense, the sea grinding to a halt. "What do you mean?"

"You know…" She plays with her pendant, lifting it to her mouth, holding it between her lips.

"No, I don't."

She lets the *B* drop back to her chest where it gleams like a third eye.

"You said you wanted him dead, Gabby." Her voice is a whisper, her eyes shining intensely like they did before. "And I told you I knew a way to make it happen—knew a guy."

"No. That's not true," I say, panic washing over me. I think of her knifing the man's chest, the animal sound of pain, the thud as his body hit the ground.

Behind us, the door swings open in a swell of heat and noise, two yachties appearing, sweaters draped over their shoulders. They barely notice us; one of us too old, the other too boyish. We wait, their brogues crunching on sand.

"It's true… Damn!" She clicks her fingers, as though this is a lightbulb moment. "I knew I should have recorded it!"

I gaze at the stripes of the deckchair, the lines blurring. "I don't remember…" I begin weakly, trailing off. Behind her, the sea shifts unnervingly, the lanterns jangling in a sudden gust of wind.

"Well, I do. Clear as a bell. You told me to do whatever it took—that you'd use the kids' investments if you had to." She grips my arm, her jacket buffeting, swelling, like devil's wings. "Which is funny because that's exactly what Fred did too, only for different reasons."

"That's not true. I'd never—"

"Yes, it is! You even told me the name of your investment broker. Something North, right? How else would I know that?" She looks right at me, and I can't see past her eyes, her pupils bigger than the sea, her grip on me so strong I'm bolted in place. "We're the same, Gabby. Dad taught us to be ruthless, to do whatever it takes to survive, and that's what we do."

"No, I'd never have asked you to hurt Fred."

"And yet you did." She shakes her head as though I'm a lost cause. "You told me how small he made you feel, invisible; the way he was sniffing around younger women. And it pained me so much because no one should be made to feel like that."

"You're lying!" I tug my hand away. "Don't touch me!"

Her brow creases. "I just wanted to help—to make up for

the past. I swear." She reaches for me again and this time I hit her hand away.

"Get away from me!" I turn around then, so fast that my head reels, my heel grinding on wood, searching for Jam's face.

I nod to her.

"Was that the signal?" she asks, a strange look on her face. Disappointment.

I don't reply.

"Because if they find me, then I'll have to tell them about you, about why I did it." She taps her pocket, removes her phone, a web of cracks on the screen. "Hang on, maybe I did record it after all… I'll have to check."

I stare at her in horror. "What are you talking about?… You don't—"

"Have proof?" She smiles. "So, you admit it's true?"

"No. Not at all. You're making this up. You're sick—you need help."

"You and me both, sis."

Shuddering, my eyes lift searchingly to the horizon, to the end of the road, the darkness—the direction the police will arrive in. She notices, withdrawing quickly, standing on the steps.

She looks even smaller now, her features pinched and cold. "I guess this is goodbye? Well, you take care now, Gabby." She blows me a kiss and then turns, running noiselessly, and in a heartbeat, she's gone.

Behind me, the door opens again to a crescendo of noise and Jam appears, drawing close to me. "They're on their way, Gabs. Are you okay? What did she want?"

"To talk," I say, staring in the direction that she disappeared into.

"Well, you were brave—braver than I'd be," she says, taking my hand. "But you need to get inside in the warmth now. You're freezing."

Back at our table, she gazes at me, waiting for me to speak.

When I don't, she says, "Why didn't you signal sooner, hey? You were ages."

I shrug limply.

"What happened?" She cups my hands, warming them. "What did she say?"

My stomach backflips in guilt.

"What is it, Gabby? You can tell me."

No, I can't. Freeing my hand, I take a gulp of my milky cocktail. Then I turn to look outside, scanning the decking. The police haven't arrived yet. "She'll be long gone by the time they get here."

"That's what I was saying. We should have rung sooner." She looks at me quizzingly. "It's like you wanted her to get away or something."

"Of course I didn't," I reply, my stomach turning guiltily again.

Her expression softens and she pats my arm. "Look, don't worry about it, hun, okay? They'll find her. It's not your job. Just relax and forget about it for now." She drums the table with her hands. "I'll get us some more Santas."

As she goes to the bar, I turn to look outside again, thinking of that cracked phone screen, imagining the police getting hold of it. I picture the man's head hitting the concrete—Fred's twisted body beside the bicycle cage.

Dread overcomes me—a ghastly sense of doom. I clench my hands, my breathing shallow. I shouldn't have gone outside to talk to her, should have phoned the police right away.

Or shouldn't have phoned them at all.

What if they find her? What if she's telling the truth?

46

It's quiet on the beach as I run. I don't listen to music anymore; I like to know what's happening around me. Instead, I focus on my steps, the sun rising on the horizon, a tangerine glow on the sea.

I can't quite catch a full breath—can't get enough air into my lungs; not since I saw her two weeks ago. It's like something's sitting on my chest, weighing me down. So I go slowly, watching my feet, hoping my heart is strong.

Shaun resigned yesterday and I accepted it wordlessly. I'm not going to analyze it—what I could have done differently; how he might have tried harder, given me more respect. I could draw parallels with Fred, connecting dots that aren't there, but I'm moving on for the sake of my sanity.

As I approach Rumors, my phone beeps. Pulling it from my armband, I read it.

Can you talk?

Turning, I look all around me—at Rumors, the promenade, the dunes. I can't see her anywhere. I hesitate and then my phone rings, startling me. I almost drop it onto the sand.

Answering it, I stand facing the sea.

"Gabby?" she says.

I flinch defensively. There's a dead crab near my foot, its bleached belly facing upward, claws extended. I kick seaweed onto it, covering it.

"What do you want?"

"A favor." Her voice sounds shrunken, the line crackly, muffled. Maybe she's left the country. I hope she has.

"What is it?" Everything is clenching, knotting—my hands, stomach, knees—my heart still racing from running.

"It's Mom..." The line breaks, distorts, her voice coming in and out. I don't catch every word. "...Wondered if...check on her now and then?"

Her mother? Frizzy?

Out to sea, a cormorant plummets rocket-like into the water, disappearing. "I can't hear you," I try.

"Give you her address... Easy...remember. Ready...? It's The Gables, Torridon... Message you too."

The cormorant surfaces. I watch as it flies to a rock, dries its wings, a sinister shadow against the sky.

She comes in clearly now, delivering every syllable. "No prizes for guessing why he called it that." She laughs. "Told you he was obsessed! Gables. Gabby. Do you hear it?"

I do. But the last thing I need is more evidence that he loved me, given what she did to him.

Troubled, I bite my lip, gazing at the hazy waterline—a huge cargo ship passing. "I'm sorry, but I have my own family to take care of. It's not fair of you to ask."

"Not fair?" Her voice sounds brittle. I imagine that look in her eyes that scared me from the start. "You've gotta be kidding me...after everything I've done for you?"

A trickle of sweat runs down my neckline, down my back, and I shiver, considering hanging up.

"It's no big deal, Gabby. Just an occasional visit. She's called Sara, in case you've forgotten, although I bet you haven't."

No, I haven't. I gaze out to sea again, thinking of the frail woman I hated so much because I saw her as the cause of all my problems. If it weren't for her, my beautiful mom would still be alive.

But that wasn't true. My dad would have found another Sara just like that, as he proved on more than one occasion.

I'm sorry for Frizzy, for everything, but I'm not going to be coerced into this.

I watch the cargo ship, its steady course. "No. I'm not doing it. Leave me alone."

And then I hang up, my heart racing in warning. I don't know why it's warning me, what I'm supposed to heed. Yet, it's done now and I'll block this number and the next. She won't be able to get to me anymore. If she sets foot in this area, the police will find her, arrest her, because this time I'll phone them right away—won't delay.

I set off running again, toward the orange clouds, telling myself that I just need to keep going—that everything's okay. That life will settle down and things will move on, stabilize, as they always do eventually.

But I know somehow that that's not quite true. Because there's something I'm missing, something I'm denying myself still. It's been out of reach right from the start, yet it's going to catch up with me. One of these days, when I least expect it.

At home, the house greets me without so much as a creak or moan. Still in my running gear, I sit on the chair beside the console table, not far from the empty rack that once held so many shoes in so many colors and sizes. Yet, it's okay now. I've changed, am changing. I have to.

I take a deep breath as the line connects and I find that it's no longer restricted—that I can fill my chest without fear or constraint.

This is what letting go feels like.

"Hello?" he says.

My heart twists with regret, like it always will at the sound of his voice. "Hi, Fred. How are you?"

He gives a nervous laugh. "Back at work, actually."

"Oh, you're there right now? Shall I—?"

"No, it's okay. I'm going in later. Reduced hours at first, just to see how it goes."

I shuffle my feet. "Good, well, that's good."

"Yes."

There's a long pause. The house gives me space, waiting. I imagine it completely empty—the way it was when I first saw it.

"Fred, I don't want to fight anymore. I want to sell the house. Split it fifty-fifty. Okay?"

His reaction is so unexpected I goose bump all over.

He's crying, little stifled sobs.

"Okay, Gabby," he says. "Thank you."

I nod. "I'll speak to you later… Good luck at work."

And I'm about to end the call, when he says, "Gabby?"

I press the phone to my ear, listening. "Yes?"

"I'm sorry."

47

I sit by the pool, sipping red wine, nibbling olives from a jar for dinner, my puffy coat zipped right up to the neck. It's not the warmest of evenings, the winter oaks startled-looking, the threat of frost in the mist, yet I'm aware that my days doing this are numbered, so I've taken to sitting out here whenever I can.

It only occurred to me recently that all those years I thought this was my favorite spot because it was near the palm trees, or the perfect position to watch Will and Alice. Whereas in fact I was like a dog grieving its master, resting loyally near the handprints he left behind.

In the driveway, the for-sale sign gleams. Jam is handling it—assured me that although this time of year is typically slow, a property like this will sell in a flash. I'm hoping that's the case, that it slips away, a well-oiled transaction. I've already started sorting out the attic; ordering removal boxes; house hunting.

Shifting position, I pull the blanket higher up my legs, thinking of how I was sitting like this the first time I met Ellis. It's been one month since I heard from her. I'm praying she's gone for good. Yet, the silence feels eerie, too good to be true.

I gaze over at the side gate instinctively, looking for her, taking a long drink of wine. Above me, a couple of bats circle against the inky sky. In the distance, the sea shifts, whispers.

I don't know how I know it's going to happen, but I do. Somehow, I was waiting for it all along, like I always knew this moment was going to come.

Beside me, the metal table buzzes, vibrates, as a message appears. Slowly reaching for my phone, putting on my reading glasses, a nasty feeling shrouds me—the same dread that I felt the last time I saw her.

It's from a withheld number.

There's no message, no words. Just an audio clip.

My heart's going so fast it hurts. I consider throwing my phone across the lawn, into the darkness. I don't have to engage with her. I can block it; delete. But I'm not going to do that.

I press Play.

There's a rumbling, rustling sound: background noise of Rumors, and the sea. And then her voice.

So you're sure about this? Because once we press go, there'll be no going back.

My response is muffled, distant.

Yes. I want him to pay for what he's done.

Her voice is a lot closer than mine.

Because this guy won't mess around, you understand?

I picture her, recording this conversation, her phone concealed. Keeping it as collateral if things went wrong. Which they did.

He'll kill him, Gabby. With no trace. And that's definitely what you want?

I hold my breath, waiting for myself to reply.

And it's then that I remember what I said, what happened that night. The memory is so vivid I hear the words before my recorded voice says them.

One hundred percent… Do it… I want him dead.

Hanging my head, I stop the recording.

My mind whirls back through that night, every detail, no dark corners, no blank spots. Just the ugly horrendous truth.

I wished him dead and then we planned it.

Gripping my phone, my knuckles whiten. I don't know if I really meant it—was confused, frightened, devastated the day Alice left—but Ellis did. She meant it, recorded this, held me to account, took me at my word.

I don't know how I'm ever going to forgive myself, how I'll ever get over witnessing her stabbing that man—the sight of Fred on the verge of death. But I know that when it came to it, I saved him. I didn't hesitate, not for one second.

There has to be some good in that, in me. Doesn't there?

I'm wondering what to do with the recording, about to delete it, when a message appears.

Let me know how Mom is when you see her x

She's going to hold this over me for the rest of my life. I'll never be free of her. I'll forever regret the night I went to Rumors, tried to drink away my empty nest and marriage, and made a pact with the devil.

The palm trees rustle, the baby oaks shivering as a breeze sweeps across the garden from the sea. I draw my blanket closer, the awnings rattling and shaking behind me, and I gaze up at the night sky, a canopy of darkness that seems closer now, bearing down on me. And then there's a noise and I jump, staring in horror at the side gate.

But there's no one there.

★★★★★

ACKNOWLEDGMENTS

I would like to thank the following people; their encouragement and support have been priceless. Thank you to everyone at Peters Fraser & Dunlop literary agency, especially my wonderfully cheerful agent, Sam Brace, and Rebecca Wearmouth, head of international rights. To the entire team at Park Row, HarperCollins US and Canada, including the copy editors, proofreaders, publicists, marketers, and salespeople, who work so hard in support of their authors. Also to the fabulous design team for the most beautiful cover. Special mention to my editor, Erika Imranyi; it's no exaggeration to say that this book wouldn't have happened without you. Thank you to the authors and bloggers who endorsed the book; and to my readers, who make the long writing hours worthwhile. To my dear friend Sally Pasche: I dedicate this book to you. Our poignant conversation about empty nests was the spark that ignited the story. And finally, to my friends and family. Thank you. I love you.